Acclaim

"The hockey ice might be cold, but the romance is warm and cozy, and the characters will melt your heart in this charming story of second-chance love."
—BECKY DEAN, author of *Love & Other Great Expectations*

"Augustine, in her signature wit, creates a story full of laughter, swoon, and, of course, hockey. With arching themes of grace and second chances, the reader is sure to fall in love with not only the main characters but also with the beauty of growth and change."
—DREW TAYLOR, author of The Politics of... series and the Designated series

"A clever, heartfelt story that instantly transports readers to that beloved small-town feel with characters that instantly steal the entire show. A must-read for all contemporary romance fans!"

ANNA AUGUSTINE

—AJ Skelly, bestselling author of The Wolves of Rock Falls
series and Magik Prep Academy series

On Thin Ice

On Thin Ice

Quill & Flame
PUBLISHING HOUSE

Anna Augustine

Quill & Flame
PUBLISHING HOUSE

On Thin Ice

Dedicated to Abby Augustine—my sister without whom this story wouldn't be.

Thank you for brainstorming a hockey romance with me Easter 2021 at our dining room table and for subtly needling me to write this story. Tanner and Molly were born from your love of hockey, and my love of teaching.

I love you to the moon and back, little sis. This one's for you!

PROLOGUE

Molly

"It would be amazing, Mols. I think I might get some offers. There were scouts at the game Saturday." Tanner drapes his arm around my shoulders as we lounge in the back of his pickup, staring up at the billions of stars that dot the spring sky. A few lingering crickets sing as I snuggle closer, tucking my fingers under the light flannel Tanner has over his hockey t-shirt. It's the team he loves most in the world—the Minnesota Wild.

"Even though you lost?" I ask, not trying to poke a wound, but genuinely curious. Most scouts like to sign players who help get the winning goal, who play hard and aggressively. And sure, the Cloverfield Cougars had only lost by one goal. They'd held the Richmond Wardens to three and had come from behind to tie the score in the second period, only to lose by one goal in the third—right at the buzzer, nonetheless.

Tanner shrugs, though I can feel him stiffen, his coiling muscles belying his frustration. "Coach didn't seem to think it would matter. I played hard, led well. We'll see."

I can't imagine what Tanner must be feeling. In a month, he graduates. He'll be off to college in the fall as scholarships to play college hockey are already lining up for him. But I know pro is his dream.

"Well, if you want to know what I think..." I sit up on my knees and lean my forehead against his. "I want my boyfriend to hang out a bit longer in Cloverfield. Because I have one more year of high school, and I don't want to lose him to the NHL this soon. Someday, but not yet."

Tanner smiles, but there's something in his eyes I can't name. And it scares me because I don't know if it's good or bad. All I know is it's a look that makes my stomach flip and my heartbeat escalate.

Rather than figure it out, I close the distance between us and kiss him.

He tangles his fingers in my hair as I lean back, now settled into his lap. "I love you, Molly Pruitt."

"Tell me again." I giggle as he waggles his brows.

"I. Love. You." Between each word, he presses another kiss to my lips.

I sigh. "Good. Because I love you, too."

He somehow tugs me closer, and I forget all about hockey scouts and the NHL. Rather, I let myself get lost in Tanner's kiss, in the gentle way he holds me. There's nothing to worry about. He's a senior. Who signs a senior right out of high school, anyway?

Six weeks later...

Dear Mols,

So, I have an offer. The offer of a lifetime. And I wasn't brave enough to tell you. I've been drafted by the Houston Comets, and I've accepted. By the time you get this, I'll have already left.

I'm certain I'll be back someday. When that happens, I hope you can forgive me and accept that this is best for both of us.

I'll miss you.

Tanner

I stare down at the paper in disbelief. *He's gone?* I pull out my cell and punch a button, willing Tanner to pick up. But it goes right to voicemail. I swallow the burning sensation of tears down my throat and hit Tanner's contact again. And again. And again.

But he doesn't pick up.

I crumple the letter in my fist, a strangled scream tearing from my throat as I drop to my knees on the soft carpet of my bedroom.

"You don't get to just walk out!" I swear as I throw the paper across the room. My heart shatters in my chest, aching like my knees when I wipe out on the ice. I'm not sure how much time passes before Mom steps into my room. One look at my tear-stained face, and she's on the floor beside me. "What's wrong, Molly?"

"He left. He left, and he didn't say goodbye." I burst into tears, and Mom pulls me into a hug.

"Tanner?" she guesses, and when I nod, she whispers, "Oh, Molly. I'm so sorry."

He'll be back. This isn't forever. It's just for now. Tanner will be back soon.

Three months later...

Months pass. School starts and then come the whispers. The giggles.

Tanner and Ava—my best friend—had both graduated the year before and now, I'm left to brave the halls alone. No one understands my love for the "boy sport." Even though I am a figure skater, hockey is my first love. Or was. Until a certain boy ruined the game for me forever.

I hug my binder to my chest as I duck into the bathroom. A couple of my fellow seniors are putting on lip gloss and giggling as I enter. Selina, one of the most popular girls, stops and pouts cruelly. "Oh look, girls. It's Miss Hockey herself. What, Tanner got tired of you that quickly?"

I bristle. "We were together for almost a year."

"*Almost.*" Selina twirls a strand of her black hair around her finger. "But he still up and left. Did you know about his offer, Haley?"

"Yeah." A pretty blonde smiles, but her expression is colder than frostbite. "A lot of the players and their families heard the news. Too bad you didn't rank up there, Molly."

The lump returns. "Maybe he didn't want to hurt me by leaving."

"Maybe." Selina leans closer, her dazzling white smile sharp as her eyes narrow to slits. "Or perhaps you were a distraction, a moment of weakness, and he realized he could do so much better than you, Molly Pruitt."

The tears are so close now, and I hurry out of the bathroom and down the mostly deserted hall. I don't know where to go, but I need to be alone. I have to get *somewhere.*

"Molly?"

I freeze, then turn and fly into the arms of my old literature teacher, Mrs. Dunn. Tears trail down my cheeks, and I choke back hardcore sobs.

"Molly, honey. What's wrong?"

"He didn't say goodbye." I let the sobs shake me as Mrs. Dunn guides me into her empty classroom. She holds my hands as I tell her about Tanner, about him leaving, about the last three months without him. I'd stayed curled up in my room most of the summer, drowning my sorrows in books, Ben & Jerry's, and true crime podcasts.

"Now, I'm here, and I don't know what to do. Everyone is being so mean." And not only about my crappy breakup, but Mrs. Dunn doesn't need to know that factoid.

Mrs. Dunn squeezes my hands. "You raise your chin and march right through this year like the brave woman you are. You have dreams, Molly. Don't let Tanner steal them away, too."

"But it hurts." I sniff.

"It will," she agrees. "But you also need to move on, honey."

Breathing in deeply, I nod. "Okay."

"Good girl."

I stand, hugging my old teacher before facing the door.

Screw you, Tanner Bradshaw. I swallow the ache in my throat. *I'm going to make a name for myself here in Cloverfield. And you're never going to be part of it again.*

CHAPTER ONE

Five years later...

Molly

"Today, I am confident. I am ready for this job," I state as I straighten the collar on my blue blazer and roll back my shoulders. In no way do I feel ready. My first year as a teacher, and I'd miraculously landed my dream job at Cloverfield High as the literature teacher.

You will make them respect you!

Yeah, right. *Respect.* Like any of the fourteen-to-cighteen-year-olds I'll be teaching will actually care about old books that even I found duller than dull at times. I push my tortoiseshell glasses up my nose and eye the stack of reading material that the state kindly *suggests* I teach in my lit class. As if. Perhaps a few of them I'll make my students read. But I believe in the old adage my mom trumpets about like a battle cry—if you love what you are learning, you'll remember it. I want my students to *love* learning as much as I love teaching. And that means teaching and learning what *I* love.

I latch my briefcase and scoop up my stack of books. Shutting the door to my room with my hip, I precariously inch my way down the carpeted hallway and the stairs with tottering steps. I breathe a sigh of relief when I reach the front entry without a disaster. I share the house with two roommates and am thankful they left the hall devoid of shoes and other hazards today.

It is a struggle to navigate out the door. I barely manage to close it with my foot. My heel catches on a crack in the sidewalk, and I almost fall on my face, but I manage to steady myself. How I was so graceful balancing on thin blades atop an icy surface will forever remain a mystery to mankind.

With a huff, I shove my armload of things onto the seat of my car before sliding into the driver's side.

"Man, am I out of shape," I mutter to myself before buckling up and blasting the AC. It isn't terribly hot for late August in Iowa, but it is warm enough for a thin sheen of sweat to build on my brow as I back out of the driveway and onto the road. The radio plays the news—an update on Tanner Bradshaw, hockey player extraordinaire, and the injury that had landed him in the hospital for months.

I click it off. I don't want to hear a word about Tanner Bradshaw or hockey in general. I keep up on it solely because both my dad and Gramps love it. It's the one thing we have in common. Otherwise, I eschew it as much as humanly possible. Hockey dredges up memories that are better left dead and buried, six feet under.

I pull into the staff parking lot and gather up all my things again. A quick trip to my classroom will be needed before hurrying to the gym and the mandatory district staff meeting. I blow a strand of my honey-brown hair off my forehead as I swipe my key card and let myself in the side door.

Blast these infernally long halls! I think as I make sure the door clicks closed behind me. It likes to stick—nearly as cantankerous as the head janitor of our building, Bob.

"Can I help with that?" a low voice asks over my shoulder.

My heart leaps into my throat as I spin around. Precariously balanced as they are, my books topple over, thudding dully against the mismatched tiles that march up and down the hall. Stifling the curse that wants to spring forth, I kneel to retrieve them.

A nice pair of brown loafers fill my vision as my scarer bends down to help me. "I'm so sorry! Let me—"

That voice. I look up, my gaze colliding with startling blue set in a tan face. Dark-brown hair that curls across a furrowed brow. I haven't looked into this face in years. Five years, to be precise. The year that Tanner Bradshaw had been drafted by the NHL right out of high school. The town had been thrilled, ecstatic even, when they'd heard the news. The woman who was madly, irrevocably in love with said player? Decidedly less so.

Tanner's eyes widen to match mine. "Mols! Is that you?"

Words. You need words, Molly. But all that escapes my lips is a squeak.

"How—what are you doing here?" he asks.

I shove a lock of hair out of my face and push my glasses back up my nose, my motions jerky. "I work here. What are *you* doing here?"

He flinches at my frosty tone. "I'm—"

"You know what? Never mind." I angrily grab my books from him and add them to the stack before I heft them into my arms. I had vowed that I wasn't going to waste time pining for him like some lovesick teenager—even though that's what I had been for my entire senior year—and that I was going to buck it up and face life head-on—which I more or less did. I got my degree. I got a job I am excited for. And no surprise reappearance of a long-lost lover is going to change that. Period.

Being rude isn't in my nature, but I'll make an exception for Tanner. I tighten my hold on my books and push around the man in question, not willing to squander any of my words on him.

"Hey, Mols?"

The nickname irks me. I skid to a halt, my back to him, and wait for whatever he has to say.

"Which way to the faculty meeting?"

"Why?" I draw the word out. The hair on my arms stands up straight, my chest tightening as I slowly turn around to stare at

Tanner again. Really take him in. He has on a light-blue linen shirt, the sleeves rolled to his elbows—seriously, that should be illegal because men kill with that look—while khaki pants and the dark-brown loafers I'd noticed earlier complete his ensemble.

Dang it, why do you still have to be cute? I inwardly groan. He couldn't have a couple of teeth knocked out or a crooked nose? Nope, he still has to resemble Michelangelo chiseled him from marble.

Tanner smirks—the left side of his mouth tilting higher in a way that I used to find endearing. Now, it just makes me want to punch him in that perfectly sculpted nose. "I work here, too."

"What?" My arms grow weak and the books tilt forward precariously. I hug them closer to my chest, staring at my ex with an open mouth.

He shoves his hands into his back pockets, shifting his weight to one side. "Yeah. They hired me."

"To do *what*?" I nearly shout but manage to find a shred of self-control. "You're a freaking hockey player!"

"Ex-hockey player." His smile turns a touch self-deprecating, and he takes a step toward me. It's then I notice the limp. Lips twisting in a grimace, he hobbles up to me. "I injured myself last year, remember?"

"Wow, you think I keep up with you and your career? How cute." I won't admit that I have, unintentionally, stayed up with him and his stupid hockey playing. I managed to avoid the radio broadcasts and the magazines in the checkout lane for the most part. The one informant I couldn't avoid was Gramps. He loved

Tanner from the moment I started dating him until the day Tanner hightailed it out of here. If I'm being honest, I think Gramps still loves him. Tanner is Cloverfield famous, after all—and that's better than winning the Stanley Cup in a lot of ways.

"I'm leaving now." I don't know why I announce that fact, but there is no taking back the words. Turning away, I walk as gracefully as I can down the hall and to my classroom, where I fumble to unlock the door, my arms still weighed down with the books. A glance over my shoulder shows me that Tanner still stands by the side doors, arms crossed and looking far too smug, even from the other end of the hallway.

Setting the books by the wall, I unlock my door and fling it wide. I scoop my books into my arms while holding the door open with my foot. And then I retreat like the absolute coward I am.

Chapter Two

Tanner

The door with the word *Literature* printed out in the green and black letters unique to Cloverfield High clicks shut behind Molly Pruitt—my one-time girlfriend now turned painful memory.

She looks good today. Really good. In a white jean skirt, pinstripe blouse, and a navy-blue blazer, she is the epitome of professional chic—nothing like the tomboy I'd left behind five years ago.

I run a hand through my hair. I'd been an idiot at nineteen, itching to get out of Cloverfield, Iowa and make a name for myself. Pushing aside family, friends, and community, I'd taken off to

Texas and jumped into training with the Houston Comets with vigor. It'd been four great seasons, filled with camaraderie, excitement, and yes, fame. I'd been the golden boy, held up and lauded as one of the most valuable assets to ever cross Houston's door.

Then one hit, one play, and I was gone. Kicked to the curb like trash on garbage day. I rub my leg. The ligament had been torn in two places. While I'd undergone extensive surgeries and therapy, I won't be able to play again—not without straining my leg further.

I *may have* played up my limp slightly for Molly's sake. Now I stride with purpose, knowing exactly where the gym and meeting are. The panicked look on Molly's face had been worth the little white lie, though.

You're cruel, one part of my conscience chides. But the cheeky side of me—the one who liked to goad my opposition into fights on the ice and my sister into wanting to throttle me—lets my smirk shine through as I saunter into the gym and slide in beside Eli Cho, the football coach.

In Cloverfield, hockey is a big deal. Or at least, it had been when I was in school. Somewhere along the way, Clover-High lost the spark for the game. A pity, since we are one of the wettest sections of Iowa, with plenty of ponds and lakes to skate on in the wintertime. It helps that we are only an hour or so south of Minnesota—where hockey is king.

It's why we can afford our own skating rink, ironically named *the Rink.* We're central to a number of smaller towns that have hockey teams. They travel in to use the Rink for practices, tournaments, and other events, including the traveling troupe of figure skaters.

The college being here is another assist. We love our Rink, and I think the town would sooner go bankrupt than give it up.

I pick up a pen that sits on the table and click it rapidly. I am already planning plays in my head, the stick becoming an extension of my arm as I move the blade to guide the puck down the smooth sheet of ice toward the net. I'll revitalize the sport in Cloverfield. I'll bring it back to life. I'll—

"Would you cut that out?" Eli snatches the pen from my hand, wagging it in my face. He is a couple of years older than me. I knew him from when I'd been a part of 4H and other local events. He'd also been the star quarterback his senior year, leading the team to the state championship. And here he is now—the coach. He eyes me, his black eyes acute. "They scraping the bottom of the barrel for coaches now?"

The words shouldn't sting. My pro team almost made it to the final round of the playoffs last year—which is more than his scrappy high school football team can say. They hadn't even made it to the playoffs. Not like I had checked the records for all of Cloverfield's sports or anything before agreeing to be the hockey coach. Of course not.

Although, I can't goad Eli too much. For how bad the football team sucks, the Cloverfield Cougar hockey team hasn't been much better. They haven't made it to state since the year I graduated.

I clear my throat and force a grin I'm not feeling to my lips. "Apparently. They hired you, too."

Eli scoffs before a small smirk turns up the corners of his mouth. "Touché, Bradshaw."

Feedback echoes around the gym as Principal Skinner steps to the front. He grins, far too happy for eight o'clock in the morning. He wears a green polo with the Cloverfield Cougar emblem embroidered over his heart, and his eyeglasses are perched on top of his balding head.

"Welcome back, staff!" he booms through the microphone, nearly deafening the half of the staff who chose to sit near the speakers. "Is this going to be a great school year or what?"

Or what, I think, my gaze wandering over the tables and the teachers sitting at them. Almost as if my eyes are magnets, they pull my gaze toward Molly. She is sitting with the English teacher, Ava Kendell, whose bright red curls bounce as she nods along with Principal Skinner. Molly is furiously scribbling in a notebook, her eyes flicking up toward Skinner every so often. I shake my head. She hasn't changed at all. Ever the studious one, she strove for the 4.0 grade point average with the tenacity of the most dedicated team member on the Comets. I've never wanted anything that badly—not even hockey if I am being honest.

"And now to greet our new staff!" That jerks me back to the present. Skinner gestures around the tables. "When I call your name, please stand. Molly Pruitt has been hired as our junior and senior literature teacher."

Molly stands, smiles, and waves. Her gaze meets mine as she scans her coworkers, and I catch the momentary anger that flares in her blue eyes before she sits.

"Lydia Jenkins?"

Three more staff members—whose names I quickly forget—are called and introduced before Skinner calls me to stand. A few people whisper—a couple of teachers get that starry-eyed look of wonder on their faces. I hate that look, but I force a smile and wave at my coworkers.

Fame, you suck, I think melodramatically as I plop back into my chair, my leg aching up into my hip as Skinner continues to call names. In total, there are eight new teachers, three new paraprofessionals, and one new cook.

"All right everyone! Time to get everything ready for the first day tomorrow." Skinner clasps his hands together and shakes them over his head as if cheering. "Dismissed!"

The whispers grow to talking, and I slowly stand, letting my leg get used to being vertical again.

"Tanner, wait a moment!" Skinner hurries over to me. "I have something I need to tell you."

"Oh?" I raise a brow. *This can't be good.*

"Yes. See, the office that used to be Coach Reynolds's?" He clears his throat several times and rubs the back of his neck.

"Yes?" I draw out the one-syllable word, unease blooming in my chest when he hesitates further.

"Well, you see, it had some of the pipes from the girls' bathroom on the east side of the building in the wall." Skinner shifts, not looking at me.

"And?" I prompt when he doesn't elaborate.

"Ah, well." He rubs the back of his neck and then blurts. "They have a leak, and sewage has backed up into what's supposed to be your office."

Words fail me and it takes a lot of self-control to not gag. I remember when our sewer backed up into the basement. I'd only been six, but that's not a smell one forgets. Like, ever.

"We're temporarily putting your office in the back of Molly Pruitt's classroom until we can get the pipes fixed." He gusts the words out in one breath. The words freeze me to the spot. Noticing my hesitation, Skinner continues rambling. "She said last week she didn't mind, and she has one of the larger classrooms in the building."

Last week. Before she realized I was the new coach.

When I still don't reply, Skinner forges on. "It's either that or dealing with a septic smell in your office, which I didn't think you'd want."

"No, but" —It's my turn to clear my throat— "I'm not so sure this is a good idea, sir."

"Oh, it will be fine! Better than fine since you'll get to see how your boys interact with others in authority." He waggles his eyebrows—something no sixty-year-old man should ever attempt—and says, "Besides, I seem to remember you and Molly being a thing back in high school."

I wince, wishing people would forget that particular piece of trivia of my life. *Our* lives. "That was a long time ago, sir. And we didn't exactly part on the best of terms."

Skinner shrugs. "Well, it's either that, or you'll have to camp out in Janitor Bob's closet."

I sigh and run a hand through my hair, properly disheveling it. "You're not giving me much of a choice, now, are you?"

"No, not really." Skinner chuckles and clasps my shoulder. "It'll be fine, Tanner. Trust me."

Yeah, I think, my hand rubbing up and down my stiff leg. *Everything will be just fine.*

Chapter Three

Molly

"I hate that meeting," my friend, Ava Kendell, states emphatically as she glides beside me. We are striding out the large double doors of the gym, back toward our classrooms.

Ava teaches English. Growing up, she'd been a grade above me in school and had done four years of college in two—hello, over-achiever—for the sole reason of landing the English position at Cloverfield High once old Mrs. Burg retired. Ava is the type of person to know what she wants and goes for it. She's been that way for years. But the moment I specifically experienced it was when I first met her my freshman year. For whatever reason, she chose to befriend the quiet, introverted girl that was me on my first day in Clover-High and relentlessly pushed me until I had no choice but to accept her friendship. She has been the peanut butter to my jelly ever since.

She links her arm with mine as I unlock my classroom door. "How's your room looking?"

"Pretty good." I smile as I swing the door open and gesture around. I got low cubby shelves at a thrift store for next to nothing. Family and friends helped buy the sets of classic literature books I needed that weren't supplied by the school since I was allowed to go a little off script for some of my unit studies. Cloverfield is small, with an average of twenty kids per class. Some are larger, some are smaller—but that meant I needed thirty of every book I wanted to teach in a school year. And with the help of grants, generous family, and excited friends, I'd been able to stock my classroom with all the new books, maps, posters, and everything else a first-year teacher could dream of.

"Oh, it's so cute!" Ava bounces on her toes, the graceful figure skater in her coming out as she spins around my classroom. The coffee shop motif I'd gone for gives the room a cozy feel. My desk chair is chocolate brown, while the desk mat, wireless keyboard, and desk organizer are all dark teal. The border around the bulletin board matches the color scheme with a light mocha brown mixed in. Flowers and lamps are scattered over the top of the bookshelves. All in all, it is a snapshot of me. I want my students to see me for me, but I'm also going to make sure they respect me—even if I am only five-foot-three and about as intimidating as a chihuahua.

I refuse to glance at the far corner. Refuse to acknowledge who will be sitting at that small desk in the back where I won't be able to look away. I'm in Denial Land—and shall happily reside there as long as humanly possible.

"Are you ready for tomorrow?" Ava's freckled nose scrunches as she watches me from where she is perched on the edge of my desk. Her black leggings show how defined her legs are. Her lean frame, willowy arms encased in a sheer cardigan, and bouncing red hair gives her an ethereal vibe that I low-key envy. I am on the curvy side, short, and way more awkward around the human population than my athletic, outgoing friend.

"I think so." I plop into my desk chair, pushing away all the negative thoughts and memories. They are the last thing I need before my teaching debut. "I've never taught without another teacher in the room."

Ava snorts. "You'll probably have some of the special ed teachers floating in and out of here. I swear, the number of kids that need help goes up every year."

"A lot of them just need a little TLC." I pick up a pen and click it on and off in rapid succession, imagining what the school day will be like tomorrow. My first day with students. Lesson plans, teaching, exciting the kids about literature. I lean back in my chair, closing my eyes with a sigh, and try to release the stress in my shoulders.

"Hey." Ava draws out the word until it is five times too long. "I have a question for you."

I crack open one eye. "Yes?"

Ava is pulling at one of her curls, letting it bounce up before catching it between her thumb and forefinger again. She does it five or six times before she blurts, "I want you to be my assistant coach for figure skating this year."

"Not happening." I sit up, my jaw tensing until I think it might snap.

"Molly—"

"No. I can't." Not with Tanner Bradshaw working here. It was bad enough running into him when I walked in the door this morning, but the thought of going back to the Rink? To see him *there*, in a place with so many memories? So many stolen moments? I can't do it.

But Ava doesn't understand. She'd been away at school already when Tanner left, when my world came crashing down around me.

She rolls her eyes, leveling a glare that could leave a WWE wrestler in tears. "This has something to do with Tanner, doesn't it?"

Okay, maybe she knows more than I think. I slump back against the chair, feeling as though I'd run a million miles in the summer sun. "Please, just drop it, Ava."

My friend taps her bright pink nail against the desk. "There's no need to get defensive."

"I am *not* defensive," I snap.

Ava huffs a breath and raises her brows.

Because my tone is totally defensive. That's the thing about Tanner. He makes me irrational in so many ways. I thought I had dealt with him, pushed him out of my heart and mind. But bumping into him this morning? All the hurt and pain had rushed in like a tidal wave. Call him Miley Cyrus because he came in like a wrecking ball and shattered my carefully constructed walls. While I don't have a choice but to work with him, staying away from the Rink is the one thing I *can* do to control this situation.

"All I ask is that you think about it, Molly. It might be good for you." Ava stands before I can interject. "Come on! Let's go to Sweetie's, get some coffee, and finish up our lesson plans."

Conceding defeat—this time, anyway—I nod and gather up my binder and briefcase. Clicking the lights off one by one, I pause in the doorway.

Tomorrow, you'll be full of students! A giddiness swirls in my stomach, and I smile. This is why I spent four years studying and crying. This is what I'd dreamt about since *my* first year in lit class. Tomorrow, it will all be worth it.

I turn off the overhead lights and follow Ava out of the school toward her silver smart car. Sliding into the passenger seat, I snap my seatbelt into place with a sigh. A headache is starting to form behind my eyes, stress eating at me like termites in wood. My mom often says I am wound as tightly as a corkscrew. She isn't wrong.

Ava pulls out of the teachers' parking lot and starts the short drive to Cloverfield's local café.

Sweetie's is owned and operated by Sweetie Esperanza, an Italian woman with a gift for creamy coffees and heavenly baked confections. It is both a blessing and a curse that I can stop at her little café on my way to the school every morning before work.

Ava pushes inside, the little bell above the door jingling merrily, and strides right up to the counter, with me on her heels.

"Ava!" Ms. Esperanza coos as she steps up to the register. Her black hair is pulled back into a low bun at the base of her neck, and her beautiful Italian complexion seems to glow as she wipes her hands on her dark-purple apron. "How's my favorite English teacher?"

"Fabulous, Ms. E!" Ava all but chirps in reply. "You're looking positively radiant today!"

I barely resist the urge to roll my eyes at their antics. The two have some unspoken battle as to who can compliment the other more. I can't remember when it started, but I refuse to get involved. Rather, I let Ava place our orders as my gaze wanders over the chalkboards and pictures that Ms. Esperanza has mounted on the walls. The chalkboard signs all boast ridiculous fall sayings like *It's Fall, Y'all* or *Hello, Pumpkin.* Some have quotes about autumn from *Anne of Green Gables.* There were even a few poems from Dickinson and Frost.

But it's the pictures around the quotes that draw my attention. They change as frequently as the writing on the blackboards, boasting shots from local photographers, both professional and amateur. I gaze at a beautiful red maple tree framed by a foggy field, a cherry red barn between golden cornfields, bales of hay dotted over a small hill, and a colorful farmer's market stand. But the one that arrests my attention is an old photo of a group of Clover-High students at the line dance the town hosts the first Friday of every November. Old Mr. Richards would clean up his barn, string lights from the rafters, and all of us would mosey on over and learn line dances late into the autumn night.

That year, I'd gone with my new boyfriend, Tanner Bradshaw. We'd danced and laughed. He'd kissed me for the first time that night, under the stars as we snuggled in the back of his old Ford pickup. He'd told me he was falling in love with me, and that—

"Earth to Molly! Come in, Molly, are you there?"

I jump and turn, nearly crashing into Ava's chest in my haste to escape the painful memories. She doesn't know how much the breakup broke *me*. No one really does.

"Geez!" Ava's reflexes save our drinks from hitting the floor. "Where were you? Mars?"

"Something like that." I shake my head, trying to re-erect the walls that started to crumble that morning.

"Okay, then." Ava raises one brow and thrusts one of the paper cups toward me. "A caramel latte with an extra pump of caramel."

"Perfection!" I sigh, letting the strong scent of coffee whisk away any lingering memories of Tanner Bradshaw, line dancing in a barn, and first kisses under a blanket of stars.

I sigh as I kick off my shoes and shove them into the bin that sits under the coatrack in our entryway. The sound of chatter comes from the kitchen, and after setting my briefcase on the bench that runs the length of the short wall, I hurry toward the scent of baked goods.

My two roommates are laughing and chatting amiably. Susan is shoveling chocolate chip cookies onto a cooling rack. Dozens of other types are already scattered across the counters, ranging from red velvet to pumpkin to sugar cookies—all for the local farmers' market on Thursday. Flour coats the tiny table set up in the middle of the room that holds her fancy mixer. Susan's blonde hair is piled into a messy bun on the top of her head, a headband with baked goods printed on it barely holding back her flyaways. Her brown eyes—as dark as the chocolate chips in her cookies—sparkle as she laughs at something our other roomie, Emily, says.

"Dolly Molly!" Emily welcomes in a singsongy voice. She gestures me over to the barstool she sits cross-legged on and then waves a hand dramatically at a plate of broken cookie pieces. "Dearest Sue said we can eat these less-than-perfect specimens of her baking exploits."

"Have you been watching regency shows again?" I ask, sliding onto the second barstool and picking up an oblong-shaped pumpkin cookie. It doesn't have Susan's cream cheese frosting on it—a pity—but it is moist enough to melt in my mouth regardless.

"No, rather reading them." Emily smiles, her hazel eyes dancing. "Out loud, of course. Because darling Charlotte should be cultured."

"She's three months old!" Susan rolls her eyes.

Emily shrugs her thin shoulders. "What better time to educate? When they can't move and can't tell me they don't like it!"

Her phone rings, and she rolls her eyes as she picks it up. "What is it now, Mr. Markel?"

I swallow back a chuckle. Emily is a nanny for a super wealthy man in town. He just became the sole guardian of a baby girl after her parents died in a car crash. The man has absolutely no clue how to care for his goddaughter and is always calling with questions. Emily, however, loves mothering the infant and takes it all in stride.

After ending the call, Emily flicks her shoulder-length black hair out of her face and asks, "How was the meeting?"

"Fine." I grab a slightly crisp chocolate chip cookie and break it in half. The thought of Tanner's sparkling eyes and lopsided smirk invades my mind again. "Boring."

Susan looks up from her pan of cookies before she waves her spatula at me. "Spill it!"

"Spill what?" Emily looks between Susan and me. "What am I missing?"

"Nothing!" I protest at the same time Susan says, "Everything!"

"There's nothing to tell!" I say, far too much vehemence to the words. When Susan cocks her head and raises her brows, I roll my eyes. "Okay, fine. I *may* have bumped into my ex, but that doesn't mean—"

"Wait, wait, wait!" Susan drops the spatula and throws her hands into a time-out signal. "Isn't your ex *the* Tanner Bradshaw?"

"*What?*" Emily shrieks, standing up so fast that the metal barstool topples to the floor behind her. "Your old beau is *Tanner Bradshaw?*"

I glare at Susan, who has the decency to blush. Very much on purpose, I had kept the fact that the famous Cloverfield hockey player was once my boyfriend from Emily, who has the tendency to one, overreact; and two, play matchmaker to every single man and woman in her life.

"Okay," Susan shakes her head, "but how did you run into Tanner Bradshaw here in Cloverfield? Isn't he still under contract to the Houston Comets?" Susan moves to the sink where soapy water fills one side.

"Can we just back up to the fact that you *know and dated Tanner Bradshaw?*" Emily clutches at her chest and sighs the biggest sigh I'd ever heard. She blinks and braces a hand against the counter. "Oh, now I'm dizzy."

"Serves you right." I cross my arms and lean against the counter. "And to answer Susan's question, I don't know, and I don't care. He's been hired to coach the hockey team."

"He's living in Cloverfield?" Emily asks.

"Working at the school would tend to mean he is!" Susan huffs. "Well, so much for the avoidance technique, Molly."

"Yeah." I press my lips thin at the reminder that I won't be able to flip the channel whenever I see Tanner's face anymore. Can't turn the magazine around or click off the radio when his voice rumbles through. He'll be sitting in the back of my room, watching and judging my every move. I'll be utterly, completely stuck.

Deciding not to bring up that unfortunate detail with my roommates, I play with the crumbs on the counter. "Ava also asked me to be her assistant figure skating coach."

Susan studies me with a narrowed gaze as she starts placing dough on the cooking tray. She knows a lot about my post high-school drama since she'd gone to Cloverfield Community College with me and has been rooming with me for the last four years. Emily joined us two years ago when she'd gotten her preschool job and moved to Cloverfield.

"You figure skated?" Emily's eyes sparkle.

"Yeah." I look away, pain carving a hole in my chest like a cavity in a tooth. "But I haven't been on the ice in five years."

Something in my tone must warn Emily to stop asking questions. Or maybe it is the look Susan is shooting her way. Either way, Emily picks up a snickerdoodle off the reject plate and shoves it in her mouth.

"It might be good for you, Molly." Susan shrugs. "But that's up to you."

I push back from the counter, the cookies turning to lead in my stomach. Forcing a smile, but not saying a word, I hurry up the stairs and into my room. I settle into my tiny wingback chair before staring out the narrow window that looks out over our block. Mr. Needlemire—our next-door neighbor—is out working in his yard again, and sweet Ms. DeWhit from across the street is watering her beloved plants that wrap around her porch. But my mind isn't on the neighbors. It isn't on Susan and Emily's chatter and laughter that floats up the stairs. It isn't even on the first day of school tomorrow.

Rather, my mind is stuck on a pair of bright-blue eyes, unruly brown hair, and a lopsided smirk, all of which threaten to drive me crazy once again.

Chapter Four

Tanner

I can smell the cinnamon before I open the door of our single-story, ranch-style house. With pretty green shutters against white siding, a swing situated in the front yard between the two towering maple trees, and a plethora of flowers in a bed along the side of the house, the whole place screams comfort. *This* is home, even after five years away.

I step through the door. The open living room and kitchen make the space feel bigger than they are. Both are nearly spotless, the lodge motif that is uniquely my mom making the whole atmosphere feel homey. My eyes skim over the caramel-colored sofa, the coffee-colored recliner, and the large wooden bookshelf before coming to rest on Mom. She stands at the kitchen sink, her hips shaking to the country song playing on her old stereo. The crooning voice laments about how when momma ain't happy, ain't nobody happy. I never found that to be true in my house, however, because I honestly can't remember a time when my mom was truly mad. She'd get upset, as is only human, but she never stayed that way for long.

"Hey, Mom." I lean down and kiss her cheek. Even at twenty-four, I am her baby boy. She welcomed me home with open arms after my injury, letting the basement become my "bachelor pad." Although, I am fairly certain she is trying to remedy *that* specific title despite her continuous denial.

"How was the first day at Cloverfield High?" She looks up—way up—at me as I lean against the counter and chomp into an apple. At five feet even, she doesn't quite reach my shoulder. Her graying dark-brown hair is cut to her chin, and her eyes are a deep umber color. I inherited Dad's eyes, though, and the pain of missing him hits me every time I look in the mirror.

I switch the apple to my other hand and rest my elbow on my crossed arm. "Why didn't you tell me that Molly Pruitt is one of the new teachers at the high school?"

My mother is nothing if not a master at emotions. Whenever I think I have her pegged, she'll do something that will totally blow my theories of what she is thinking and feeling out of the water.

Now is one of those times. Her eyebrows rise in what appears to be genuine surprise as she turns, her right hip leaning up against the sink, and she studies me. "I didn't know. What is she teaching?"

"Literature."

A slow smile spreads across Mom's face. "Fits her."

"Yeah, it does," I begrudgingly admit. "But that means I have to work with her!"

"And?" Mom's brows rise again, and she crosses her arms with a *harrumph*. "You're the one that left, Tanner James, and you're the one that has to face the consequences of that action. If that means getting back in Molly's good graces, then you'll find a way." She pats my cheek, her calloused, workworn hands still damp from the dishwater. "You always were the tenacious one of this family."

She says it like it's a good thing, but I know it's not great being stubborn. There are times to be pigheaded. Times to push the limits, rile the enemy, poke the bear. Use whatever colloquialisms you want, that is me many days. Even on the Comets, I was the one who would annoy the defense into lashing out, earning themselves a penalty.

But I don't want to be tenacious with Molly. I know I hurt her. I hurt her badly. How am I supposed to make up for that? I walked away five years ago only to show up in a place that is practically *hers*. How is that fair? I feel like the intruder.

"It's going to be hard to earn her good graces back," I state, finishing off my apple in an attempt to ignore the gnawing sense of dread in my gut.

"Oh?" Mom questions as she wipes off the counter. I throw out the apple core, wipe my hands off, and begin to put the clean dishes away from the drying mat. Like the ever-patient mother that she is, Mom waits for me to elaborate.

"Principal Skinner may have cornered me today and forced me to move my office into the back of Molly's classroom."

"You're stuck in the back of Molly's classroom?" Mom pauses in her work, then snorts a laugh. Her eyes crinkle at the corner, and she shakes her head, barely holding in more.

"Apparently!" I throw my hands up, nearly dropping a plastic container and unintentionally juggling it to keep it from hitting the tile floor. "It's only temporary. A pipe backed up and flooded my office, and they can't get a plumber out to fix it for a while. It's not funny, Mother!" I protest when Mom's laugh breaks free.

"Oh, yes, it is!" Her eyes sparkle with mirth as her laugh lines deepen. "And it will be quite interesting, too."

"You think?" I say drily, but her humor ignites a bit of my own and I smile.

"Are you heading to the Rink tonight?" she asks as she carefully folds the towel and hangs it over the stove bar.

The Rink sits in the middle of the town. It is almost like the town sprung up around the stadium, paying homage to the sport of the city—hockey. It has banners featuring the championships of the colleges and universities around Cloverfield, as well as the local community college wins. It's also home to Spin, the local figure skating team, and—of course—Cloverfield's very own Cougars.

The Rink is run by Rick Pruitt, Molly's grandfather. Though he is eighty-six, the man has more spring in his step than me—even before my injury. He is often on the Zamboni, smoothing out his beloved ice, or running the ticket and concession counters when the Rink is open to the public—which is about every night that there isn't a game or competition going on.

Thankfully, when I bumped into Rick a few days ago while scoping out the Rink again, he'd been thrilled to see me. Hugged me, in fact. His weathered face appeared to have genuine joy on it, but I could have just been fooling myself. I'm not the best judge of character sometimes.

I grimace before turning my attention back to Mom. "Nah, the Rink can wait until tomorrow. I'm going to turn in early, I think."

"Are you going to want dinner, or are you fending for yourself?" She cocks her head to the side. "Taysleigh and the kids might stop by tonight for dessert, too."

I smile at the thought of seeing my sister, niece, and nephew. Three-year-old Hayley is a ball of uncontainable energy. With golden curls that match her daddy—my brother-in-law, Jacob—and eyes that I swear can grow three times the size that should fit in her head, she is too adorable for words.

Henry is one year old and a warm, squirming ball of adorable. With his daddy's cobalt eyes and Taysleigh's dark-brown ringlets that no kid should have, he is the exact opposite of his sister in looks. But he has just as much uncontainable energy. I often joke with Taysleigh that when he starts walking, the world better watch out. Henry and Hayley will be able to single-handedly level Cloverfield in a matter of hours, I am certain.

"I may pop up." I smile and peck her cheek. "Especially if dessert is your pumpkin bread?"

Mom smiles. "That nose of yours."

She reaches up as if to pinch my cheek, and I duck her hand, moving to the side of the fridge and towards my escape to the basement.

"Call me up when Tays gets here!"

"Aye, aye, Captain." She moves to the oven, missing the fact that I freeze at the old nickname.

I had been the captain of the Cougars and then the Comets. It aches more than the pain in my leg that it isn't my title anymore. I'm not in charge of anything but a group of ragtag high school boys who want to play hockey. Who am I without my title of captain? Without my team at my back and the lights in my face?

Who is Tanner Bradshaw without hockey?

I stifle a yawn as I button up the front of my burgundy dress shirt. Taysleigh stayed far later than I anticipated, especially with the littles. My head aches, and I want to tumble back into bed. But a glance at my old analog clock shows I have about five minutes before I need to be at the high school.

Rubbing at my face to wake myself up, I sling my satchel over my shoulder and grab my loafers. I am as put together as I can possibly be. One last glance in the mirror, and I hurry out of the tiny bathroom. My little kitchenette boasts a single-door fridge, a two-burner stovetop, a microwave, and the most important necessity—a coffee pot.

Bless timed start. I sigh as I pour the hot, black brew into a stainless steel travel mug with a Minnesota Wild sticker slapped on the side, and twist on the top. I may have played for the Comets, but the Wild was the team that had me falling in love with hockey and will always be the team I cheer for.

Clicking off the appliance and the lights, I navigate past my small flatscreen and love seat and head up the stairs to the mudroom. I pause in the narrow hall, my leg starting to ache from the twelve steps from the basement. The mudroom has hooks on one wall and a bench to sit and put on shoes, coats, and winter gear when the snow flies. I slip my feet into my shoes and do a final once-over.

Phone. Check. *Bag and papers.* Check. *Life liquid.* I raise the mug in a salute before fishing my keys out of my pocket and marching out the door to the car.

My basic sedan might not be much to look at, but it gets me where I need to go. I never understood my teammates and their obsession with the newest, fanciest cars. Yeah, they can afford it. Heck, *I* can afford it. I really don't even need to teach, not if I invest the money I earned from my four seasons playing for the Comets. We'd made it to the conference final last year, losing our chance at competing for the Cup during double overtime in game seven.

That helped boost the money in my savings tremendously. Getting into the playoffs guarantees more money than our contract—a bonus for playing well and going further than the other teams.

That money went to refinishing the basement into an apartment. It helped Mom fix up the upper floor, too. I don't need a job—honestly, I don't even need to live with Mom. But I could tell she was lonely. And family comes first. Always.

Those are the reasons I am pulling into the teachers' lot at the high school at the unholy hour of seven a.m. Because I don't want to get lazy and entitled. I'd been handed a gift in the shape of a hockey stick, and I want to pass that passion and skill on to whichever kids want to play.

And there's going to be so many of them. I tighten my grip on the wheel, staring at the large building as trepidation swirls in my gut. They will all know who I am—or was. I led my team to the playoffs, and then that stupid injury in the conference final happened. It's what's keeping me from playing now.

I slowly make my way up to the doors of my old school. It takes everything in me to step into the office, where Mrs. Maize grins cheekily at me.

"Mornin', Tanner." She has that slight midwestern drawl that the older ladies who've lived most of their life here seem to acquire. I can't deny that I love it, although I am glad Mom appears to have missed the memo—doesn't fit her at all. But for ladies over sixty, it almost seems to be mandatory.

"Morning." I smile. "Is Principal Skinner in?"

"Yep." She gestures toward the door, and I step into his office.

Skinner is bent over some paperwork, scratching his pen against the bottom of the page before looking up at me. "Ready to start your new job?"

I hope I hide my wince as I nod. The thought of being in Molly's space for hours on end has me on high alert. I'm like the cheetah I saw the other day at the zoo. It paced around and around, clearly wanting out and yet completely stuck. Hello cage, call me cheetah.

Skinner pushes to his feet and motions for me to follow. "I'll show you to Molly's room."

"Sir, I really don't think this is going to work." I didn't dare grab Skinner's arm, though my hand flexes before it drops to my side. I need to get a grip. This is *Molly*.

Although, she can hold a grudge. On second thought, maybe she's the cheetah, and I'm the poor glob of ground beef on the rock, waiting for her to pounce. I rub my throat; it hurts to swallow.

"Why not?" Skinner's bushy brows rise as he pushes his glasses on top of his head.

"Molly and I…" I *really* don't want to spill my tragic love life at the feet of my boss. "We didn't part on the best of terms."

"You said that yesterday. Are you saying you can't be professional?" His forehead wrinkles as his eyebrows hitch up.

I grit my teeth. "This isn't exactly what I signed up for, sir." I tack on the title for good measure. Ticking off Skinner is no way to start my year. Because that would be my luck. Not only did I lose my hockey career, I also managed to get fired day one of my new job. The great Tanner Bradshaw, everyone!

Skinner crosses his arms. "I am aware of that, but we all have to be flexible. I know this isn't ideal. We are working to fix the office situation. I know you want to focus more on hockey, and being in another classroom isn't what you were planning on. But this school is a family, and we have to work together to help these kids learn, first and foremost. Everything else comes second."

I bite back the retort about coworkers being family. There is only one person on my team that I am still barely in contact with—and I've only officially been gone from Houston a month. No, *family* family—blood family—they're the only ones you can count on to always be there, no matter what. Mom, Taysleigh, Jacob, and the kids are that for me. I don't need any more *family* that will simply bail when I stop performing the way they want.

I dare to level a glare at my boss, but before I can reply, Skinner says, "I suggest you find your professionalism, Mr. Bradshaw." For being a head shorter than me, he somehow manages to pull himself up enough to meet my gaze.

Skinner gestures to the Literature room. "Good luck with Miss Pruitt."

"You're not coming in?" I ask, surprised.

He flashes me a cheeky grin over his shoulder as he trots back to the offices.

"Sweet mercy."

Considering I'd seen Skinner stare down five nearly grown seniors one year when they got into a serious brawl in the halls—let the record show that I'd been a witness, not a participant—watching him now, I am starting to suspect he is petrified of his own staff.

Which, to be fair, adults are scary. But being famous meant I had years of dealing with mics and reporters in my face. I'd dealt with all sorts of humans, and I can safely say I prefer anonymity. So, I got Skinner's reluctance.

Didn't mean the thought of facing Molly alone didn't scare me half to death.

I groan, refusing to give into the Hulk-size tantrum that I want to throw, and take a fortifying breath. Then, I push through the door and into Molly's surprisingly cozy classroom. Coffee posters hang on the wall, a scented wax melt burner is plugged into the corner and emitting a vanilla and coffee scent while softly glowing lamps are positioned around the room to welcome me in. Molly has the desks situated five across and five deep. They face her desk, which is in front of a large whiteboard. To the right of the board is a smart TV with a cord stretching to Molly's laptop, which she is currently hunched over, typing furiously.

"Good morning." Does my voice sound squeaky, or is that only me?

Molly's head snaps up, her blue eyes narrowing.

Yep, I'm definitely the ground beef.

"What do *you* want?" she asks, the words frosty.

To be anywhere but here. I clear my throat. "Skinner said I'm using this room for my office."

Her face smooths, but I can see the muscle in her cheek bobbing in and out with her barely suppressed frustration. "Fine. I was hoping you'd set up in the Rink, but I can see I'm not that lucky."

My shoulders relax, but only slightly. "So, we're good?"

"Yes." She scoops up the stack of papers, her eyes narrowing as she lightly taps them against the desktop to level them. "But just so you know, Tanner, I don't put up with being contradicted nor questioned in front of the students. You have a problem?" She slams a hand against her desk, leaning forward. "You come talk about it with me. No running to Skinner or anyone else."

The ties on the top of her blouse fall forward, brushing the top of the desk, and my eyes follow them, unable to handle the coldness of her eyes. I stride further into her room, struck again by how *Molly* everything is.

"I always meet confrontation head on." I lean over her desk, close enough to feel her breath, my voice dropping to a whisper as I gaze over her shoulder. "That's what made me such a good enforcer on the ice."

"Yeah, sure you do." She snorts, turning her back to me to write something on the board. I take a moment to appreciate her style that morning. She has on a lacy cream-colored top tucked into a black skirt that hits her midthigh with sheer black tights under it. Maroon heels click with each step she takes, the color matching the cardigan that hangs over the back of her desk chair. Her honey-brown hair is secured with a large, black jaw clip, and she tucks a few loose strands behind her ear as she caps the marker and turns to me.

"Your desk is in the back corner." She eyes me for a moment. "And just so you understand me clearly—I'm not happy with this."

"I know." I do. I truly, truly do. And I don't like it any more than she does. This stupid solution of Skinner's is cutting into my planning time for team strategy, practice planning, and...

Ah, who am I kidding? If I get to sit in the back of a classroom and listen to Molly drone on and on about some of her favorite books, then my workdays are going to be glorious.

I still curse myself every day for walking away—for being a coward and a chicken and a wuss in all the things that actually matter. I ran from the one person who has ever truly seen me for who I *am*, not what I *do*.

Because the truth is, while I don't know who I am without the captain's *C* on my shirt, I'm beginning to realize I sure as heck don't know who I am without Molly Pruitt in my life.

CHAPTER FIVE

Molly

We have on matching outfits.

I swallow back the bile that threatens to climb up my throat and into my mouth as I turn from Tanner and write a welcome on the whiteboard. I tried to do it on the stupid smart TV but can't get the dang thing to work. I'll have to email the tech department and ask for help later.

Right now, the issue at hand is to keep from strangling both my boss and the imposter in the back of my classroom.

They say time heals all wounds. I don't know who *they* are, but they need a swift kick in the head. Because one look at Tanner, and I'm struggling to breathe at the weird mixture of anger and attraction bubbling in my chest.

I'd been attracted to the man ever since my freshman year. But it wasn't until he was a senior in high school that he took notice of me as more than a friend. I was the underclassman with the thick glasses and less-than-stylish fashion sense. I'd been a tomboy. Ratty jeans and faded t-shirts were my go-to for horsing around on the basketball court or on the ice with my brothers. They'd been the ones to convince Dad and Gramps to let me tag along to the Rink every weekend to skate and race and play the sport I loved.

It had been Mom who finally put her foot down. She didn't care if I skated, so long as I gave figure skating a chance. Since I loved hockey too much to give it up, I'd agreed. And that became my second love—figure skating. It was the same cold ice, the same balance and strength, but channeled in a way that made me come alive. Mom said it was my inner beauty flowing out through the skates. I still don't know if I believe that, but ice skating woke up a dormant part of my soul. The ice and I were one. And it was glorious.

Tanner had done the same thing for me. He'd awakened a part of me buried under the whispers and judgment of my peers. He'd seen me, even dressed in ratty jeans and oversized shirts. He had said he loved me as I was, but then he left.

And that memory makes the anger worse. Because I don't want to be attracted to the man who walked out on me—on us—and said it was for the best. Nothing good will come from that.

I am still shaking as the warning bell rings, and I turn around to face the students flowing into my class. My black pen finds its way into my hands, my thumb clicking it on and off in rapid succession. Skin crawling from all the eyes on me, my gaze flicks to Tanner, who is sitting at his corner desk, a fake smile on his face. His meets mine, stealing my breath again.

You hate him, my head reminds me in an attempt to settle my heart that's doing an Irish jig at having Tanner in my room.

Shoving all thoughts of the past into the dark recesses of my mind, I force my smile onto my face and smooth a wrinkle out of my top.

"Good morning, class. I am Miss Pruitt, and I will be your literature teacher this year." My eyes wander over the students. Most look half asleep, and since it's eight in the morning, that could very well be the case. Almost as if they have a mind of their own, my eyes land on Tanner again. He's half-slouched in his seat, arms crossed over his chest. The action pulls the shoulders of his shirt taut, revealing his muscular arms.

Stop it! I all but scream at myself as I return to teaching.

"This year, I hope to show you some of the wonders of classic and modern literature. My desire is to instill in you a love of literature and reveal beauty that can be found in all levels of books—from middle grade to adult. That being said, we will be starting the semester off with a short middle-grade unit, reading books such as *The Lion, the Witch, and the Wardrobe, Anne of Green Gables, The Giver,* and *Tuck Everlasting.*"

A hand shoots up. Oh, dear. I know her. Gloria Steinfield. Her father is on the school board and a royal pain in the posterior. I cross my arms and lean against the front of my desk as I eye the girl. "Yes, Gloria?"

She seems taken aback that I know her name, but she smiles a saccharine grin and asks, "Are these books on the list of recommended state reading material for *high schoolers?*"

You know they're not. I literally just said they were middle grade! I stifle the words with a smile of my own. But before I can speak, Tanner pipes up.

"Miss Pruitt just told you that it's a middle-grade unit, Gloria. And I do believe it's your *teacher's* discretion to choose what you'll read in literature class." He leans forward, elbows on his knees, and I feel mine start to wobble. All the students' heads turn toward Tanner, and he smiles. It's his fake one, the one he puts on for the reporters and his coaches when he is less than pleased.

I hate this smile. It's not Tanner. It's him hiding, pretending to be okay when he's not. And I hate that I still recognize it after so many years.

Clearing my throat, I wave toward Tanner, saying, "Everyone, this is Mr. Bradshaw. He's the new hockey coach and currently has his office in the back of our room."

A boy—I think his name is Sebastian, but I'd have to check my roster to make sure—was slouching in his seat near the front.

Hearing Tanner's name has him straightening and turning toward the former NHL star. "Wait, you're *the* Tanner Bradshaw?"

Why do people keep doing that? Emphasizing the *the* is ridiculous! He's just Tanner.

I scowl when Gloria's mouth turns into a cherry lip gloss *O* of surprise and awe. The entire class turns to stare at my ex, who sits up straight and meets my gaze as I cross my arms.

Tanner reels in the starstruck students. "Yes, I am Tanner Bradshaw and yes, I'm the new coach. But this class isn't about me and hockey. It's about literature. Now, if you'll direct your attention back to Miss Pruitt, it's time we got started."

"Thank you." I incline my head slightly, a small smile springing onto my lips as Tanner's authentic grin appears.

Would it be so bad to forgive him? a part of me wonders, but now isn't the time. Clearing my throat, I launch into the first class of the school year.

The class is going rather well if I do say so myself. I hand out a syllabus with the material we'll be covering in class, as well as a list of books I think every senior should read. It doesn't mean they will, but I will give extra credit for each one they read and write a report on—particularly the ones listed under classic American and British Literature. Even I have to admit that a number of those are boring.

A few of the students look up from their papers with giant grins on their faces. All I want is for kids to have a healthy breadth of literature under their belts. That's what my old literature teacher had done for me, and I aim to continue her legacy.

The bell for the end of the period rings, and the students leap up, shoving their papers into bookbags and slinging them over their shoulders. I watch, already exhausted, as they shuffle out the door.

That was only first period? I stifle a groan and take a long sip of my lukewarm caramel latte.

"You did good, Mols." Tanner steps up to my desk, rapping his knuckles against it.

He looks everywhere but at me. Why do I want him to look at me? It is like his baby blues are the sun, pulling me and everyone else into orbit around him. It is infuriating and irresistible.

You will resist it, Molly Elaine Pruitt, because he broke your heart once already. He's not allowed to do it again.

Yet, the moment his eyes meet mine, I know it's hopeless. I'm caught in the riptide of his gaze, and there's no breaking free.

Tanner clears his throat. "I didn't overstep, did I?"

I blink. No, he didn't. I actually appreciated the help. But there is no way I am ever telling *him* that. I might not be able to ignore his gaze, but I sure as heck can avoid puffing up his already overinflated ego. "It was...fine."

That infernal smirk twists his lips. "Fine?"

"Yes, fine! Do you need hearing aids?"

He chuckles, and I'm yanked to the past. To the first day I officially met Tanner James Bradshaw. The day he took hold of my heart.

Being a freshman sucks.

You're at the lowest end of the pecking order. You're the fresh meat in a pack of starving wolves. You're the gum on the proverbial heel of literally everyone—including those who were supposed to be in your corner.

I hunch my shoulders, hoping Ryder's old jean jacket hides me as I shoulder through the mass of students in the hall. I'm attempting to locate my literature class, but it's proving impossible. Tears gather in the corner of my eyes as I glance at my watch. I have to blink rapidly before I can see the numbers. Only an hour left until the end of the day, thank heaven. I'd been late to two classes because I got lost in the craziness that is the hallways of this annoyingly large school. Thankfully, both teachers had given me some grace.

The warning bell rings right as I find the doors and push inside. Every head turns. I stop so abruptly that the door slams into my back, causing me to stumble forward and trip over my shoelace that had come undone at some point during the day. I fall, my bookbag slipping off my shoulder and spilling all over the yellow tiles.

I want to dissolve into sobs as I push to my knees. Can this day get any worse?

"Here, let me help," a kind voice says. I blink up into sparkling-blue eyes, the kind that are impossible to look away from. The boy flicks a strand of hair off his brow, smiling a lopsided grin that has a dimple appearing on the left side of his cheek. "I think you might be in the wrong class?" he offers, still smiling.

"Is this literature?"

"Yeah, but it's honors lit."

"Then I'm in the right class." I duck my head, shoving my pencil case back into my bag. "I'm a few years ahead in literature."

He laughs, and it's low and deep and seems to race across my arms like warm water in the shower. I peek up at him through my curtain of hair, a smile of my own tugging on my lips. "I'm Molly Pruitt, by the way."

"Oh, are your brothers Ryley and Ryder?" He pushes to his feet and offers me his hand. It's callused and rough, a comfort against my thin fingers.

I nod, realizing I'd failed to answer his question. "Yeah, they're my brothers."

"We play on the Cougars together." The boy shoves his hands into his back pockets. His sweatshirt hides his frame, but if he plays hockey, I'm certain he's in shape. Coach Reynolds accepts nothing less. The twins complain about it daily.

"I'll have to catch more practices then." I force a smile. Reynolds won't let girls play on his team. I know. Even though I checked, and there's nothing in the Iowa High School Hockey Association rules about it, he is adamant it's not safe.

"Do you play?" He motions for me to follow him.

"Not for the school." I can't bite back the bitterness before it leaches into my words. "But I play on our pond in the winter. My brothers, Dad, and I."

"Not your mom?" He plops into his seat which is next to an open one that I slide into.

I snort. "She's more into figure skating." Which is fine. Figure skating is hard work, nothing to scoff at. But I'd much rather be cross-checking dudes into the boards and whacking them with sticks than doing a double axel.

He laughs right as the tardy bell sounds, and the teacher sails in.

I realize I never got his name...

"Mols?"

I shake my head, scowling at Tanner whose brows are raised in what I hope is fear. But it's likely he's laughing at me behind that shocked exterior. The man always knew how to make fun of me in the gentlest way possible—which infuriated me while making me laugh right along with him. He helped me embrace my quirks. Now, they seem all the more glaring in the light of his twinkling gaze.

Tanner cocks his head to the side, crossing his arms so the fabric of his shirt pulls against his well-muscled biceps once again. It should be illegal. Or at the very least carry a hefty fine for...indecent exposure toward an angry female?

"When's your lunch?" he asks.

"I don't know, and even if I did, I wouldn't want to eat it with you." I jut my chin out, trying to hide the way my heart is racing, and my hands are shaking—not only from Tanner's... Tanner-ness but also from that memory. Why, oh, why, did *that* specific one have to return after five years of suppression? I didn't miss him for the last five years, and I sure as heck don't need any more friends in my life, now.

"Okay." He smiles, but his dimple fails to appear as he slings his bag over his shoulder. Not that my poor heart could have taken it. Dimples are my kryptonite. "I'm headed to look at the equipment the school has for me in the gym. I'll be back after the next class."

With a nod, I turn to my computer, pretending to not notice the way he stares at me for a long second before striding out the door. My body shudders, and I pillow my forehead on my crossed arms.

This is going to be one heck of a long school year.

Chapter Six

Tanner

After the final bell of the day, I practically sprint from the building, slouching forward in my car to lean my head against the steering wheel. That had been a living hell. Trapped in the back of Molly's room, watching as the woman, I up and left, talked to students about her greatest passion. It was as if I'd been ripped through time back to high school when Molly had been a bubbly tomboy who loved hockey, skating, and of course, her books.

I breathe deeply, sucking in the hot leather interior, and hold it. My mind is racing. It doesn't happen often, but when it does, this is the only trick I've found to calm myself down. Just as my chest begins to ache with a painful intensity, I let it out in a slow, measured count, releasing the tension that's wrapped itself up and down my spine in its viselike grip.

"I need coffee!" I declare to the cactus bobble on my dashboard. His sunglasses and pink flower wiggle as I flick it and start the car.

Pulling out, I head to Sweetie's and order my usual—an iced vanilla latte with an extra pump of vanilla flavoring. Breathing deeply of the sweet treat that is vastly different from my normal black coffee in the mornings, I turn and head back to my car. The Rink is calling, and if I'm being honest, I'm ready to be on skates again.

Since the surgery to fix the tendons in my leg six months ago, I haven't let myself skate. The fear of wrecking all the healing and therapy I'd gone through had made my legs shake and my heart race.

My chest still aches at the thought of lacing up and hitting the ice, but the rest of my body coils with eager anticipation at the thought of racing across the slick surface of the Rink, of holding a stick and smacking pucks to the far net simply to relieve the tension twining through my arms and back. I want to fly—but my wings have been cut. The thing that brought so much joy is now the cause of so much pain.

My traitorous thoughts flick to Molly. The way her eyes glow as she talks about literature. About Poe and Lowry and L.M. Montgomery. She used to look at me that way.

But you thoroughly burnt that bridge. I curse, punching the top of the steering wheel. If I had to describe nineteen-year-old me, I would say I was a boxer, and Molly's heart had been the punching bag. I was the blade of a skate, cutting up the pristine surface of her life. The nail in the tire, the bulldozer to the building, the jackhammer to the concrete.

Before my analogies can get worse, I grab my duffle bag from the backseat and head into the Rink.

Rick had given me a key when he heard that I was the new coach for the Cloverfield Cougars. I step through the door. The cool temperature fills my lungs as I breathe in the scent of stale popcorn and sweat—a smell that strangely feels like coming home. Any apprehension I have about this job melts away like ice in the sunshine.

I'm hit by an old memory; one I didn't even realize I had stored away.

I sit on the bench, watching a couple other freshmen cut across the ice, hitting pucks, and performing maneuvers I can do in my sleep. My hands feel sweaty in my gloves. My stomach churns as I watch one guy blast the puck into the net, the goalie helpless to stop it.

This is my first tryout for the Cloverfield Cougars. Before now, I've played for years in junior leagues. All through elementary and middle school, hockey has been my sport. It is like breathing. The thought of not getting to play for my school? I can't stand it.

"Bradshaw!" Coach Reynolds calls. "You're up."

I jump the bench wall and skate to center ice. A few of the current team members set up for some three-on-three. Two guys who look eerily like each other stand on either side of me. We make up the opposing team.

Coach Reynolds holds the puck up, and I slide into place for a face-off.

Gentry—the team captain last year—sneers as he bends down, stick at the ready. "You're going down, Bradshaw."

I smile as Coach drops the puck, and I slap it over to the guy on my left. He takes control and drives down the ice like a bat out of hell with me on his right, the other guy on his left.

"Ry! Over here!" my team member calls, and Ry shoots it to him. He glides closer still as one of our opponents drives hard toward him.

"Here!" I shout and feel the puck hit my blade. I turn—keeping control of the puck as another player tries to swoop in from the left—and take my shot.

I'm still not entirely sure how it happens, but somehow it makes it in. A cheer rises from the bench. I grin as Coach Reynolds claps and says, "Very good! I'm impressed."

"So am I!" One of my teammates skates up. "Ryley and I have been playing together since diaper days, but you fit right in with us."

"And you're only going out for the team now?" I ask pulling off my helmet and swiping at the sweat on my upper lip.

The guy grins. "We had other hobbies for a long time. But since Gramps owns the Rink, we decided it was time."

"Wait...you're Rick Pruitt's grandsons?" I shake my head. "Wow! I would have thought he'd have had you on the ice by the time you could walk."

"He did!" Ryley—Ry—says with a laugh as he skates over. "Mom, however, didn't love the idea of contact sports in elementary school."

"She's not wrong," the other guy states with a low chuckle. "I'm Ryder, by the way."

He holds his hand out, and I shake it. "I'm Tanner. Tanner Bradshaw."

That was the day I became friends with the Pruitt twins. The day I got placed on the Cloverfield Cougars. The day that changed everything.

With a sigh that pushes back the memories, I turn on my phone flashlight and maneuver to the ticket counter. There is a master switch for the lights, and I push it on, the *chunk* of the lights echoing through the empty building. It's amazing the memories this space holds for me. My first hockey game in Peewee League. My first time watching a professional league game. Watching my one and only figure skating competition...but I don't want to think about that. I can't let myself think about that. It hurts. My stupidity makes my head ache, and I need to be with it.

With the lights on, I move to the locker room where I change into my track pants and Houston Comets sweatshirt. Then I lace on my skates. I stare at my feet for a solid minute and question my sanity. Am I ready? I love hockey and kids without a doubt—otherwise, I definitely wouldn't be here. But is it really time to bury my professional dream and teach high schoolers?

I slide onto the ice and feel my leg muscles tighten. Taking a couple laps, I work on loosening my body while it screams at me for not stretching it in months. I find my rhythm, allowing my imagination to produce muffled cheers of a crowd. They roar in my ears along with the whistles of the refs, the swish of skates against the ice, and the slashes and *thwacks* of the sticks as my team and I fight for position of the puck. I pause my warm-ups, sliding to stand in the middle of the ice and breathe in the frosty air.

The memories I've been trying to keep at bay rush me. The Comets, the Cougars. Both my teams—so different, yet so similar. The games, the coaches, the crowds, the cameras, the reporters...

Desire knifes through my chest—white and hot—and I groan, burying my fingers in my hair. It's a longing I can't satisfy. Yeah, I can coach until I'm so old that being on the ice could result in a broken hip, but I'll never be a *player* on the ice ever again. I'm done. I'm not the legendary hockey player that gets to play for seasons upon seasons. I'm not a Jaromir Jagr or a Joe Thornton. I'm a nobody. A washout.

I turn and skate again, hard and fast. I can outrun the memories, the longing, the pain. If I move fast enough, work hard enough, I can leave it all behind me. It will go away if I can run, run, run, and never look back.

"Lookin' good there, ol' man."

Rick Pruitt leans against the opening to the ice, and I slide to a stop beside him, wincing at the dull throb that shoots up into my hip. That was probably a dumb move.

"Who you calling old, Rick?" I chuckle as he raises a brow at me. "I'm a young whippersnapper."

"Ha. In spirit maybe." His grin grows, taking up so much of his face that his eyes nearly vanish in the mess of wrinkles and bushy gray brows. "But I have the body you wish you had!"

I can't help but laugh. Rick is skinny—probably too skinny. But he stands straight and tall and has a swagger that must come with the confidence of being over eighty and knowing no one will tell you *not* to do something. But a wisdom radiates off Rick, too. Like he sees and knows more than everyone around him. Which, to be fair, he probably does. The man can be downright freaky sometimes.

"Doesn't practice start tomrrow?" he asks as I waddle to the benches and unlace my skates. The muscles in my leg object the movement, but I ignore them.

"Yeah. Trying to see how long I can stay on the ice before the leg starts to protest." I glance at my watch, scowling when the display lights up. Only an hour. Not nearly long enough.

"Tanner, let me tell you something my wise wife told me back when I was probably a bit older than you and broke my leg." He settles beside me on the bleacher and clasps my good leg until I turn to meet his gaze. "Healing takes time. Whether physical, emotional, or mental, it's a process. To rush it can hurt you more in the long run."

Why does it feel like he isn't just talking about my messed-up leg? I breathe in deeply before slowly exhaling. "I know. I won't push myself on my leg."

"Good." He slaps my shoulder with a grin. "And just remember, I'm here if you ever need to talk. Healing, coaching, life, I'm pretty well-versed in it all." He grins, his cocoa eyes sparkling in the dim lights of the Rink. "And I'll never turn down extra help in the fixing department."

I laugh as I place the guards back on my skates and shove them into my bag. "Good to know. Thanks, Rick."

"You heading out?" he asks as I sling the strap over my shoulder.

"Yeah. Need to get more coffee and go over what I need to order for equipment so I can put in a request form." I grimace. Paperwork is the one side of coaching I am dreading.

Rick smiles sympathetically. "That was my Elsie's job before she passed. Now it's Mabel." His brow furrows, and he turns a little pale at the mention of his daughter-in-law. "She's a lot more nitpicky than my El ever was."

I chuckle, a small pang of sorrow hitting my chest at the memory of Elsie Pruitt. She'd been a whirlwind wrapped in a hurricane trapped inside the bottle that was her five-foot-three frame. With her sea-green eyes and red hair that gave Anne Shirley a run for her money—and that none of her kids nor her grandkids had inherited—she was a feisty, kindhearted soul. She'd all but adopted me as her grandson when she'd heard that all of my grandparents had died before I was born. She didn't take no for an answer, was stubborn to a fault, and all around was a lot like me. It broke my heart when I heard from Mom that she had passed away my first year on the Comets, but since she wasn't family, I hadn't been allowed to come home for the funeral.

I swallow down the all-too-familiar lump of regret and force a smile for Rick. "I bet. If Mabel is still as stubborn as Molly, I bet you have loads of fun."

"I do indeed." He grins, looking far too much like that cartoon boy hatching a plan with his stuffed tiger to attack the girl down the street, and rubs his callused hands together. "And yet my son backs me one hundred percent."

I laugh for real and shake my head. "Good luck with that, Rick."

"See ya around, ol' man." He winks and saunters off.

Chapter Seven

Molly

The next morning comes, and I walk briskly down the hall with a study pack for the first book in the middle-grade unit tucked under my arm. I'd settled on a simple first book—*Tuck Everlasting*. Short, but with a solid message for the readers. Simple language, but with an impactful story. I smile as I hum a few of the tunes from the little-known musical as I push into my room.

I draw up short when I see Tanner already in his corner. His hand is buried in his hair, his shoulders hunched as he scribbles something in a journal open on his desk. It doesn't look like anything important, but seeing as I don't want to interact with the infuriating man any more than strictly necessary, I move toward my desk. I curse my choice of footwear—four-inch red heels to offset my black blazer and slacks—when Tanner's head snaps up.

"Good, you're here." He smiles, soft and hesitant, like he expects me to lash out.

Smart man. "Where else would I be?"

His smile hitches up on the left side, and I turn away, settling my packets on my desk as an excuse not to look at him.

"Good morning," he says in reply, standing and shoving his hands into his navy dress pants. He walks over, and I barely notice him favoring his bad leg. But I still notice and mutter a curse under my breath because I did.

Tanner settles onto the corner of my desk and watches as I unpack my briefcase. "How was your evening?"

"It was fine." I interlock my fingers and settle them before me as I straighten to my full height. "Yours?"

"Went to the Rink. Skated a bit to see how my dud can keep up." He pats his left thigh with a self-deprecating scoff. "It can't."

I am not sure what he wants me to say to that, so I settle on, "Sorry."

He shrugs. "Crap happens. Life goes on. You either move with it or get steamrolled by it."

Bleak outlook, but I can't imagine an injury happening that will knock me out of my dream. I clear my throat as the bell rings. "Ready for the day?"

Red alert! A caring question! Retract! Retract!

Tanner nods, but a fake smile settles on his lips as students pour through the door. He turns back to his desk, his shoulders slumping.

What the heck? Did my brusque answer hurt that badly? It shouldn't have. Our conversation was small talk. What was he expecting? I rub the back of my neck and sigh. Why are relationships—wait, no! *Friendships.* Why are *friendships* so hard?

Gloria sails in, disrupting my thoughts in a swirl of bubblegum-pink skirt, cotton candy-colored blouse, and a white cardigan. I blink, wondering when the world decided kids could just skip the awkward phase of bad haircuts, ugly clothes, and gaudy makeup. Gloria looks like the China doll my Grandma Elsie had given me for my thirteenth birthday. A little too perfect and polished to be real.

She settles in the exact middle of the classroom. Center of attention. Center of control.

My stomach flips as I smooth my hand over my jacket, straightening it as the final bell rings and the class settles into silence.

"Good morning, everyone. Today, we're going to go over the synopsis of one of my favorite stories, *Tuck Everlasting*." I grin as I pull up a slide with various cover art for the book.

Before I can start, Gloria shoots her hand up into the air, her eyes far too big and innocent for anything good.

"Yes, Gloria?"

"This book wasn't on the recommended list." Her hands are interlocked into a fist and set on top of her desk. She smiles, but it doesn't reach her eyes and makes my skin crawl. "In fact, my mother and I checked, and this is commonly taught in fourth grade. *Fourth grade*, Miss Pruitt."

"Be that as it may, Gloria," I manage through gritted teeth. "This is my classroom. If you have a problem with it, go talk to Principal Skinner. But I have passed these lesson plans by him as well as the other teachers. They have all approved of my plan to teach you common middle-grade books that you may or may not have read in elementary school.

"Furthermore!" I hold up my hand when Gloria opens her mouth. "I have gone to school for literature and looked at the rules for this district." I smile an equally false grin back at her. "I only need to teach five of the recommended books, which I plan on doing. The rest can be whatever I see fit. Will that be all?"

She nods, her gaze hardening when I return it with one of my own and turn back to the board.

"As I was saying, this modern classic has been lauded as a book that is both honest and intelligent in the way it grapples with the issue of aging and death. Since its publication in 1975, *Tuck Everlasting* has sold over five million copies."

I fall into rhythm, going through the overview of the novel, and the individual characters. All too soon for me, the bell rings, and the kids file out of the room. I'm shaking. The high that is gushing over some of the best literature I've ever read sends adrenaline coursing through me. I grab my coffee, gulping a few great swallows as I struggle to calm down.

Although, I'm not certain caffeine is the best choice for a calm-down beverage.

"You come alive when you're talking about books, Mols. Did you know that?" Tanner's smooth voice wraps around me, only causing my tremors to increase. "It's fun to watch."

Traitor, I think to my body, scowling at the creamy beverage through my travel mug's lid. To Tanner I say, "I do know, but I don't want to hear it from you."

He pauses as if he might say more, but he answers with, "You better watch out for Gloria. She seems like trouble."

I bristle. "She is. She's a royal pain in the butt."

"I seem to remember that every class had one of those in high school." He laughs, the sound wrapping around me like a longed-for hug. My back is still to him, and, oh...do I ever want to turn. Want to let him wrap me in his actual arms. They were my safe place my junior year. A place I could be myself. No one telling me what I should or shouldn't do or should and shouldn't be like. I was simply Molly when I was with Tanner.

And yet...he'd walked away. I wasn't enough.

"Thanks for the advice. I'll keep an eye on her." I straighten up and force myself to turn and face him with crossed arms. I won't hug Tanner. Won't launch myself at him. Even if I want to cross that bridge, he burned it years ago.

His jaw, with just a slight bit of stubble across it that I totally don't notice, flexes, and he nods. "Good."

The next group of kids waltzes in, and I prep to teach another class. More young minds to mold and nurture. But I find it harder than first period. My eyes keep wandering to the hunched shoulders that pull the jade-colored dress shirt taut. The hair that he ruffles each time he buries his fingers into it.

And with each passing glance, my temper grows.

You're not allowed to fall back in love with him, Molly Elaine Pruitt. You're not allowing yourself to be hurt again.

CHAPTER EIGHT

Tanner

I head to the Rink after work, eager to meet my team and get to practicing. Partly for the sport itself, but mostly to distract myself from Molly's anger and the restlessness in my soul. It annoys me if I'm being honest. Because it shouldn't be this hard. I was the one who walked away, and I should be over Molly Pruitt. I dated in Houston. Nothing serious, nothing like the feelings Molly stirred up in high school. But I ruined that. Rick said healing takes time, but I don't know if either of us can heal while I'm here in Cloverfield. That might just be too big a wound.

I'm lacing up my skates when the shouts of boys entering the Rink reverberate through the steel rafters. I step from the locker room, feeling my bad leg tighten from balancing on the blades of my skates.

Four young men amble in as if they own the Rink. Two of them look identical, and I blink to make sure I didn't fall and hit my head. Mischievous brown eyes stare at me under mops of curly brown hair. With tanned complexions, towering height, and wide shoulders, they remind me of some of the guys from my high school days—the ones that all the girls went crazy for.

Next to them is a sandy-haired beanpole of a kid with a face full of freckles. He doesn't look like he has an ounce of meat on his bones, but he has a large grin and a loud laugh that make a smile of my own bloom. His blue eyes sparkle in the dim lights of the Rink.

The last boy leans against the boards, his beefy arms crossed over his chest. His ebony eyes hold a world of secrets, and a dark air dares anyone to pry. Which is exactly what I want to do. He looks like he could use a friend.

"Hey, fellas." I step out of the shadows and toss a grin their way. They eye me, assessing me for weakness like a pack of wolves. Oh, I remember being a punk like them. Daring anyone to question me and my skills. It took a domineering presence, one that meant business, to keep me in line back then. Which is exactly what I plan to be. I straighten and cross my arms, still smiling. "Ready for practice?"

"You the new coach?" The kid against the boards asks, pushing off of it to stalk over to me. He's maybe an inch taller, but I won't let him intimidate me.

"Yep." I meet his steely gaze head on. "And I will be addressed as such—Coach or Coach Bradshaw. Got it?"

I wait a beat before turning toward the rink. Pulling off the blade guards, I slide onto the pristine ice. I relish the sound of the steel against the frozen surface, same as yesterday. *Swish, swish, swish.* My eyes flutter closed as I do a lap around the rink. The stiffness remains, but it bends with a bit more ease today. But only a bit.

Don't be an idiot, Bradshaw. Don't jack it up worse, or Mom will have a fit.

I slide to a stop by the door and raise my brows. "Skates on."

The twins spring toward their duffels and retrieve their skates, lacing them on with an impressive speed. Sandy is right behind them, but Angry Boy hasn't moved.

"You plan on playing?" I ask, leaning against the doorframe to try and appear nonchalant.

"You suck or something?" he asks.

My brows shoot skyward. "Excuse me?"

"You heard me. Why'd the NHL let you go?"

"Lay off, Kai!" Sandy says from behind me and the safety of the ice. "Coach hasn't done anything to you."

Kai is scowling at Sandy. Though I may look calm to them, inside my heart is racing. This isn't a situation I'd mentally prepared for. I'm not entirely sure what I'll do if a brawl breaks out between these two. There's no way I can beat the brawn of Kai without backup.

"This ain't between us, Leo. It's between me and the *coach*," he says, his lip curling on the title like he's saying a curse. "I didn't ask for you to come and replace the last coach."

"Is that what this is about?" One of the twins rolls his eyes. "Because he replaced your ancient grandpa, you're gonna get kicked off the team?"

Oh, fantastic. I stifle a sigh. I had wanted Coach Reynolds to do the introduction to the boys, but a heart attack and a few broken ribs from the way he'd fallen when that happened had him stuck in a nursing home. I can understand the hostility from Kai to a certain extent. I don't think I'd be very nice if some upstart replaced my relative either.

Running a hand through my hair, I say, "Listen, Kai. I got injured last year. Messed my leg up pretty bad. But I can coach. You have to know that I got my team to the playoffs and game seven of the conference finals last year. I'm sorry I replaced family, but I'm here now to craft a winning team. We could make it to the playoffs, maybe even state if we push hard enough."

"You think?" Sandy—or Leo, I guess his name is—asks.

"I know." I meet Kai's gaze, seeing a million things the kid isn't saying, but that I'm not smart enough to read. "But we need the best players."

Kai scoffs. "Well, you ain't getting me."

He storms off, muttering under his breath as he does.

"Well, you three." I turn and skate to center ice. "Where's the rest of the team?"

The twins shift, and Leo chuckles. "They'll come once they know they can trust you."

Ouch. But also not unexpected. While it sucks that not more showed up for day one of tryouts, I purposefully planned three days for this very reason. I need them to trust me. Need a team.

I wave my finger at the boys and ask, "And you three do already?"

"We might have lost a bet." One of the twins winces. "Sorry, Coach."

"For losing a bet, or for the others not being here?" I chuckle and wave away the question. "On second thought, don't answer that. I'd like to escape here with some dignity."

The twins' matching smiles appear, and one of them skates forward. "I'm Luke. It's nice to meet you, sir."

I shake his hand as his brother moves behind him. "And I'm Carter. It's an honor to meet you, Coach Bradshaw, sir."

"And I'm Leo, but I guess you figured that out." The kid is skating backwards, hands clasped behind his back. "This is my first year trying out for varsity."

"Well, as of right now, I'm planning on giving you all starting positions since you're the only ones who bothered to show up."

Luke shrugs. "I've started most of my high school career."

"What position?" I skate over to the bench and sit down. My leg protests, and I swallow a wince as I pluck up the clipboard Rick left for me.

Luke leans against the edge of the board. "Left defense was primary, but I'm pretty good at both sides of defense and forward as a left wing."

"I'm usually a forward—at least at a JV level." Leo swings over the bench wall, perches on the edge, and kicks his legs as he watches me write.

Carter props his elbows next to his brother. "I'm a goalie."

I eye him. "I'd like to test that."

He nods and says nothing more.

"So...practice?" Leo grins.

"Practice," I agree.

Chapter Nine

Molly

The hiss of the espresso machine echoes around Sweetie's as I sink into a booth and open my laptop. I glance out the front window and wait for my computer to load. There's nothing I'd rather do than hightail it back home to veg in front of the TV or with the new book that arrived yesterday (Susan had given me a hard time about it since my shelves are bursting at the seams, and books are stacking up on the floor around my bed). But alas...there are lessons to be planned. It might only be the second day of school, but I aim to keep up on them. If I learned anything from student teaching, it was that.

Taking a sip of my caramel latte, I startle as the tiny bell above the shop's door rings. A whole mess of teenage boys traipses in. The clear ringleader of the group, Owen Tucker, flashes me a smile. I babysat him when I was in high school, and he'd been a terror child. I came home exhausted every time I watched him and his younger sister, Lydia.

He hurries up the counter, leaning his elbow against the pastry case and sweet-talking Sweetie like the charmer he is. Owen is good-looking and knows it. His charm is part of the reason he was the captain of the hockey team last year.

Hockey. I glance at my smartwatch, my brows lowering as 3:45 flashes up at me. My jaw tenses. *Those little—*

I push to my feet, stalking all of my five-foot, three-inch self up to the six-foot captain. "Do you mind telling me what you're doing here?" I swing my gaze over the rest of the guys. "All of you?"

Owen turns from taking his coffee from Sweetie, his arms crossing as best he can with the hot cup. The rest of the guys take a collective step back, their eyes finding anything and anyone to look at but Owen and me.

"What are you talking about?" His brow rises, and I curse my inability to raise mine. He plays himself off as tough, but I know my silver tongue can whip him back into shape.

"Practice?" I ask. "Doesn't the first practice of the season start today? What's going on, Owen?"

"We're proving a point to the new coach." Owen juts out his chin, but I don't miss the way he flinches as my eyes narrow. "He can't just waltz in from the NHL and take over our team!"

What a little— I pinch the bridge of my nose. I'm not entirely certain why the urge to defend Tanner, of all people, takes hold of me. He's the one who took off and left me here alone. But something in me rankles at the thought of these boys disrespecting such an amazing athlete. Yes, I said it. Amazing. Sue me for admiring skill...and fine shoulder muscles.

"The fact that he is a former NHL star should be the very reason you flock to the Rink for practice today." I jab Owen in the bicep, imagining that it's my thoughts about Tanner and I'm poking them back into place.

Owen looks over his shoulder at his friends. "We don't trust him."

Can't say I blame them there, I think sullenly, while out loud, I say, "You haven't given him a chance."

All the boys cross their arms, looking like a bunch of reprimanded kindergarteners. Indignation rushes through me, and I make up my mind. "Get in your cars. Now."

Owen looks at me, his eyes filled with questions. His mouth opens, but my temper is spent. Turning my back on him, I march over to my booth to pack up my workstation—where nothing actually got done. I stack my binder, my laptop, my pencil case, and with each item I order, "Get. In. Your. Cars!"

When no one moves, I jab my finger at the door. "*Now!*"

"Where are we—" one of the boys starts, moving like he's stuck in molasses or maple syrup.

"To the Rink." I let myself feel the flip in my stomach for a moment before shoving it back into place. "You have a practice to be at."

Surprisingly, they all tromp out of Sweetie's. Although, I get a number of dirty looks as they do. The boys pile into the half-dozen vehicles in the lot. I slide into mine, taking a long draw on my latte before following behind the impromptu parade of sports cars, SUVs, and trucks.

The whole way to the Rink, I clench the steering wheel. My fingers are turning white from the pressure, but I can't seem to release my grip. This is the right thing to do. I know it is. But why is my stomach flipping like a trapeze artist on speed? My throat tightens as the giant sign that spells out R-I-N-K in big black letters comes into view. Oh. Maybe that's why. This has nothing to do with Tanner, and everything to do with the fact that I haven't been inside the Rink in over three years—ever since the twins played their last college game.

I step out of my car, coffee in hand. I take another sip and straighten as well as I can on my ridiculously tall heels. Seriously, morning Molly had a lot more faith in her ability to remain upright in these shoes all day than afternoon Molly does. But a bit of power threads into me as I stalk forward, the heels clicking against the cracked asphalt and punctuating my finger point at the glass doors of the Rink. I barely suppress my smirk as the pack of sheepish boys slinks inside.

Molly: One.

Bratty Teens: Zero.

The cool air washes over me as I follow after them, and the glass door shuts behind me with a *click* that resonates in my bones. I feel trapped. Balling my free hand into a fist, I force myself to breathe. *I'm fine,* I tell myself, yet I'm coiled tighter than a spring. I head toward the gap in the boards that leads to the ice. The hum of the lights and the chiller ring in my ears, and I remember why I love this place. Because I really do love the Rink. It's the memories that are the deterrent.

Because Tanner is everywhere here: in the stands, on the ice, under the counter in the snack bar. The whispered conversations, the stolen kisses, the first time he held my hand. Even our first official date was here. the Rink is almost synonymous with *Tanner* at this point.

And there he is, skating by the boards, blowing a whistle, and coaching three boys even though he'd been promised a team. *Coach* looks good on him. He's changed into sweats and a hoodie with Houston's logo of a fiery puck, yet he somehow manages to still look incredibly sexy in the casual wear. His skates glide with an ease I envy. There is no way I'll be that coordinated if I ever put skates back on.

Stop it! You're angry at him! But I'm not. Not really. It's more that I'm sad, remembering what we'd had. What we'd wanted and dreamed of before Tanner's delusions of grandeur actually came true.

I cross my arms over my chest and inhale sharply of the frosty air before striding onto the ice.

Don't faceplant. Don't faceplant! Because that would be a Molly entrance and we're going for strong and confident. Not...whatever I am right now.

"Hey, Coach. I brought your delinquents."

Tanner's head whips toward me, his gaze tugging me closer. But I resist. Barely.

"What are you talking about?" he asks. His forehead wrinkles, and one side of his mouth raises just a touch higher than normal.

Dang, he's attractive when he's confused. I moisten my lips with the tip of my tongue as I point with my thumb over my shoulder. "Your team, Coach."

Tanner glances behind me, his confusion melting fully into his crooked smirk. It twists the heart he took a chunk of when he ran off to Houston.

"So, the mighty Molly Pruitt got the team to the Rink." He braces his hands against the edge of the boards, his smirk turning into more of a grimace. "Thanks."

I turn to watch the team slide onto the ice. They all cast glances at Tanner, wariness on their features. Jutting my chin toward them, I state, "You're going to have your work cut out for you. They've told me they don't trust you."

"I'm aware." He shoves his hands into his back pockets and glides toward me. "But I'm not scared of challenges. They rather appeal to me."

He's close, so close I can almost feel the heat radiating off of him. I gulp. I'm fully aware of the effect this man has on me. Fully. Aware. And that's the problem. Because what if there is a double meaning to his words? I shake my head and force a smile.

"Well, have fun with that." I turn, shuffling toward solid ground. How had I been a figure skater? Although, I am in four-inch heels. Add in Tanner Bradshaw staring at my back and yeah, this equation is just an accident waiting to happen.

"Hey, Mols?"

I freeze, sliding a bit at my abrupt halt, but I refuse to look at him. If I turn, I'll throw myself into his arms—yeah, that's the effect of the Rink on my psyche—and honestly, I am trying to maintain a modicum of dignity here.

The gentle *swoosh* of the skates is accompanied by a soft question. "Hidden in any cupboards lately?"

Shoulder against shoulder. A hand entwined with mine. The smell of musty wood, cotton candy, and fresh pretzels. The memory slams into me, and I almost crumple at the force of it. I have to get away. From Tanner, the ice, and the dull *thwacks* of sticks against pucks.

I manage to slide off the ice without twisting my ankle and hurry down the dark hall to the Snack Counter. I have to see if it is still here, still like the memory burned into my mind so vividly. I fumble with my keyring, find the right one, and let myself into the small kitchen space where Grams had served snacks, candy, and soda to all the fans. My breath rushes out in a giant exhale. This place hasn't changed in fifty years. The old, scuffed cabinets still boast the bright-yellow laminate counters on top of them.

I lean against the door, staring at the corner cabinet like I am seeing a ghost. I kind of am...the ghost of a hockey season long since past.

I tug my legs closer to my chest, pressing my face against my bony kneecaps. My sobs are mostly muffled by the noise in the Snack Counter. Grams is busy taking orders and shouting at Gramps to get a pretzel with cheese. Ryley and Ryder are out on the ice with their college team, Mom and Dad in the stands cheering for them. No one notices me squirreled away in the corner cabinet.

Sixteen and small enough to fit under a cabinet. Sixteen and with only one friend—who is headed for college in a few months. Sixteen and the butt of a number of cruel and inappropriate jokes at the behest of the seniors.

A light knock sounds on the door, and I crack it enough to see blue eyes and a lopsided smile. "Can I come in?"

I shake my head, but with no way to hold the cabinet closed, Tanner Bradshaw pulls it open and somehow contorts his massive body inside with me. Thankfully, the cabinets don't have walls between them, nor do they have shelves. Tanner's knees brush the top of the counter, and he scoots until his back hits the wall, though his legs are still curled to his chest.

"What's wrong, Mols?" he asks. His knee bumps mine, sending chills down my arms and neck.

"Nothing." I sniff, betraying the depth of my emotions.

He shifts and his shoulder presses into mine as he settles against the wall. "It's not nothing if you're hiding in the Snack Counter. Trust me, I know."

I laugh, snuffling in an attempt to stop the tears that are still sliding down my face. "You sound as if you're speaking from experience."

"Oh, I am." He leans closer, his voice dropping to a whisper. "I'm a pro at hiding."

"Oh?" I reply weakly.

"Yeah, and I can give you an example if you want." His hand brushes against the back of mine, and I sense him shifting closer—though I'm not sure how in our already cramped space.

"Um...sure?" My voice squeaks, and I hate it. "How do you hide?"

"The question should be *what*, Mols." Laughter taints his words, and now I know he's teasing me.

I huff a breath of exasperation. "Fine. *What* have you been hiding?"

"I've been trying to hide the fact that I think you're the prettiest girl in the school." All humor has left his voice. Warmth slides through me, but this isn't embarrassment like it had been out in the Rink. This warmth has my toes curling in my boots and a small smile blooming on my lips.

Tanner's forehead bumps my temple, his breath warm against my cheek as he asks, "Will you go on a date with me?"

I freeze. Tanner and I are friends—of a sort. While I like that he thinks I'm pretty, another part of me shivers at the thought of anything more with him. Because that means things have to change, and I hate change. Crossing the line of friendship feels like the tearing up of something classic and comfortable and refitting it with itchy, awkward newness.

Yet sitting under the cabinet, in the one place that has ever made me feel special and unique, without the lights and the bustle and the chaos of the world around us, with Tanner Bradshaw at my side saying he wants to date me...it has me leaning my head against his shoulder. For just a moment, I dare to let my walls down and embrace the change.

After a few minutes, I swallow and ask, "You don't think...you don't think I'm a—" I whisper the vulgarity I'd heard in the Rink's stands.

Tanner's body coils with anger. "Who said that about you?"

"It's not important." I grab his arm as he shifts forward, likely off to break some noses. "Tanner, don't."

He pauses. "Is that really what you want, Mols?"

"Yes."

With a sigh, he leans back.

I settle my head on his shoulder once more, a single tear escaping my closed eyes. "Will you please stay here with me?"

Despite the darkness, he reaches out and threads his fingers with mine. "You sure you want that?"

"Yeah." I swallow the lump in my throat and squeeze his hand. "I'm sure."

The buzzing of my cell in my back pocket jerks me back to the present. I stare at it for a full ten seconds before focusing on the caller's name—*Susan Fenton.*

I fumble with it for a moment before hitting *accept.* "Hello?"

"Where the heck are you?"

"I'm at the Rink." I choke on the name, but Susan's squeal of delight keeps me from going into full-on panic mode at the memories. "Why are you squealing?"

"You're taking Ava up on her offer, right?" Susan clears her throat when I don't immediately respond. "Right, Molly?"

"Not...exactly."

"Then what, exactly?" I can picture Susan propping one fist on her hip and glaring at me, even on a phone call.

"I was bringing some delinquent hockey players to their coach."

A long silence stretches, and I pull the phone away to check and make sure the call didn't drop. "Sue? Are you there?"

"You and Tanner are at the Rink with just the hockey jocks?"

I hate when she calls them that. She doesn't understand hockey or the guys who play it. Though I've never really bothered to correct her either. Susan has always been more into men who can match her wit, who aren't scared of her verbal crossfire and who fire right back.

"I'm with the *hockey players* and their *coach*." If I think about Tanner as the kids' coach, it will be easier to navigate whatever our professional relationship has to be. Because I refuse to fall for the same man twice. Especially when he crushed me so badly the first time.

Been there. Done that. No thanks.

"Well, get your butt home," Susan orders. The sound of the oven beeping carries over the phone. "I made your favorite cookies, and if you're not home in the next hour, I'm eating them all."

"You made peanut butter cookies?" I grin. Susan can't eat peanuts. It isn't a deathly dangerous allergy—cross-contamination is fine, which is why we even dare to have a jar of peanut butter in the house in the first place. But for her to make a cookie she can't sample first is a sign of true love and devotion.

"I did. So, you better hurry." She sounds grumpy about it.

I laugh. "I'm coming! Don't kill yourself."

Saying goodbye, I turn, fling open the door to the Snack Counter, and immediately slam into a chest.

An incredibly solid chest.

I'm only saved by a hand catching my waist while my palms land on pecs I have no business touching. I gulp as the spicy scent of pine and spearmint envelops me—a scent I'm well-versed in. My eyes slide closed.

Oh dear.

Oh dear, oh dear, oh dear. This is bad. So very bad. But...why does it feel so good?

I feel Tanner's chuckle through my palms. It races up my arms, settling in my chest. I don't want to step back. This is like the corner cabinet all over again. It's safe.

But Tanner is anything but safe.

"Twice in two days?" he asks. "Are you trying to throw yourself at me, Mols?"

That breaks the spell.

"Don't you wish, Bradshaw!" I snap back, stepping out of his arms so fast my spine hits against the doorframe. I stifle a curse, rubbing at the sore spot that will probably bruise my ridiculously sensitive skin. But it's worth it because I get to see the surprised look on Tanner's face as his eyes widen, and one brow hops up.

I forgot you could do it, too! I bemoan the fact that I can't raise my brow before sliding around him. "If I don't get back to my house, my roommate is going to kill herself with peanut butter cookies."

"Wait, she'll what?" he calls after me, causing a laugh to slip out. It's great to bewilder him again. I haven't gotten to do that in ages, and I laugh again when I picture his wide-eyed confusion. I fairly skip out to my car.

But then I freeze, my hand on the door handle.

No way! I fell for it! I fell for the smooth laugh, soft eyes, and those charming looks. I absolutely refuse to let him sway me.

He left once before, and he could easily do it again, I remind myself, with a nod of agreement to...me.

Steeling my heart against the charismatic ex-hockey player will be hard, but I will manage. I won't get hurt again.

Chapter Ten

Tanner

She is a whirlwind. I watch Molly's retreating form for a moment before heading back to the ice. The boys already have their sticks out. No pads, which is fine. I'd rather see their accuracy shooting before we get to the defensive side of things.

"Alright, boys," I call, leaning against the rail around the bench. I only catch Luke and Carter's attention. Luke whistles and motions to me, and the rest of the team skates over and stops in a semicircle around me. My stomach clenches at the varying degrees of expressions on their faces. Some smile, some scowl, a few have warily guarded looks as they size me up.

This is a whole different game—being a coach. Ineptness presses against my shoulders. But one thought of Molly's blazing gaze as she marched these boys to the Rink has me shrugging off all disparaging thoughts as I stand a bit straighter. My leg twinges in protest, but I ignore it. Now isn't the time to get cold feet—although, my toes do feel a touch frosty at the moment...

Crossing my arms, I study the twelve boys before me. It is a good variance of sizes and builds. I can already tell that Owen leads the pack, but Luke is a silent challenger to his dominance. The boys respect Luke, and I think I may be able to work with that.

"Well, *Coach*?" Owen asks, a slight curl to his lips.

I meet his gaze, and my retort flees. His eyes startle me. They're a hazel color—more green than brown—except half of the iris of his left eye is a deep mahogany.

Owen scoffs and rolls his disconcerting eyes, snapping me from my stupor. "You done gawking?"

"Yeah." I clear my throat as a few chuckles ripple through the boys. "First, I want to thank you all for deciding to give me a chance. I'm not your old coach, but I hope I can lead us to the championship in March."

"We'll do our best, Coach!" Leo whoops.

With a chuckle, I heft a five-gallon bucket of pucks over the barrier. "I want to see you shoot."

Owen's gaze narrows. "Don't you want to know what position we play?"

Seriously, who does this kid think he is? Little punk better get it through his thick head real quick that he may be captain, but he's not in charge. I'm the one who calls the shots.

"I know what I want, Owen. Take turns passing it down the ice and shooting at the goal."

With another eye roll, Owen snaps at a skinny kid with shaggy brown hair. The kid grabs a puck, pausing a minute to say, "I'm Wyatt Stephens, Coach."

I nod and jot his name down on my clipboard besides Carter's, Luke's, and Leo's.

Begrudgingly, I admit that Owen looks like he was born on skates. He glides across the ice with a subtle grace that's unusual in guys his size. He stops a few feet from the net as Wyatt drops the puck.

The scrawnier kid handles the puck for a moment before passing it to Owen. He skates down the ice as Owen follows, the puck moving fast under his blade. Owen slaps it to Wyatt, who easily takes control once more as Owen races down to the net. Wyatt passes, and Owen slams it into the net. They glide over to the rest of the group, eyeing me as they do.

I drop my gaze to my clipboard, writing my observations even as I keep an eye on the former captain of the team. He crosses his arms, the shaft of his stick tucked into his elbow.

"Good. Next," I call, not giving the arrogant little turd a second glance. He tenses, but I don't acknowledge it.

As he skates to the far side of the ice, I rub the back of my neck.

This is going to be one heck of a long year.

I flop onto Mom's sofa with a groan. Propping my foot onto the coffee table, I lean forward to rub at the tense muscles. Sweet mercy, this is annoying. I used to skate every day. Even if I didn't have practice, I used to skate around the arena or rink we were playing at and just...think. Now, two days on skates has the scar tissue flaring in irritation and me stifling a barrage of curses at the stupid luck of one bad hit.

Mom putters around the kitchen, sighs escaping her like she's a deflating beach ball. I know what this is. She wants to berate me for pushing myself too hard but is refraining. Barely.

After the tenth sigh, I can't take it anymore. Propping my arm against the back of the sofa, I turn and raise my brow at her. "Something on your mind, Mother?"

She cuts me a searing look of reproach. "Don't get sassy with me, boy. I can still turn you over my knee."

My gaze rakes over her slight, five-foot frame. I am easily double her weight. With a snort of a chuckle, I state, "I feel the sudden urge to be sassy. It could be interesting."

"Hush it!" She laughs as she grabs the kettle and fills it in the sink. The laugh peters out into another sigh as she stares out into the backyard. Fields lay behind and beside us on our dead-end road. It's quiet. Tranquil. And it's slightly stifling when one is used to city life.

But in some ways, I wouldn't trade my quiet home for anything. I like being back in Cloverfield. I like the small town with our bowling alley, ice skating rink, library, post office, and eight-block main street. I like going to our tiny grocery store and inevitably seeing someone I know. I like the people that bustle in for skating in all seasons, for hockey in the fall and winter, for the football games, and the holiday parades. I love Cloverfield!

However...

I remember a musical Mom and Taysleigh made me watch when my sister was in high school, and I was in eighth grade—*The Music Man*. There's a song where the ladies of the town are gossiping about the poor librarian who only wants the townsfolk to be more literate. To them, however, the books are horrible. (I was given this synopsis after loudly complaining that I didn't understand what was going on, because *for real*, who breaks into singing at every turn? Totally ridiculous!)

That scene perfectly reveals what Cloverfield is like. Everyone knows everybody's business, and there's no escaping it.

And that gets really old, really quick.

Mom sighs again—is that the eleventh or twelfth time? I've lost count—and it shakes me from my thoughts. With a dramatic sigh of my own, I ask, "What is wrong?"

She sets the kettle on the stove and taps her fingers against the handle. Each beat accelerates my heart. Mom only takes this long to answer when it's something serious. The silence that stretches this time is so lengthy that I'm certain I'm going to suffer heart failure if she doesn't answer me soon.

"Are you sure it's good to be coaching?" she blurts.

I blink. That isn't what I was expecting. "What?"

"You seem exhausted, honey." Mom's dark brows furrow, and she busies herself by grabbing a mug for her tea. "I'm not sure it's healthy for you to be pushing your leg so hard so soon after your surgery."

"I am tired," I admit with a grin to soften the words. No use getting Mom's mama bear instinct raised. "But it's the good kind. It's hockey, Mom. It's all I've ever wanted to do. I'm not giving it up. Besides, it's fun."

Except for trying to get eleven teenage boys to give me a chance.

"Then why do you have that furrow that means you're worried and stressed?" She steps up behind the couch and pokes my forehead.

"I inherited both my worry and the furrow from you. *You* get it when you worry over Tays and me. Guilt by association, Mom. You don't get to reprimand me for worrying until you stop worrying about us. Ow!" I laugh when she smacks the back of my head lightly.

"You're sassing me, boy." But her laughter fades back into worry when she says, "I'm serious, Tanner. If this coaching job is going to cause you stress, then—"

"Mom." I grab her hand. "Any job is stressful. But I love the ice, and I'm not giving up." I feel her fingers tighten around mine and squeeze it in return. "I'll be fine."

The kettle shrieks. Mom fills her mug with the water and turns back around as I'm rubbing my propped-up leg. Her brows raise in a way that makes me feel guilty for pushing myself so hard—seriously, do moms go to school for *looks*? Because my mother seems to have an entire arsenal of them. I pull my tablet out of my satchel and click open my document app, eager to get away from her prying eyes.

"Do you want some tea?" Mom asks.

"Sure," I reply, grabbing my clipboard to stare at the names of the boys I have listed.

Luke Grady is a dead-on beast at defense. And Carter Grady wasn't wrong—he is an exceptional goalie. I can see no reason to *not* keep him as one.

Leo is a good forward. He is light, quick, and able to turn on a dime. He carves up the ice like an animal.

Now, Owen Tucker. There is a kid who knows he's good at his sport. And therein lies the problem. I bite my lip and tap my index finger against the side of my tablet. I'm not sure what to do with him, because while he's an excellent shot and a great player, the arrogance threatens to drive me nuts.

And it's not only about our clash of personalities either. Owen is a driving force of the team. Possibly *the* driving force. If he says no to me, the rest will follow. He's the pied piper of the Cougars.

Yet, through all of that, I see leadership qualities in Luke. They're raw, untrained, and definitely overshadowed by the overbearing personality of Owen, but they're there all the same.

"Here, honey." Mom hands me a large mug with the Cloverfield Cougars logo on it. I can smell the sweet fragrance of my favorite blueberry tea and smile at her as I take a careful sip of the steaming beverage.

As Mom settles on the sofa, the boys rotate through my head.

Luke, Carter, Leo.

Owen, Liam, Seb.

Wyatt, Mateo, Kai...

"Hey, Mom. What do you know of Kai Reynolds?" I ask. I'd been gone long enough to not remember all the people in and around Cloverfield. Especially with the new factory that had been built three years ago. It brought in a host of new families and kids, making me feel like a stranger in my own hometown sometimes.

Mom clicks her tongue. "That's a sad story. You remember Grant Reynolds, right?"

I think for a minute before nodding. Grant had been in my grade in school, although the only time we really interacted was in sports.

"Well, Grant had an older brother, Travis. They lived up in Montana somewhere. Anyways, four years ago, Travis and his wife got in a head-on collision. It killed them both and left Kai behind. He came to live with his grandparents—Grant's parents."

"Wow." I drop my gaze back to my clipboard. "Poor Grant." To lose your brother like that—so unexpectedly—sounded horrible. At least Dad's death had given us some warning.

"Yeah." Mom tucks her legs under her. "And poor Kai."

I glance up at her before tipping my head to rest against the back of the coach. "He looked so...mad, for lack of a better word. He stormed off, furious that I'm replacing his grandpa."

Which, with the information Mom just told me, makes sense. I mean, Coach Reynolds had been the head coach when *I* had been on varsity. It was high time for him to retire, but that didn't make it easy for the boys left behind on the ice. Loyalty runs thick through our veins.

"Mom, how do I get the boys to trust me?" I rub my face with both hands. "Right now, I have three of the eleven on my side." *Possibly four, if Wyatt is as nice as he seemed today.* But Wyatt is under Owen's thumb, and I don't trust Owen one bit.

"Just be your lovely self and kick their butts." Mom grins as I shoot her a skeptical look. "Honestly, Tanner. I think you're going to have to be tough with them before you can be their friend. You're close to their age, but you're their coach first. You want them to trust you, but you also have to be firm. It's a fine line to walk."

You're telling me. I sigh and take a long sip of the tea. "I thought this would be easy. Natural. It wasn't hard to lead the guys on the Comets. It felt like breathing. This? This is a whole other level of leadership. Especially when they hate my guts for replacing Reynolds."

"Well, I have faith in you." She pats my knee before scooping up the remote and clicking on an old sitcom—effectively ending the conversation. I smile at her. She cooked, cleaned, and kept Taysleigh and me in line when we were living at home, but when it came to the more difficult conversations, she'd always left that in Dad's ballpark. With him gone, she's trying. And I'm thankful for her steady presence.

I turn back to my list, and my last conversation with Molly springs to mind without my consent. Her standing in the middle of the snack counter, her eyes riveted on the old cabinet. Had she been thinking about us, hidden away under it all those years ago? Remembering when I'd asked her to go on a date? Regretting that she'd said yes?

I can still remember her hand in mine. The indignation that filled my chest when she'd whispered the awful name a group of guys had called her. The way her body pressed against my side while her head rested on my shoulder. Molly doesn't know it, but that was the moment I realized I was in love with her.

My heart kicks up a notch, and I lick my suddenly dry lips. Sweet mercy, I shouldn't be thinking about Molly. I glance at Mom, worrying that she'll notice my shifting. She is too busy watching John Stamos, thank goodness.

I glance at my tablet and swear under my breath. I was an idiot to walk away five years ago, and I'm an idiot now. Is there any hope in trying to win her back? I'm not naïve enough to believe that second-chance romances work in real life. They're fine for the Hallmark movies with the cookie-cutter plots, but reality rarely favors the moron—of which I am king.

But maybe there's hope for a second-chance *friendship*. I pull up my school email and compose a letter to Molly, my tired brain formulating a weak and desperate plan. My finger hovers over the *send* button before I save it as a draft and click off my tablet.

Better to save desperate for when I can think clearly.

Chapter Eleven

Molly

Mornings come far too early. My alarm blares the six a.m. wake-up call that ten-thirty p.m. Molly had thought was just a *stupendous* time to get ready for the day. *Newsflash!* It isn't!

I hit the snooze button and roll onto my stomach, tucking my arms under my pillow as I screw my eyes shut against the morning sun. My dreams hadn't been kind. Going to the Rink had dredged up far too many memories.

Of figure skating.

Of helping Gramps and Grams in the Snack Counter.

Of Tanner.

Of first dates and hand-holding.

I curse under my breath, ticked that Tanner got under my skin. Again. He's old news. An old fling that I'm not going to waste another minute thinking about.

But still...

"Where are we going?" I bounce in Tanner's truck, the red bandana wrapped over my eyes blocking out anything around us.

Tanner has my hand captured in his, his thumb sending butterflies zipping around my stomach as he rubs lazy circles over my knuckles. He laughs, and they turn into a cyclone of excitement because we had made Tanner Bradshaw *laugh*. Seriously, is this a dream? How is he *holding my hand?*

"If I told you, that would totally defeat the purpose of the blindfold, Mols."

I grin. I can't help it. I love it when he calls me *Mols.* I love hearing him laugh. I love his cologne. It's kind of a pine scent with a hint of spearmint—spicy yet sweet, totally Tanner.

"Fine." I sigh, but I can't help bouncing a bit more.

"We're almost there," he promises, his hand squeezing mine. "Sweet mercy, Mols. I didn't know you were this impatient."

"I'm not. Normally." It's only that going on my first date ever with *Tanner Bradshaw* has me all sorts of jittery.

The truck turns into a parking lot, and Tanner is soon parked and pulling the keys out of the ignition. "Okay, wait right there."

He hops out, but the door closes so quickly that I can't get any clues as to where we are. I bounce a bit more. Where is our first date?

What if he tries to kiss me? Butterflies leap into my throat, choking me. What if Tanner tries to kiss me? What do I do? I've never been kissed before. Am I a good kisser?

Heat climbs up my neck as the door clicks open.

Tanner's voice fills the cab. "Ready?"

"Yep." My voice comes out a squeak, and I pray fervently that Tanner can't read my mind.

His large hand closes around mine, and he helps me to the ground. My high tops crunch against loose gravel as he guides me into a large—and cold—building.

"Here we are!"

Wait. Are we—?

He tugs off my blindfold, revealing the freshly Zamboni-ed ice as clear as crystal. Only a few of the lights are on, casting the ice in a low glow that's...super romantic. My skates lean up against the boards by the opening that leads to the ice, a single lavender carnation—my favorite flower—next to them.

I can't speak. I can't move. Tears prick my eyes as I stare at it. Then, from somewhere, a slow waltz blends with the hum of the chiller.

This is absolutely the sweetest.

"Molly?" Tanner's hands land hesitantly on my shoulders. "Is this...okay?"

"Okay?" I croak, turning to bury my face against his chest. "This is perfect. Oh, Tanner! This is my absolute dream first date."

I hear him exhale as his arms tighten around my back. "Good."

We stand there for a moment before he asks, "You ready to skate?"

I nod, and Tanner helps me lace up my skates.

We skate for hours, hand in hand, dancing across the ice to songs Tanner picked for me as we laugh and talk. It's a dream. A beautiful dream that I never want to wake up from.

With another groan to emphasize how very *not* ready I am to be awake—and how much my dreams sucked last night—I stumble to the bathroom. Thirty minutes later, I step out looking much more put together. With my makeup in place, hair pulled into a high tail, and my plaid dress slacks with a black shirt, I feel like a powerhouse.

"Watch out Clover-High! Miss Pruitt is in the house!"

With a small laugh at that, I push my glasses up my nose and slip into my heels. Running through my mental checklist, I grab my bags and head down the stairs. I have time to run to Sweetie's for coffee today. So I can justify grabbing myself one of her salads for lunch instead of packing something.

Nodding at this thought process, I hurry down the stairs and grab one of Susan's cookies for my breakfast. Yeah, yeah, I'm so healthy.

I'm checking my watch as I step through the door of Sweetie's. The hissing of espresso machines and the quiet murmur of half-awake patrons wrap around me. I smile as I look up and nearly collide into the broad back of the person in front of me in line.

"Sorry!" I begin before noticing who it is.

Tanner smirks, his hands shoved into his army-green windbreaker. "I think you're making it a habit to run into me, Mols. Literally."

"Har har." I roll my eyes with a scowl. "Because I wanted to see you again, Bradshaw."

His brows hitch up to match his lopsided smile. The smile that does weird stuff to my breathing. I close my eyes. I can't handle his stupidly handsome face when caffeine deprived.

"You alright there, Mols?"

His voice is warm. Dang it! Why does it make me feel like a perfectly warm, toasty marshmallow?

"I'm fine, I'm meditating." I'm *what?* Where the heck did *that* come from?

"Meditating?" Humor laces his words, and I can picture his blue eyes laughing at me. "Is this a new endeavor?"

"Yeah,"—as of thirty seconds ago—"and it's remarkably relaxing. You should try it."

He grabs my arm and helps me shift forward. The brave thing to do would be to face him, open my eyes, and deal with the issue head on. But I'm not brave. I'm the Cowardly Lion of Cloverfield, and I'm hiding behind my winged eyeliner and mascara.

"Doesn't meditating usually involve...you know...quiet?"

"Not my kind. You can do it anywhere." I breathe in deeply and exhale. "Think about things that make you happy. Coffee, sunshine, not being in line with you."

He chuckles again as we shift forward once more. And oh boy. My dream comes back, unbidden. We'd laughed that day at the Rink on our first date. Sure, we'd laughed plenty before that when he'd hung out with my brothers and me, playing hockey on the pond outside of town. But it had been different that day. We'd been different. And just like then, his hand sends shock waves rippling up into my shoulder and neck.

I want to rip away—because how dare I remember how happy we'd been, how in love. But I refuse to open my eyes. Refuse to face the fact that Tanner is talking to me—like a friend, no less—and that when I look at him, I remember our past and melt like a chocolate chip from one of Susan's cookies.

"Do you still order caramel lattes?" Tanner asks, pulling my thoughts from gooey chocolate chips and the pressure of his hand on my bare arm.

"Do you still order vanilla?" I ask instead of answering his question.

But instead of getting angry like I want him to, Tanner simply chuckles and mutters, "Touché."

It would be a whole lot easier to stay mad at him if he would just retaliate. Why is he so nice all the time?

Isn't that why you fell in love with him? I push that annoying question away to ponder later. Much later.

"Tanner!" Sweetie's faint Italian accent swirls over the hum of the coffee machine and the low murmur of the people at the tables. "I'm glad you stopped in! We have those vanilla bean scones fresh out of the oven. Oh." A note of confusion touches her words. "Are you and Molly here together?"

"No!" We deny as one. Tanner clears his throat, and I pipe up. "We...ah...ran into each other."

"Molly, *cara*." Her voice drips with concern. "Why are your eyes closed?"

Before I can say anything, Tanner interjects, "She's meditating."

"I'm done now." I open my eyes as my cheeks begin to burn. Blinking against the soft glow of the Edison bulbs strung behind Sweetie, I smile at the woman. "Can I please have my usual?"

"A caramel latte with a double pump of caramel?" Sweetie asks as her smile appears, crinkling her espresso-brown eyes as she writes the order on a paper cup.

"Yes, please."

"And for you, Tanner?" She sweeps her arm at the chalkboard menu.

"I normally just have black coffee in the morning, but," he cuts a glance at me, a challenging gleam in his eyes, "I can't be one-upped by Mols, here."

I scowl at the nickname—or maybe it's at the return of the butterflies in my stomach hearing Tanner use it.

And that only earns me another smirk from the man. "I'll have a hot venti vanilla latte with a pump of white chocolate, please, Sweetie."

Sweetie laughs out loud, a great booming laugh that's at odds with her size. She shakes her head at Tanner as he joins her in laughing, then writes his order on the cup and hands it to her barista. "How's school going?"

"Good." Tanner smiles, leaning his shoulder against the tall, glass display case with all of Sweetie's pastries. "Hard to believe it's only been three days."

I shift from foot to foot, keeping my gaze locked onto my black heels. I want to ask him a question, yet I also want to keep him at arm's length. Asking a question could lead to more, to conversations, to confessions, to forgiveness. I don't want to forgive Tanner. I want to hold on to all the feelings I'd had when he'd first left. Nurture the bitterness rooted deep down. Because holding on to that seems better than opening up myself to hurt again. But my mouth has a mind of its own. "How did practice go yesterday?"

A pause fills the space between us, so minuscule most others might not catch it. I flick my gaze up for a heartbeat to see Tanner's blue eyes focused on me. They remind me of the ocean on a bright, sunny day. Yet something lurks in their depths. Something I'm not equipped to name; nor do I want to.

"It went well." The pause breaks under the pressure of Tanner's words, and I find I can draw a full breath once more.

"Here's your coffee, Molly. And yours, Tanner."

"Thanks." I take a sip and sigh, a small smile on my face. "Perfect as always, Sweetie."

She chuckles with a shake of her head. "On the house this week for school staff."

"Thanks." I move toward the door then turn back, remembering why I'd decided to come to Sweetie's in the first place. "I need a salad for lunch."

"Of course! Chicken bacon ranch?"

I grin with a nod. She knows me so well I should be embarrassed. But I can't be. Because all of us grew up coming to Sweetie's. To study, to chat, to cry, to hang out. She'd been everyone's sister, aunt, mother. She was someone safe to turn to, a place to go to hide away from the wild world we all lived in.

"That's seven, *cara*," she says as she hands me the plastic container.

I fish the cash out of my wallet and hand it to her before waving and heading out the door. My mood sours when I see Tanner waiting beside it. "What? You have to follow me everywhere now?"

His brows raise. "Pretty sure *you* followed *me* into Sweetie's this morning. Besides, I think we're parked next to each other."

He's right. Although, I'm a bit surprised by his choice of vehicle. It's a plain gold sedan.

Humble, still. I cut a glance at Tanner. The car is nothing like the flashy, cherry-red sports car I'd been imagining. In fact, the little car looks like it belongs next to my baby-blue hatchback.

I clear my throat at *that* particular thought and say, "Well, see you at—"

"Can we try and be friends, Mols?" Tanner asks abruptly. His eyes go wide, like he hadn't meant to say that out loud.

"Tanner—"

But before I can say anything more, he turns and hurries to his car, turning over the engine and peeling out of the parking lot like the devil himself is on his heels.

"Well, I guess some things don't change." I sigh and close my eyes, deciding that maybe public meditating isn't such a bad idea after all.

CHAPTER TWELVE

Tanner

The school day is incredibly long. Listening to Molly going on and on about books like I hadn't just dropped the bombshell of friendship on her pricks at my pride. Shouldn't she be as shaken as I am? Because I'd freaked myself out so badly that I ran. Again.

Standing in the line at Sweetie's showed me what has been absent in my life for five long, lonely years.

I have a Molly-shaped hole in my heart. Although, I hadn't realized that's what was missing for so long. Through all the games, the money, the press conferences, the fame, I've been pining for my best friend. The one I'd run away from and who I kept running from until a busted knee and early retirement forced me to turn around and see all the carnage I'd left behind.

The bell rings, signaling the end of the school day. I throw everything into my bag and hurry out before Molly can say anything.

Before I can stick my foot further into my mouth.

When I arrive at the Rink, a few of the boys are already there, skating and smack-talking as I change into sweats and a sweatshirt.

"Alright. Let's do a little playing." I glance at my clipboard. "Owen, Carter, Leo, Mateo, and Seb on the left side. Luke, Liam, Wyatt, James, and Jacob on the right." I blow my whistle, and the boys scatter.

I climb onto the bench and watch as they play. They're aggressive, quick to get a penalty, and sometimes to flat out fight, even with their team members.

Owen slams Luke into the boards, knocking the slightly leaner boy onto the ice. Owen bends over and says something that has fire shooting out of Luke's eyes as he struggles to get to his feet. They don't listen when I blow the whistle, and I can see tempers getting ready to boil over as the boys begin to take sides.

"Boys!" My voice rattles around the open rafters of the Rink, and another shrill blast on my whistle finally gets their attention. "Everyone to the left side of the Rink." When they hesitate, I snap, "Now!"

They shuffle over, and I channel my inner Herb Brooks. Mean. Unyielding. Coach before friend.

"Bag skate," I order, blowing my whistle as the boys groan. A bag skate drill means that the players have to skate in a sprint from the goal line to the near blue line and back, then to the red line and back, to the far blue line and eventually from goal line to goal line. Once they complete the drill and are all lined up on the goal line, I blow my whistle. "Again."

Five times I make them do it until they're puffing for air, and sweat is trickling down their foreheads. Owen glares, still full of hot air, apparently, but the rest look justifiably cowed.

"Bench." I jab my finger over my shoulder, not giving an inch.

They all hurry over and grab their water bottles, guzzling, gasping, and looking exhausted. Good. Maybe they'll stay cooled off for a bit now.

I slide back and forth in front of the bench, arms crossed. "I'm not sure whether to be impressed or mortified at what I just saw."

"Coach?" Leo raises one of his blond brows.

Thumping my clipboard against my side, I try to think of the right words. You say the wrong thing completely, and they're going to eat you alive. Say the *right* thing the *wrong* way? Same outcome.

"You're aggressive, and that's fine. But you've got to channel that aggression. Just beating up on every opposing player that comes at you is a good way to lose the game."

"Oh, and you're an expert?" Owen snorts and crosses his arms.

"Yeah," I state blandly, "I am. And if you have a problem with it, you can go do five more bag skates."

Owen rips off his helmet and jabs a gloved finger at me. "I'm not buying it. You may have played for four seasons, but you never made it to the Cup. You never amounted to anything! And then you crawl back here and expect us to listen to a single word you say about *our* playing?"

"Shut up, Owen!" Luke launches to his feet, the tension that had left during the drill filling the Rink once more. "He knows more than you and your big mouth!"

A stream of expletives explodes out of Owen, and he launches himself toward Luke.

For a moment, I'm shell-shocked—unable to move or say anything. What is going on? We're not on the ice. This isn't supposed to happen. But a shout from Rick—who'd been sweeping around the seats—jerks me into motion.

"Enough!" I push between them, almost getting hit in the process. "Stop it, or I'll kick both of your sorry butts off this team!"

Luke chills, but Owen's eyes promise pain as he glares first at me then at his teammate.

"I have half a mind to still sack you." I stare at the former captain. Yes, absolutely *former*. If there had been an inkling of allowing him the honor, there's no way now. He clearly hasn't earned it. "But for now, I'll only suspend you two games."

"What?" Owen's mouth falls open. "What about him?"

I look at Luke. "Your outburst wasn't much better."

"I'm sorry, Coach." Luke drops his head.

"I forgive you, Luke. Consider this your first and only warning. I'm trusting that you'll do better from now on."

"I will!" He nods emphatically.

I turn back to Owen. "You, on the other hand—"

"I'm the best player you got!" he interrupts.

"Yeah, you are," I admit with a nod. "But you're also not willing to listen. You are short-tempered, surly, and I can't have someone like that leading my team."

"What are you saying?" Liam, one of my defensemen, asks slowly.

With a deep breath, I look at the rest of the team. "I mean that Owen isn't captain anymore."

The boys all begin talking at once, and I wait for them to settle down.

It finally takes a shout from Rick before they all fall silent and watch me once more.

"I was looking over my list last night. I have strong players, supporting players, defensive. But only one showed true leadership. And I decided this before this little episode, just so you all know." I turn toward the young man whose head is still dropped with his gaze fixated on his skates. "Luke is going to be the team captain this year."

"Coach?" Luke asks softly, his eyes meeting mine. "You're sure?"

"Yeah. I'm sure." I clasp his shoulder. "Because this? This is humility. You are a fine example of that, and you lead your team with a quiet leadership that doesn't demand attention. I want to cultivate that this year. If you'll let me."

A long silence settles over us, and I swear all the boys lean toward Luke and me, waiting.

Luke finally smiles and gives me a small nod. "Yeah, Coach. I'd like that."

The team cheers, and Luke's smile grows.

"Good." I squeeze his shoulder as much as I can through his pads.

Red infuses Luke's cheeks. "Thanks, Coach."

"This is ridiculous!" Owen cries, his hands balling into fists. "I'll talk to the athletic director! I've been the captain for two years!"

"And you haven't earned it this year," I declare. "I'm sorry, Owen."

I hold my breath, waiting for him to flip out even more.

But all Owen does is scowl and sit back on the bench. Mateo, who is sitting next to him, slides a bit closer to Jacob. I can't say I blame the kid.

"Okay, more drills! Let's go!"

We do a few drills, a couple laps around the ice, and a maneuver or two. As the boys head to the lockers, I can't help but chuckle. They're an even more tired and sweaty group than normal. Good.

"Coach?" Luke hesitates beside me as I unlace my skates on the bleachers.

"Yeah?" I look up.

He has his hands on his hips, his brows furrowed. "Why me?"

"Pardon?" I stop tying my shoelaces and give him my full attention.

"Why did you choose me to be the captain? I know what you said in front of the guys, but...I'm not a leader, Coach."

Does he not see it? The way the guys gravitate toward him, the way he takes command on the ice without saying a word. If Owen is a bulldozer, Luke is the quiet tide, pulling and guiding his peers to the right path.

But I can't just tell him that. He has to see it. See how his persistent desire for excellence causes his team to look to him.

I brace my elbows on my knees and study Luke. "You don't think you're a leader, huh?"

"No, sir."

"Hm." I nod my head for a minute. "Well, you're proving my earlier point about humility. And ultimately, it's my choice to make."

Luke sighs. "Okay."

He doesn't seem convinced. And I need boldness from him. Need him to be confident as he leads the others.

"Tell you what, why don't we try this? You're team captain through the regular season. If you still don't see yourself as a leader by Christmas, we'll talk about who should replace you. Deal?"

Luke shifts. "You're that confident in me, Coach?"

"Yeah, Luke. I am." I meet his gaze. His brown eyes are hesitant and unsure as they flick back and forth between mine. Gosh, he reminds me of me. Of starting out on the ice in grade school, rising through the ranks, and eventually, leading guys older than me to a state title. It'd been terrifying. It'd been amazing. It led me to where I am today.

I smile at the boy. "There's something there, something I think I can bring out if you'll work with me."

Luke hesitates. "But Owen—"

There it is. The real reason he's not comfortable leading the team. Owen is a bully, pure and simple. And if there's one thing I can't stand, it's a bully. I wince when a memory rushes me. A memory I'd forgotten until this moment.

I stalk out of the Rink. It's my senior year, and I'm hyped on the high of another win for the Cougars. We'd played our hearts out.

Now, off the ice, all I can think about is Molly. Molly Pruitt. My brain is looping our date from last night. Of skating and laughing and talking. Of holding her hand.

But one thing stands out even more. The confession she'd given me just a few days earlier while hiding in the kitchen cupboard. A confession about a couple of guys calling her awful names. It makes my blood boil even two days after the fact. I can't say I didn't take a touch of my aggression out on the ice tonight, imagining my opponents were the jerks who thought they were cool for degrading another human being.

I catch sight of one of the jerks now. *Speak of the devil...* He's leaning against his truck, waiting for his brother to come out from our game, a cigarette between his fingers.

Show time! "Hey, Mason! Waiting for Lewis?"

"Yeah." He eyes me warily. Wise guy, though he's still a few tacos short of a fiesta platter.

"So. I heard you talked to Molly Pruitt last Friday." I shove my hands into my pockets, though they really, *really* want to rearrange this guy's too-straight nose.

"Who?" Mason asks, exhaling a plume of smoke.

I grit my teeth and try not to breathe too deeply. "Molly Pruitt. Ryley and Ryder's sister?"

Slow recognition dawns in his gray eyes, and my jaw tense further. Gosh, I hate this guy.

"Oh, you mean the little—" He spits out a word that spikes my blood pressure.

"Yeah, her." I step closer to him, invade his space so he knows I'm serious. "Only if you *ever* call her that again—to her face or behind her back—and I hear of it, you're gonna have to have reconstructive surgery."

Mason snorts. "You and what army?"

Now, listen, Mason easily has five inches and thirty pounds on me. His shoulders are huge. *However,* I have five years of Taekwon-do on my side. Granted, that was in my early elementary school days and before my parents took seriously my plea to try out for hockey. But it's got to be like riding a bike and will all come back once I tap into it.

Right?

Well, I'm going with that.

Before Mason can react, I grab the wrist that holds his cigarette and yank him forward. Twisting his arm around, I get it up and behind his back, pressing a pressure point that—for whatever rea-son—I remember quite clearly—to make him drop the cigarette.

He struggles, but the element of surprise is on my side, and I quickly have him very thoroughly pinned. I slam him against his truck, anger making me want to hurt him.

But then I'd be no better than him. And I *will* be better than Mason McCormick.

"Leave. Molly. Alone." I push him more firmly. "Got it, Mace?"

"Got it. Lay off, Bradshaw."

I step back warily. But all Mason does is brush at nonexistent dirt and spit in my general direction before sliding into the cab.

I smirk, brush my hands together, and head to my truck.

That, my friends, is how to deal with a bully.

I smirk at the memory before turning my attention back to Luke.

"Let me deal with Owen. You just worry about becoming the captain I know you can be, okay?"

My captain nods, his smile making a momentary appearance. "Sure thing, Coach."

"Good. Go hit the showers."

Luke nods again, turning and loping off for the locker room.

With a long exhale, I let my head loll forward and brace my hands behind my neck. I am right there with Luke. I'm not a leader; I'm not a coach. I am an ex-captain who is still every bit as uncertain and terrified as the day he was given the title in the NHL and expected to lead. The kid who was scared to ask the girl he loved to follow after him into a world he wasn't sure he'd ever belong in. And now, once again, I am being thrust into a position where people are depending on me. People I can let down. People I can hurt.

"Good words there, Tanner."

I sit up, the world tilting from the sudden head rush before I blink Rick into focus.

He chuckles. "Sorry. Didn't mean to scare you."

"No, it was my fault. I was lost in thought."

The banging of a door has us turning to wave to the boys as they head out, their hair dripping as they laugh and shove one another.

"See ya Friday, Coach!" Leo calls, walking backwards in front of Carter.

"See you, boys! Stay out of trouble, you hear?"

They jeer at that and laugh some more before the Rink falls back to the eerie silence interrupted only by the humming of the cooler.

"So, where did that little speech to Luke come from?" Rick asks as he stares out at the ice we'd broken in. He'd have it clear and clean before the end of the day. Rick is nothing if not meticulous in his care of the Rink.

"It just...came." I shrugged a shoulder.

"Do you believe it?"

"What?" I turn toward the old man. It is easy to forget he is Molly's grandpa until I look into his eyes. They sparkle with mischief and joy—like Molly's when she talks about books.

"Do you believe what you told Luke? Because I knew from the day you hit the ice that there was a leader in Tanner Bradshaw.

Reynolds saw it, too. That's why you were captain senior year. The Comets saw it; that's what got you drafted right out of high school. Molly saw it when you decided to date her." His bushy white mustache twitches. "Might want to use it now to try and smooth things over with our Molly girl, hm?"

"I don't think she likes me at the moment." I bury my fingers in my hair and sigh. "Besides, she's grown a smart mouth on her. She wasn't that sassy when we were teens, was she?"

"No, she wasn't!" Rick laughs. "College was good for her. Got the jitters out of her backbone and replaced it with one of steel. But don't let her fool you, Tanner. She's still a softy when it comes to those she cares about."

He winks, and I scowl. "That's not me, Rick."

The insufferable man raises his hands with a wide grin. "Whatever you say, Coach. You headed out?"

"Yeah." I stand and wince at the pain in my leg.

"Want to ice that first?"

I shake my head. It's spinning faster than a top, and I want to simply fall into bed. How is it not even the end of the first week of school?

Rick clasps my shoulder. "Alright. I'll see you Friday."

It's not a question, but I respond with a nod. I shoulder my bag before limping my way out the door and to the car. I pause, staring out over the setting sun. Why does my gimp leg feel like an accurate representation of my life all of a sudden?

Shaking my head, I climb into my car and head home, not at all ready to deal with *that* line of thought.

Chapter Thirteen

Molly

I grab two of Susan's peanut butter cookies as I fly out the door Friday morning. It has been a long week of getting to know the dynamics of my class, preparing lessons, and avoiding Tanner at all costs. And now, I'm late because my alarm didn't go off this morning.

Tanner fills my mind as I drive as quickly as possible down Main Street toward the high school. It's been impossible to avoid the man. He keeps popping into my space all of the time. He showed up at Sweetie's Wednesday morning, and also yesterday afternoon when I went to lesson plan. He's started to eat his lunch—a disgustingly healthy one most days, too—in the room so I either have to go mingle with my coworkers or eat in his presence. He's a phantom at the back of my class, always in my peripheral and at my side whenever I need help.

It's infuriating.

It's endearing.

It needs to stop.

The bell rings as I stumble into my classroom. I hate being late. My students all turn to watch me from their seats, and heat floods my cheeks. I pull on my teacher smile as I straighten my cardigan and slide my hands over my pencil skirt. "Sorry for being late, class."

"Are you going to make it a habit, Miss Pruitt?" Gloria asks from the front row. A saccharine smile that curdles the cookie in my stomach twists Gloria's glossed lips, all while her eyes spell my demise. I hadn't had time for coffee and can feel the pounding ache building behind my eyes and at the base of my skull.

"No, Gloria. I'm not." I glance at the back, noticing that Tanner isn't there. His presence is the best thing to keep the big-mouthed girl in line. But I guess I'm going it alone today. A strange pang of loneliness hits, but I push it away. "Alright class, please pull out your copy of *Tuck Everlasting*. As I said yesterday, we're finally ready to begin reading the book. Please turn to the Prologue on page three. Ben, will you read it for us?"

We began to dissect the prologue, discussing the complex idea of time and lives crossing lives that Natalie Babbitt wove into the first four pages of her middle-grade story.

"Do you really think one life, one choice, can affect so many people, Miss Pruitt?" Sebastian asks. "I mean, I'm just one person out of eight billion. Am I really going to touch that many lives?"

I glance over them all. "You've touched twenty-one lives right here, Seb. I've touched the same twenty-one. Later today, you'll interact with the hockey team and Coach Bradshaw. The choices you make, the words you say, they have a ripple effect. Like we'll see with Winnie and the Tucks, what we choose to do with our lives makes a difference."

"Like when Coach Bradshaw up and left you, Miss Pruitt?" Gloria asked innocently, that same fake smile on her face.

"What?" I ask coolly, despite the heat beginning to crawl from my chest up into my neck.

"Mother told me you and Coach were a thing in high school." A trail of whispers and *oohs* follow that declaration. "What ripple did *that* choice have?"

My hands shake as I brace them against my desk. Memories I've already been failing to keep at bay pound through me.

The barn dance.

The cabinet confession.

The first date at the Rink.

The kisses.

The promises.

The abandonment.

Clearing my throat, I meet Gloria's flinty gaze. "That is none of your business, Gloria."

"But you still like him," she insists. She stands and struts around the room, perfectly in her element as Queen of Cloverfield High. I grit my teeth as she continues, "I've seen the way you look at him. Part loathing and part *kiss me senseless.*" That elicits a chuckle from the rest of the class. "You do know there's a policy against staff dating, don't you, Miss Pruitt?"

"Where does it say that, Gloria?" a boy near the back calls. I'm too shaken to figure out who.

"Mother told me. It's old, but I'm sure Principal Skinner would find it most interesting, don't you?"

"Sit down, Gloria," I order.

She turns, brown eyes on fire. "I'm not done."

"Oh, yes. You are." I stalk over to her and jab a finger at her chair. "Sit. Now."

She waits just long enough to have the class shifting at the silent standoff before sitting. She tucks a lock of her long sable-colored hair behind her ear before folding her hands on top of her un-opened copy of *Tuck.*

I'm shaking, adrenaline coursing through me as I instruct the kids to read chapters one through five and write a summary to be turned in tomorrow. They jot down the homework notes as the bell rings.

Forcing a smile to my lips, I stand at the door until every last one of my students is gone. Slamming it shut, I burst into tears as the memories flood me.

One stands out above the rest; one I've fought for years to forget.

I smooth my hand over my skinny jeans, my palms slick with sweat. Mom laughs as she finishes the second French braid and ties it off with a cute red ribbon to match the left one.

"You look adorable!" she declares.

My nose wrinkles. "I don't want to be *adorable*. I want to look hot."

Mom sighs. "No, you don't. You already got yourself a guy, and he's sweet and thoughtful. All you need to be is you, Molly Elaine!"

I glare at her, hating when she uses my middle name. But she's right. Tonight, I'm going with Tanner to the November Barn Dance, and nothing is going to take away my joy about that.

Grabbing my red and black flannel shirt, I button it up over my black tank top. Cuffing the sleeves up—because it's a guy flannel with ridiculously long sleeves—I tug my jean jacket over it.

Mom laughs when I produce cowboy boots from the closet. They were five bucks at the thrift store and exactly my size. "Look at you. You're a regular cowgirl!"

I laugh and then hear the doorbell ring. Butterflies soar as I grab my tiny backpack purse and fly down the stairs. Dad, Ryley, and Ryder are all standing in the entryway talking to Tanner, and I pause in the upper landing to listen.

"Take care of her." Dad's voice is cold, but not uncaring. "If you hurt her—"

"You'll have to deal with all of us," Ryder finishes.

Ryley adds, "Dang right, you will."

I walk the rest of the way down, smiling at my family as Tanner's eyes sweep over me. His smirky smile appears, curling warmth blooms in the pit of my stomach.

"You look beautiful, Mols." His voice is a bit breathy, and my smile grows. I could bask in his admiration all night. But we have places to be.

"I'll be home by eleven, Dad," I promise, hugging him quickly before grabbing Tanner's hand.

"Ten!" Ryley calls after me while Ryder chimes in with, "Nine is better!"

I laugh as I scramble up into Tanner's truck and heave a sigh of relief. "I thought we'd never get out of there!"

He just laughs and twines my fingers with his.

He's strangely silent on our drive over to the barn, his thumb rubbing absentminded circles over my knuckles. The butterflies and warm, sunny feeling slowly bleed out, anxiety sinking its claws into my mind and around my lungs. Did I do something wrong? Is he upset at me? What's going on?

But I can't seem to voice my worry. Tanner parks and helps me out, holding my hand as we stroll up to the barn. He slips into his outgoing mode—talking with his teammates, laughing with the chaperones like he's best friends with all the parents, and just being...social. I hang on the fringe, laughing when appropriate but not really talking to anyone. Ava's out of town for a funeral, so I know no one. I hate it. Hate being in the shadows but not knowing how to step out.

"Wanna dance?"

I startle when Tanner's hand lands against the small of my back. I'd been lost in my thoughts—per the norm.

"Sure." I try and force a smile, really wanting to be anywhere but here.

Tanner grins that thousand-watt smile and pulls me onto the dance floor.

It's a slow song, and he settles his hands against my waist, holding on just tight enough to tell me he's not going to let me go. There's a security when I'm with Tanner I've never felt before, swaying slowly to some popular love song. I swallow the lump that always accompanies my tears as our foreheads touch.

"Want to go look at the stars?" he whispers. "I brought some blankets in case it's too cold out and—"

"Let's go!" I nod, eager to get away from all the eyes. I should be used to it by now. I've dated Tanner for a month, but somehow, his fame just scares me.

Tanner tugs me out of the barn, the cool autumn breeze kissing my cheeks. It's heavenly in the fall. The leaves crunch under our shoes, crisp and familiar after the awkwardness of the unknown.

We climb into Tanner's truck. He turns a knob and warm air replaces the cold. He turns onto the road as a country song fills the silence that falls over us. We drive down a back country lane and park next to an old field—all without a word. I hate it. I want to know what he's thinking. But Tanner doesn't offer me anything as he pulls a few old blankets out from the back seat. I'm not brave enough to ask as we snuggle down in the bed of the truck to stare at the stars.

We find Ursa Major and Minor; Orion's belt, too. But that's about the extent of our star knowledge. I lean my head on Tanner's shoulder as he curves his arms around me, holding me against his chest like I'm a precious treasure.

I sigh.

"Something on your mind, Mols?" Tanner asks, his voice rumbling against my ear.

"I was going to ask you that. Why haven't you really talked to me tonight?"

He hesitates. I feel it in the way his arms tighten for the barest of moments before he relaxes.

Tanner chuckles, but it sounds forced. "Because...I've had some things on my mind, I suppose."

"And you can't talk about them with me?" I sit up, hurt making me want to put some distance between us.

"What? No!" Tanner rubs his hands over his face and sighs. "Mols, it's not like that, I swear."

"Then what—"

Tanner cuts me off by cupping my cheek with his hand. My mouth is hanging open. A bug could have flown down my throat at that moment, and I would have let it. He's never held my cheek like this. Never leaned forward like he...like he...

His thumb brushes my cheekbone, lightly, tentatively. "Molly, I..."

I lick my lips as I sway forward, forcing my mouth closed as Tanner turns his head and presses his lips to mine.

I never really thought about my first kiss. I don't know why. I dreamed of holding my boyfriend's hand. Of hugs and curling up on the couch to watch a movie. But a kiss felt too sacred, too intimate.

But when Tanner's lips touch mine, it's like I'm seeing in color for the first time. It's magic. His lips fit so perfectly against mine. They move over them like I'm a new world, and he's an explorer discovering it for the first time.

Tanner's hand finds my waist, pulling me closer and angling his head to kiss me better. Deepening it as my arms slide around his neck. I press in, not wanting it to end. Because this is fun. This is exciting. This is *Tanner Bradshaw* kissing me like I'm worth it. Like I'm special.

Right now, I'm more than Tanner's girlfriend. Right now, I'm Molly Pruitt, the girl who Tanner chose to kiss tonight.

And for the first time in a long while, it feels good to be me.

Hugging my middle, I lean against the door and struggle to compose myself after that particular memory. And Gloria...she'd gotten under my skin and shook my confidence to the very core. The girl is awful, but I can't afford to tick her off. As much as I want to give her a year's worth of detention, her father basically holds the key to getting me fired. And I know for a fact that both Gloria and Mrs. Steinfield have the poor man under their thumbs, so it would happen.

Another sob slips free, and I press my fingers to my lips, not needing any of the students in the hall to hear. The memory of my first kiss with Tanner pulses through my mind again as I push to my feet and stumble to my desk. Collapsing into my desk chair, I pillow my face on my folded arms and struggle to pull myself together.

I can't do this this early in the morning. My mascara is probably a mess, and honestly! Who cares what people think about Tanner and me? We're not dating! Even if I wanted to date Tanner—which I don't—I won't let him that close again. He broke me. And I can't let that happen again. I can't and won't.

"Pull yourself together," I whisper, wiping under my eyes with a tissue as I take deep breaths to calm down.

A knock sounds a moment before Tanner pushes through. He takes one look at my face before turning and locking the door. "What happened? Are you okay?"

"No." I blow my nose into the tissue and refuse to meet his gaze. "This morning was rough."

"What happened?" he demands.

"More like who." I swallow the lump in my throat as I sit up. "Gloria was a touch vocal today. It's nothing important."

"It must have been kind of a big deal if it made you cry." He crosses his arms like he wants to argue with me, but he presses his lips together tightly.

Indignation wells up in me, and I crumple the used tissue in my hand. Who is he to call me out like this? He has no right, and I'm *not* taking his opinion. Nope. Not doing it.

But if I'm being honest, a little part of me loves how protective he looks, standing at the locked door as he studies me with that stupid concerned furrow bunching his forehead.

Pushing away *that* disconcerting thought—because we don't like Tanner anymore, heart and brain! —I ask, "Where were you?"

"Mom fell last night and twisted her ankle pretty badly. I ran her to the ER this morning."

"Oh my gosh! Is she all right?" Despite Tanner and I parting on less than amicable terms, I still adore his mom. Mrs. Bradshaw had been a confidant on the few issues I couldn't talk to my own mother about. While those were few and far between, they existed, nonetheless. She was another maternal figure who'd been steady, and I loved her for it. "Do you need to be there with her, Tanner? She might need someone there to help!"

"I know that, Molly. Taysleigh is with her now. Mom is fine." He smiles, the dimple appearing in his cheek for a flash before he sobers. "But back to you crying. What was different about today? Gloria has been a brat all week."

"She—" I bite my lip. The memory of our kiss—our high school love—sends that inconvenient warmth pooling in me again. Because if I'm being honest, I did miss Tanner while he was gone.

Gloria hinted that I watch Tanner. Do I? No. There's no way I watch him. I'm not some silly girl who longs for the old days when we'd been friends and happy. I can't be ignorant enough to want another romantic relationship with the boy—turned man—who broke my heart.

Can I?

But if that's true, then why does the idea of a new, mature relationship with *this* Tanner send butterflies soaring in my stomach? I mean, he has changed, I suppose. The last few years have been good to him in more than just his looks. I can see that he's steadier, more relatable. Watching him interact with people, I can see that false bravado he had when we dated is gone. He's still gentle with me, but there's a maturity there now, too. He still makes me laugh. And of course, he's defended me against the kids.

Though that is kind of his job, my head argues. But my heart whispers, *Maybe we can give it a second chance?*

"Mols, I'm not going to unlock this door until you tell me what Gloria said today."

Oh, right. It's not just me and my thoughts currently. Great.

I sigh. "Gloria said she would get one or both of us fired if we were dating."

His eyebrows hop up.

"Yeah."

"Why would she think we were dating?" he asks.

I shrug. "I don't know, but apparently, there's some archaic rule that says teachers can't date each other and work in the same building."

Tanner grins like the idea has never crossed his mind. "That's a dumb rule."

"Yeah, I suppose so." Butterflies zip around my stomach. Curse their colorful wings because they're making it really hard to look at Tanner without blushing.

Geez, I need to pull myself together! A pretty face smiles, and I'm a puddle at his feet.

Wait, what? No! I don't like Tanner. Not his thoughtfulness, his stupidly good looks, his strong hands, his brilliant blue eyes, his lips that are so incredibly kissable...

Stop it! No kisses! No looking at those ocean eyes.

I can feel Tanner's gaze boring into the side of my head as I busy myself sorting already sorted homework assignments. "Are you sure you're alright, Mols?"

"Yeah. I'm just dandy."

Dandy? My words are clipped, and I can't understand the swirling twisting feelings in my chest. I can't even name them. All I know for certain is that none of them are particularly pleasant. I want to scream. I want to grab Tanner by the lapels of his blazer and show him exactly what he's been missing for the last five years. I want to run away and find a different district to work at altogether. But instead, I do the single most embarrassing thing of them all. I burst into tears in front of my ex.

Chapter Fourteen

Tanner

Molly has tears running down her cheeks, and I freeze. It's been a long, long time since I've seen her cry, and I don't have a clue what to do anymore. How does one comfort his ex-girlfriend who he kind of, sort of wants to be friends with again? Do I hold her hand? Pull her into a hug?

My eyes flick to her lips, and suddenly, I remember our first kiss. The blankets, the stars, the way her lips tasted like mint lip balm. And suddenly, I want to kiss her again. Show her that even after five years, I still need her. Still care.

I vehemently shake my head as I come around her desk and tug her into an awkward hug. Molly stiffens like a board before wrapping her arms around my waist and burying her warm little self against me with another burst of tears.

The urge to kiss her overwhelms me again. She still fits perfectly against my chest. Her head nestles into the curve of my shoulder and collarbone. Her hands clasp at the small of my back, and she gives just the right amount of pressure to her hug. I lean my cheek against her head, the sweet scent of her shampoo different from the last time I'd held her five years ago. It surprises me. Molly is a stickler for consistency. To switch shampoo? Something drastic had to have happened.

I hold her, enjoying the feel of her in my arms, and try to not think about kissing her. I swallow the lump in my throat and try desperately to douse the heat building in my stomach. I don't deserve Molly. I shouldn't be given a second chance at loving her.

But...

And that *but* is a dangerous thing. It means I could screw up again. It means I could hurt Molly worse and in more permanent ways. It means I have hope.

Is hope a bad thing? What if there is a chance to try again? To show her I really do care?

Stop it, Bradshaw. You have a team to focus on.

But what if I could focus on both at the same time? The email I'd written last night pops into my mind—taunting me with the possibility of having Molly around a lot more than eight hours a day in our shared classroom.

The bell rings a warning. Molly steps out of my arms, wiping furiously at her face. "I'm okay," she lies, her eyes red-rimmed and cheeks blotchy.

"Are you sure?" I jab my thumb over my shoulder, towards the door. "We can wait to let the natives in."

She laughs at my weak humor and shakes her head. "I will be fine."

"Sweetie's, after work." I hold my finger up to stop her protest. "And then you can sit at the Rink until practice is over, okay?"

"Stop it." She glares at me.

"Stop what?"

"Stop being nice. It's not normal." She rubs her arms and won't look at me.

Interesting. "I'm not the one who's been hostile since the first day of work." I grin when she scowls. "You know I'm right."

"Well, regardless. You don't have time to run to Sweetie's before practice." She rubs a hand over her knee-length skirt nervously. "Besides, what if Gloria sees us?"

I raise a brow. Now she's fishing for an excuse to not go with me. But this isn't because of Gloria. Molly has been doing this all week long. And suddenly, I see it as a challenge, and my competitive streak flares to life. This is now a battle of wills. One I will win if it kills me. It's time to crush her feeble excuses like I used to crush the opposing team. It's time to *make* Molly be friends with me—one way or another.

More knocks sound against the door, but I ignore them. Instead, I lean against Molly's desk as she settles into her chair. "So what if Gloria sees us?"

"So," she rolls her eyes and sniffs, "I like my job and don't want to get fired."

"You're not going to get fired." Time to play my cards and see if I have a full house or a bust. "Because if anyone asks, we'll just say that I'm simply getting a coffee with my new assistant coach."

"Your—what?" Her eyes widen.

Checkmate. Wait, I was playing poker. Ah, never mind.

I brace my hands on her desk as she launches to her feet. "You heard me."

"I can't assistant coach."

"Why not? Are you going to take Ava up on her figure skating offer?"

"How do you know about that?"

"I have my connections." Ava hadn't just been Molly's friend when we were all in school. Ava and I had been in the same grade. We'd gone to homecoming together the year before Molly and I started to date. We'd even stayed in touch when we'd gone our separate ways.

More in touch than Molly and me, which is something I still regret. Maybe this wouldn't be so hard if I hadn't up and bailed on this woman in front of me.

"Ava is a traitor," Molly mutters under her breath, causing my grin to appear of its own accord. With a huff, she shakes her head.

"I'm so out of the loop when it comes to figure skating, so having me be a coach would never work."

"But hockey?"

My plan is weak, but maybe dangling the love of the sport that's been my life in front of Molly will win her over. Mrs. Pruitt never wanted Molly to play—something about Molly getting hurt. So maybe coaching will be enticing enough for Molly to spend time with me.

She's shaking her head, so it's time to add some sugar to this offer.

"Come on! You'll be great. You might not get paid, but then Gloria won't have a leg to stand on if she sees us together. We're friends who work together. That's it." *For now.* I shake the thought away. Despite wanting to spend time with Molly, there is no way we can be more. I burned that bridge years ago when I left without a word. "What do you say?"

Molly looks from one eye to the other, likely looking for the lie in my words. "You're serious." It's a statement, not a question, but I nod, regardless. "That's insane, Tanner."

"Come on, Mols. No one has ever accused me of being sane before in my life." Her snort of laughter causes my chest to tighten. "I want to be friends with you again. I...I've missed you."

A lot.

I never let myself dwell on it when I'd been gone, but I'd missed Cloverfield fiercely. Despite running from it and all the memories, deep down, I'd longed for it. Mr. and Mrs. Pruitt had been like another set of parents. Molly's brothers—Ryder and Ryley—had been some of my best friends, once upon a time. Then there was Mom, Dad, and Taysleigh. My family by blood. They'd supported my dreams but didn't like how far away it took me from Cloverfield.

But out of all the people in my hometown, I'd missed Molly the most. I missed her smile and the way she pushed her glasses up with the side of her finger when she was thinking. I missed her thoughtful insights on the world. The way she rambled on about things she was passionate about—whether that was books, coffee, or her theories about whatever show she was watching. Her voice would play through my head at night, when it was harder to run from the past, from the ache in my chest.

Standing here, in front of her, I know I don't deserve a second chance with Molly Pruitt, even if it is just in friendship. So, why am I hoping she'll say yes to my proposal? This ridiculous, off-the-wall offer to be my assistant coach?

"You are aware I haven't watched hockey in five years?" she asks with crossed arms.

Someone pounds on the classroom door, and I point at Molly as I stride toward it. "This conversation is paused until Sweetie's."

I'm rewarded when a wry smile twists Molly's lips. "Fine."

"Fine," I parrot, knowing there is far too much hope in that single word. I want this to work. Hope has me wishing to mend the trust I broke five years ago. I think I can see it, lingering in the depths of Molly's eyes. I feel her gaze finding me when she's teaching. I'm not even sure she realizes she does it, but Molly will lock eyes with me. And deep in the azure-blue rests a desire for approval.

Sweet mercy, but do I ever want to give her it. I want to build up her confidence, a trait that had been absent when we'd dated. I want to watch her unfold more and more into the strong woman that was just beginning to bloom the day I took off for Texas.

You messed up big time, Bradshaw. I run a hand through my hair as I unlock the door and head for the gym. To check the equipment, obviously. It's clearly *not* an escape from the suffocating presence that is my ex-girlfriend. Of course not.

The juniors watch me as they file into Molly's room, and I can only pray that they keep their freaking mouths shut.

Because the high school rumor mill is the last thing I need to deal with right now.

I lean against the counter at Sweetie's and tap my fingers against it as I watch Molly. She clicks her red pen and stares off into space. As soon as we stepped through the door, she plopped into a booth and spread out the seniors' summer book reports.

"Here you go, *miele*." Ms. Esperanza hands me the to-go cups. She nods toward Molly in the booth, and her brow hitches up. "Are you together *now*, Tanner?"

I quickly shake my head. Everyone loved Molly and me when we'd dated, cooing over how cute and perfect we were. Perhaps we had been. But now? Now, we're a broken, splintered disaster. Maybe even fractured beyond repair. Simply put, Molly and I are a mess.

Smiling at the kind Italian woman, I thank her and move back toward the booth. I notice there's not a spot of red ink on any of the pages.

Sliding across from Molly, I push her latte across the table. "You haven't started that yet?" She startles, her wide blue eyes narrowing when I laugh and say, "Geez, you're jumpy, Mols."

"Don't sneak up on me, Bradshaw, and we wouldn't have this problem."

Well, this level of sass is new, but I'm finding it pleasantly refreshing. I roll my eyes and gesture to the caramel latte. "Your drink, my lady."

Ignoring my sarcasm, the same way I'd ignored hers, she holds the lid up to her nose and breathes in the salty, caramelly scent. A contented sigh slips passed her lips—lips which now have a light gloss on them.

But I'm not staring at her lips. Of course not.

"This is what Heaven will smell like," Molly says.

"I'm not certain caramel coffee is a divine drink," I reply.

"Blasphemy!" She shakes her finger at me, attempting a scowl, but failing utterly.

"Nope, not blasphemy. Heaven will only serve the superior vanilla latte." I take a sip before clicking on my tablet and pulling up the list of names. I run a hand through my hair, tugging at the ends.

"Vanilla is superior to caramel? Seriously?" Skepticism drips from her words.

I don't look up, preoccupied with my team and who to put on what strings. Even after a week of watching the boys play together, I can't decide. A big part of my mind keeps straying to Kai Reynolds. He hasn't returned to the Rink since he stormed out Monday, and I wonder about him. Worry, really. I know what it's like to lose a parent, even if it's a bit of a different circumstance. I know it's been three years for him, but I still saw that wound in his eyes when I first met him. A wound I know all too well.

Losing a parent is like losing a piece of your heart. There are moments when you want to talk to them, tell them something, or ask for their advice. Then it's as if the wound is ripped open, becoming raw and sore and seeping with pain once more.

Molly's words cut through my spiraling thoughts. "Are you listening to me?"

"Yeah, mm-hmm, sure." I am, now. Watching her out of the corner of my eye, I hide a smirk with another swig of my latte.

She scoffs. "Then you heard me say that you just don't strike me as a froufrou coffee drinker?"

"What?" I ask, fully looking into her smirking face now.

Molly is cupping her chin in her palm and grinning wickedly at my affronted expression. With a shrug of false nonchalance, she drops her gaze to the papers before her. "You heard me."

"Yeah, I did. But why on earth do you think that?" My brows pull low, and I lean back against the booth. "I mean, I ordered it the other day, and you didn't bat an eye. Why is it suddenly unmanly or whatever?"

A pretty shade of pink jumps into Molly's cheeks as she shrugs again. "I don't know."

I cross my arms and lean against the table, invading her space. She draws back slightly, but that only gives me a better view of her eyes. They flick nervously, and I wonder why. We've seen each other all week. Even had some decently civil conversations. There shouldn't be this gaping awkwardness. I hugged her this morning, for pity's sake! But I can tell having me this close is making her uncomfortable. And I kind of like it.

"Yes, I like froufrou coffee," I respond. "But I also enjoy black coffee first thing in the morning. This," I gesture to my coffee cup, "is my afternoon treat for surviving having my office in *your* classroom."

I raise it in a salute and take a swig, watching her the whole time. Her eyes follow the curve of my neck, the pink turning a shade darker even as her eyes widen. "Nice," she squeaks. "Very...good."

I grin and lean forward again. "Whose report are you working on?"

"Gloria's." Her nose wrinkles, causing her glasses to slide down it when she returns to her normal expression. I watch in mild satisfaction as she pushes them up with the side of her finger—just like I remember. The clicking of her pen starts up. "It's horrible. I'm scared of what tantrum I'm going to have to endure if I have to give it a bad grade."

"Why do you think there's going to be a tantrum?" I ask, taking another swallow of my coffee.

"Her grades are all As and Bs." Molly mirrors my posture, her normally sweet floral scent swirling with caramel coffee. For a heartbeat, I let myself wonder if her lips would taste the same as the coffee.

"And?" I ask, forcing my brain back to Gloria and Molly's horrible morning.

"I'm afraid she threatens the teachers for good grades," Molly admits.

My mouth falls open. "That's quite the speculation there, Mols."

She shrugs and shoves the paper at me. "What do *you* think?"

I watch as Molly picks up another book report and begins to mark it with her red pen. There's a grace to her movements that is mesmerizing. After a minute of watching, I turn to the paper in my hand.

The beginning is awful. I flinch at every typo—I can see a ton, my misspellings are notorious—and the wording makes no sense. She rambles about something for a paragraph before it turns in a completely different direction.

"Well?" Molly asks as I hand the paper back to her.

"Yeah, that's bad."

"Told you. There's no way she got As all of last year if that's the quality of the work she turned in. Teachers have to be afraid of her. Or of her parents." Molly sighs and cups her forehead in her hand. "But I'm going to grade it the way I see fit and see what happens."

I nod. "Are you ready to head to practice? I want your thoughts on the team, *Coach* Pruitt."

She glares at me as she stacks her papers into a folder. "I never said I'd do it."

"I know. But you're going to, aren't you?" I lean closer, holding my breath as I wait for her reply.

Chapter Fifteen

Molly

I stare at Tanner, dumbfounded at his question. Assistant coach of the Cougars? Why would he want *my* help? If anything, he should be asking old Coach Reynolds. He knows the team better than me.

What in the world is going on with us? I don't have a title for...this. Whatever it is. It isn't just friendship, something I can easily identify with Susan, Emily, and Ava. It isn't what I feel for Ryley and Ryder, either. I don't see Tanner as a brother in any form of the word. But as much as I want it to be more than a brothership or friendship, it can't be.

Can it?

No. I won't let it. Because to do that means I can get hurt again. I don't want to get hurt again.

"Made you speechless there, Mols?" Tanner chuckles, snapping me from my wandering thoughts. I meet his gaze. He's so at ease. Much more than I am. I'm sitting here wanting labels and titles, and he's over there just being Tanner. Laughing, teasing, even supporting me. It's like he's fallen right back into what we were before we dated, and I'm still floundering in the deep end of the relationship pool—the rejected and bruised girlfriend.

"I—I told you at the school, I'm no coach."

"I don't want you to be simply a coach." He sighs leaning on the table again. "You have a rapport with these boys. They know you. Respect you. You stayed here for college. They've seen you around town and know your brothers. The legendary hockey team twins."

"Tanner—"

He holds his hand up to halt my protest, locking his baby-blue eyes on me with a magnetism that leaves me breathless. "I need your help, Molly. Please, be my assistant coach?"

"I have my job." I gesture at my briefcase and then sigh. "But if you promise it won't interfere with my work, then I suppose..."

"Yes?" he prompts when I trail off.

"Yeah, sure."

His grin makes his eyes sparkle as his dimple appears. He's practically glowing, and I feel a grin of my own appear on my face.

Dang you, Tanner Bradshaw. How have I survived without that smile for the last five years? It feels like the sun had been behind the clouds, and now, suddenly, I am basking in its warm, golden rays.

"Ready?" Tanner asks, slinging the strap of his satchel over his shoulders. I refuse to acknowledge how good he looks today. No man should be sexy in a Mr. Rogers cardigan, but Tanner is rocking the navy-blue cardigan with the purple polo underneath. *Purple polo.* The man is a walking model for Calvin Klein!

"Yep, totally ready!" I clear my throat and push to my feet, fumbling with my coffee, purse, car keys, and briefcase. Not at all distracted by my ex.

Ex: a prefix meaning *not* or *former.*

So, when I refer to Tanner as my ex-boyfriend, it means that he is *no longer my significant other.*

My heart still needs to get the memo.

"Here, let me help." Tanner grabs my briefcase, juggling his coffee and keys effortlessly in his large hand.

"Thanks." Does my voice sound breathy? Nah. If anyone questions it, I'll blame the caffeine pumping through my veins. "Let's go."

I sit on the bench as Tanner paces behind the boards, blowing his whistle and calling out formations and plays to the boys. They're padded up and playing a little five-on-five. Carter sits beside me.

As the goalie, he'll get more one-on-one with Tanner after normal practice. If we had one more player, we could have both of the goals filled.

The boys look good. Tanner has them evenly matched on each side. I see a lot of them play well off of each other, making a lot of options for different lines come game time. The Cougars haven't had a team like this since Tanner was a sophomore.

"Excuse me, Coach Bradshaw?" A low, young voice calls as he steps into the bench box. He's taller than Tanner, meaning he's probably pushing six-foot-three, and his smile is dazzling. He walks over to Tanner, extending his hand. "I'm Ethan Graham. I just transferred to Cloverfield from Rockhills?"

Rockhills? Oh dear. Rockhills has been the rival of Cloverfield for *years*. If we're getting a player from there, it could mean a royal pain in the butt for Tanner when it comes to keeping the team's loyalty.

Owen, who'd been on offense on the play Tanner was running, skates close enough to catch the exchange. He stumbles forward and barely catches himself. He turns sharply toward Tanner and Ethan. "We don't want him on *our* team."

Tanner crosses his arms and leans against the boards. "And why not?"

"He's the enemy."

I can't see Tanner's face, but I can imagine his brow rising as he says, "He was their top player last year. Led them to a championship, if I'm not mistaken."

Ethan smiles humbly and ducks his head. "I was on a team, sir. It takes a team to win a trophy."

My brows shoot up. *Impressive.* I already like this young man. He has a humility about him that's rare, especially for high school guys with talent.

Tanner smiles at the boy. "You're right about that. And you want to join the team?"

"If I'm not too late, sir?" Ethan turns, and I notice an equally tall and slender young lady behind him. "This is my sister, Willow. She used to play on the girls' team at Rockhills, but your school doesn't have a girls' team…"

"Are you wanting to join the Cougars?" I ask, standing next to Tanner before realizing there's barely enough space for one person between the bench and the boards, let alone two. My shoulder pushes into his, and I kneel one knee on the bench to keep from pitching forward.

"Yes, ma'am." Willow grins, her front tooth noticeably chipped "I may be a girl, but I'm tough, too. I'm not afraid to get hit, and honestly, I'm stronger and a better skater than a lot of the juniors on our boys' varsity team back in Rockhills."

I smile. Reynolds hadn't let me play in high school—although I was beginning to wonder if that was Mom's doing—but there aren't any rules in the league about a girl not being allowed to play on an all-guy team.

Tanner nods, shoving his hands into his pockets. "I'd be interested in seeing both of you in action. We have a defenseman who has also played goalie. Since he's a sophomore, he'd be a good second-string goalie and I can put you in on defense. What do you play, Ethan?"

"Right wing, though I'm pretty flexible."

With a nod, Tanner turns and blows his whistle.

I step up behind him, and whisper, "Are you sure about this? You're going to tick Owen off, and he's a nightmare when he's mad."

"Not too worried about that little punk right now, Mols," he turns, and suddenly, he's in my space. Far too close and still smelling like pine and spearmint.

I gulp and take a step back, forgetting about the bench. My arms pinwheel as I tip back, seemingly in slow motion. My head slams against the Plexiglas, and then the edge of the backboard; stars explode behind my eyes, followed closely by blackness.

But I can still hear.

"Molly?" Tanner mutters a curse as he leans over me, then he hollers, "Leo! Get some ice."

"I'm fine," I declare, but the words slur together, and I'm not sure they even exit my lips as anything more than a groan.

"Sweet mercy, you're still an adorable klutz," Tanner whispers. He grabs my hand and sits me up. Then his arm is around my waist, and I'm nestled against his broad, warm, solid chest.

Oh, good gracious. He smells even better this close. I hadn't let myself breathe deeply when he'd hugged me at school. Was that only this morning? It feels like eons ago. Because in this moment, tucked against Tanner and hearing his heart—is that how fast it normally beats? —thudding against my ear, I feel like I am home for the first time in five years.

Wait, home? I push away and force my eyes to open. The fluorescent lights stab into my brain, and I wince.

"Ow," I whisper, slumping against Tanner with a groan of frustration. "I'm an idiot."

"No, Molly, you're not," Owen growls. I glance over at him as he glares daggers into Tanner. But Tanner's looking down at me, a worried divot in his forehead that makes me want to reach up and smooth it out with my thumb.

I squash that impulse as Leo skates over and hands me an old washcloth with ice cubes in it. "Here, Coach. Are you alright, Miss Pruitt? You blacked out for a minute."

"I'm fine." Heat blooms in my cheeks as Tanner's arm tightens before he helps settle me beside him on the bench. "Just a bump."

I jump as Tanner's hand reaches up to feel the back of my head. He's gentle, his large fingers probing under my thick hair. He touches the spot, and I wince.

"I want five of you on offense, five on defense. Seb and Carter are on goal. Get going."

"But Molly—" Owen begins to argue.

I shut him down. "Do as you're told, or you can be kicked from the team, Owen. Got it?"

He scowls at me but skates past Carter and over to the side Ethan isn't on.

Willow plops on the bench beside me and eyes me curiously as Tanner presses the washcloth of ice to my head. "You two a couple?" she asks.

"No!" I declare quickly as Tanner replies, "Absolutely not!"

Willow's hands fly up in a surrender pose with a droll chuckle. "Sorry! Just looks like you are worried about her, Coach."

Tanner meets my gaze, and his crocked smile appears. "She's my assistant coach. Of course, I'm worried about her."

And for some exasperating reason, the butterflies take to shivering in my stomach again.

After practice and Tanner's thorough check for a possible concussion, I slam the door to my car and lean my forehead against the steering wheel with a long sigh. I need to talk to *someone* about what's going on. Thankfully, I have a few options.

Mom, of course, will tell me to drop the assistant coach gig and Tanner like a hot potato. She'd been furious when he'd taken off with only a letter to explain and had been the one to comfort me as I wallowed in Ben & Jerry's and true crime shows for months. She won't be much help in the objectivity department.

Then there is Ava. She likes Tanner and has never really stopped even after he broke my heart. She never gave up hope that he would come back for me. She might also be one of the reasons he hovers at work and knows my schedule so well. Again—no help.

That leaves Susan or Emily.

Emily has informed me every night that Tanner is "a nice, tall glass of water" and that I should "just drink him up before someone else does." I wrinkle my nose as I turn the key and begin to back up. Yep, that's a nope to talking to Emily.

So, Susan it is. She is the most logical of us all. Steady and dependable, she likes baking because it's both an art and a science. She's an old soul in a young body and the perfect person to turn to for help and wisdom.

I text the girls that I'm picking up pizza for dinner, and one large pepperoni later, I'm pulling into our driveway. Juggling my briefcase and purse on one arm and balancing the pizza with the other, I bump the car door closed with my hip and wobble in my heels up to the porch. Emily is waiting and flings open the front door with unabashed enthusiasm.

"Pizza!" she sings in a warbly, off-key alto that has me wincing from my headache. Her brows wrinkle as I shove the box at her. "Woah, you look horrible!"

"Thanks." I kick off my shoes and hurry into the kitchen as my temples pound. I need ibuprofen, and I need it now. I throw four into my mouth and swallow. After having my wisdom teeth out, I know it is the most I can take and be safe.

Susan pops her head into the kitchen as Emily slides the pizza box onto the stove and opens a bag of sour cream and cheddar chips. Susan hops onto a barstool and studies me. "Something happened. What happened?"

I reach up to feel the knot on the back of my head. "Tripped over the bench at the Rink and whacked myself on the head."

"What were you doing at the Rink?" Emily asks around a mouthful of chips.

"I—well, I may be the new assistant coach of the Cougars now. Yay." I wave my index fingers in the air and cut a glance at Susan. Her mouth is hanging open in disbelief.

Emily, however, is at no such loss for words. "Wait! That means you're working with *the* Tanner Bradshaw! Dude, this is just like that one romance novel, the—" she snaps her fingers, and the sound is worse than nails on a chalkboard—which is the most horrific sound known to mankind. "Oh, I can't think of the title. But it's second chance romance and sports, and that's *you and Tanner.*" She starts to squeal.

I hold my hand up, cutting it off mid-crescendo. "Em! I have the mother of all headaches from hitting my head, and all I want is pizza, a cheesy chick flick, and then bed."

"You don't have a concussion?" Susan asks, studying me like she would one of her fancy frosted cookies.

"No. Tanner checked and..." I trail off as heat climbs into my cheeks.

Emily practically has heart-shaped pupils. "Aw! How romantic is that?"

I roll my eyes. "I'm glad tomorrow is Saturday. I don't think I could handle working tomorrow."

We load up our paper plates with carbs and sugar, popping open cans of sparkling water as we settle onto the couch. Susan ends up in the middle, and as Emily clicks on *While You Were Sleeping,* I lean over and whisper, "I need to talk to you about today. Later."

"Yeah, you do." She smiles to soften her words.

I lean my head against her shoulder for a minute before sitting up and tucking my legs under me. As we laugh at the antics of Lucy Moderatz, I can't help but feel every bit as confused about my love life as she is about hers.

Chapter Sixteen

Tanner

Earlier that afternoon...

I watch Molly pull out of the Rink parking lot as I lock up. I rub the back of my neck and force some deep breaths into my lungs.

Dang, woman. I think as I walk to my car. When she'd blacked out after hitting her head, a million *what ifs* had danced through my own. *What if* she is hurt? *What if* she's going to die and you never apologized? *What if* life could have been different? *What if* you'd married her and had little hockey babies on mini skates?

Nope, not doing that. I back out of the lot and head for home. Only, home sounds horrible. I don't want to talk to Mom about this. Besides, Aunt Cheryl is there, and she'll be taking care of Mom's ankle. I shudder. I love my extended family, but Aunt Cheryl is a lot to handle on a good day. And today hadn't been the best.

Mind made up, I punch in Taysleigh's number.

She picks up on the second ring, but screaming is all I hear. I jerk the phone away from my ear as I ease to a stop at the light.

"Hayley Marie Collins! You be nice to Henry!" She sighs, sounding so much like Mom that I smile. "Sorry, Tanner."

"It's okay. You sound like you have your hands full tonight." I chuckle as I begin driving again. "How are you?"

"Exhausted. James had to work a double tonight at the factory, and I want to strangle the children. I haven't even been able to pee in peace."

"TMI, Tays." I laugh and shake my head. Taysleigh has no problem oversharing—much to Mom's mortification. "Hey, why don't I grab some pizza for dinner and come over? I have some things I want to talk to you about."

"Sure. But it'll just be me and you. The kids refused to nap today and are going to bed *right now!*" She screams the last part, and a shriek from Hayley echoes through the phone's speaker.

"Okay." I smile, already feeling better. "I'll see you in thirty minutes."

"Roger that!"

Thirty minutes later, armed with a hot pepperoni pizza, a bag of barbeque chips for Taysleigh, and sour cream and onion for me, I fumble with her door. The bag of flavored waters tugs at my free arm, but I manage to get the door open, and then kick it softly closed with my foot.

I sidestep the pile of blocks and the overturned laundry basket, making my way back to the kitchen. Every light in the house is on, and I can hear Henry wailing down the hall that's off the kitchen. Pushing the keep warm button on the oven, I slide the pizza in and shove the drinks into the fridge.

Surveying the war zone that is my sister's home, I settle on the laundry. Stretching my bad leg out in front of me as I lower myself to the floor, I begin to fold the clothes in the basket. Henry's little superhero onesie that I got him because it says *My Uncle is Super* with a cape attached to it and Hayley's princess tutu. Taysleigh's *Momma Bear* shirt and James's flannel pajama pants.

I fall into a rhythm, folding, sorting, pairing, stacking. There's something peaceful about this. Despite the screaming toddler and the food getting gross in the oven...I want this. I want a family, to settle down and have a life outside of hockey. I hadn't wanted that five years ago. I'd been scared of it, actually. But then Taysleigh met James. Their love story sucked me in, despite my teasing them mercilessly. And now, the life they have? I crave it. Crave the comfort of a home with a woman's touch and screaming, laughing, exuberant kids.

"Wow, that's a sight to behold. My baby brother, folding the laundry." Taysleigh grins from her spot leaning against the doorframe. Her chocolate-brown curls are pulled into a messy bun that sits askew on her head, and instead of contacts, her purple glasses are sliding down her nose as she pushes off the doorframe and shoves a chair back into place at the cluttered table. "Thanks, by the way."

"Sure." I stack the clothes away. "Although folding your underwear is—"

"Ah!" She holds up her finger. "No words on the undies. I have had just about enough of fart and underwear jokes today. I want grown-up conversations."

I grin. "Like the fluctuating stock market or the price of car insurance?"

"I was thinking more about your job." She bends and picks up a sippy cup from under the high chair, adding it to the leaning tower of dishes in the sink. "How's coaching going?"

I push to my feet, wincing at the tightness in my leg as I move to grab the drinks out of the fridge. "Good. Some of the boys hate my guts, but I was expecting that."

"That sounds horrible." Taysleigh adds two slices to a plate and hands it to me. "Shove the kids' coloring stuff to one side of the table, will you?"

I obey and continue our conversation. "It's not so bad. I kind of enjoy the challenge." I pause. "I may have enlisted some help."

"Oh? Who? Old Coach Reynolds?" She's distracted, picking up a bottle of blueberry-pomegranate water while juggling the bag of chips and her plate.

I grab her plate and my sour cream and onion chips as I say. "Molly Pruitt."

The bottle slips from her fingers and nails her big toe. A word that would have had Mom washing our mouths out with soap if she heard it flies off Taysleigh's lips as she hops on one foot, staring at me. "Are you insane? Are you trying to rip your heart out of your chest?"

"What?" I ask, innocently nibbling at my pizza and trying to ignore the death glare being leveled my way. "She's a coworker."

"She's your ex!" Taysleigh slams the bottle on the table. "You're being an idiot! Who asks the girl they dumped five years ago to help with..." She trails off and stares hard at me.

I squirm in my chair, playing with a stringy piece of cheese on my plate. I think I know what she's thinking, but sometimes Taysleigh comes out of left field with what pops out of her mouth, so I keep mine closed for the time being. Better safe than sorry.

"You still like her, don't you, T?" Her voice is soft, caring, and I hate it.

I rub the back of my neck and mutter a curse. "I don't know, Tays. It's not what I thought it would be, you know? Seeing her again, I can see the hurt I caused. Every time she looks at me, it's there. It's raw, and I want to fix it."

"You can't fix this, Tanner." Taysleigh's fingers close around my fist that sits on the table. "You know that, right?"

"I can try. I have to try. I can't work with her every day and not attempt to mend the rift, right?"

"Have you asked her to forgive you?" Taysleigh picks up her pizza and takes a bite, meaning I have to answer her question.

"No, I haven't. Because she can't, can she? I was a horrible person. I took off and left her a freaking letter to explain. How is that fair, Tays? How can she forgive that?"

Her brow rises, and she's never looked more like Mom in her life. "Sounds to me like you're taking the choice out of her hands. Again."

I almost choke on my bite of pizza. Had I done that when I'd left? I'd talked about the opportunity to Molly, but I guess I never did ask her what she thought. I never encouraged her voice. I certainly hadn't asked if she wanted to come with me. Fear had me running off, not looking back at the bridge I burned. If I'd asked Molly to come, would I already have the family I craved?

I glare at my sister. "When did you get so insightful? Stop it. I don't like it."

She laughs. While I got Dad's baby-blue eyes, hers are as deep and dark as Mom's. "Well, I think kids give you an extra dose of wisdom, even though you feel clueless ninety percent of the time when raising them."

"I'm sorry you had a bad day today," I say sincerely as I pop open the chip bags.

"Eh." She shrugs a shoulder and grabs one of the barbeque chips. "Kids will be kids."

I raise my lemon-flavored water. "I can salute!"

"Cheers!" She laughs as she taps hers against mine.

Chapter Seventeen

Molly

The movie is only half over, but Emily is out, snoring against the arm of the couch with her feet tucked under her.

Susan chuckles as she turns to me. The movie plays softly in the background—Lucy and Jack sliding around on the ice. "So, what did you want to talk to me about?"

"I—" I swallow. "I'm not sure how to describe it."

"Do your best with the words coming out of your mouth." She gestures to my lips. "You know, it's that thing below your nose that makes sounds so I can understand."

"But I don't know where to start," I say, giggling at the exaggerated roll of Susan's eyes.

"How about here—*you took a freaking job with Tanner Bradshaw?*" She hisses the words in a whisper, but they still make me flinch.

"Yeah, I did." And for whatever reason, that thought doesn't fill me with dread. Instead, excitement thrums against my ribs. I'm working with a hockey team! I'm a coach for the best sport in the world!

I sigh and lean my head back, staring up at the ceiling. "I know Tanner dumped me. But he also hugged me today after one of my students was a complete jerk and brought up things I didn't want to think about. Then he bought me coffee and offered me an assistant coaching position in a sport I've always wanted to be in, but Mom said no to. One that Gramps, Dad, and my brothers love and that I've been on the fringe of my whole life. Tanner is giving me a chance to..." I shrug, not knowing how to end that sentence. *He's giving me a chance to be* me. *To be a part of something I've dreamt of my entire life.* Instead, I say, "I know it means spending time with Tanner, but I think he's—"

"If you say *he's changed* so help me, Molly Pruitt, you *will* be concussed because I'll punch your lights out."

"But he is," I grab her hand to keep her from hitting me and continue, "and I'm confused. I told myself Monday that I wouldn't let him pull me in again. But he's gone right back to being my friend. I don't know what to do with that, Sue! I thought that if he ever decided to come back to Cloverfield, it would be with a girlfriend, or at the very least, he'd ignore me. Because *he* left *me*! But no, he's jumping right back in, and I—"

"Sounds like he's still in love with you."

Both Susan and I turn to Emily, who's rubbing her eyes. She yawns and her jaw pops. She looks at both of us—my undoubtedly pale complexion and Susan's murderous glare. "What? What'd I say?"

She has no idea the effect those words have on me. My mouth goes dry, my hands feel clammy, and adrenaline shoots through me. My fight or flight kicks in, and I lurch to my feet.

"He can't be," I mutter, hot and flushed even as ice slides through my veins. "He can't love me."

"He doesn't." Susan shakes her head. "He left you."

"Cold feet," Emily says, and Susan swings a pillow at her, causing our friend to fall off the sofa. "Ouch, Susan!"

"Serves you right." Susan turns to me. "I know you are still hung up on Tanner, but—"

"I am not!" I declare hotly, crossing my arms and forcing my erratic pacing to stop. I'm not *hung up* on Tanner. I can't be. He let me go and never looked back.

"How many guys have you dated since Tanner?" Susan asks, her eyes daring me to lie.

The memories of our first date, our first kiss, hiding in the cupboard, they pour through my mind, and I squeeze my eyes shut.

Emily, still on the ground, asks, "Is this a trick question? Molly hasn't been on a date since I've known her."

Susan's voice is triumphant. "See?"

Tears prick my eyes. They're right. Tanner still has my heart. None of the guys who have asked me out since have his baby-blue eyes or dark-brown hair. None of the guys understand my love of literature and hockey. No one else smiles when I ramble and listens with undivided attention. And it bugs me that they can't seem to measure up to the man who chose the NHL over me.

"Molly, I can't tell you what to do." I open my eyes to find Susan staring at me with an intensity I'm unaccustomed to. "But I know that unrequited love is no way to live your life. I've been there, done that. It's not fun. Tanner's back, fine. But hanging around him and putting yourself in a situation that can break your heart all over again isn't smart. I love you like a sister." Her voice catches, and she clears it before continuing. "And the last thing I want is for you to get hurt."

"I know." I sigh and flop back onto the couch. "I just...I want to coach hockey. Hockey has been in my life since the day I was born. Ryder and Ryley played it through college."

"Yeah, I know." There's a wealth of feeling behind Susan's words, and I turn toward my best friend.

Emily pops back onto the couch. "Not to change the topic, but are we going to address the fact that Sue said she's been on the wrong side of unrequited love?"

I study Susan. "Yeah, what's that about?"

"And *who* is it about?" Emily leans forward, eyes dancing in the dim, flickering light of the movie.

"It's old news and not worth talking about," Susan hedges.

I study my friend. Susan has been on dates since I've known her. But the fact is, they never seem to move beyond a second date. Ever. And then there's the way she stumbled over calling me her sister. There's also this little detail: I invite my roommates over for Sunday dinners at my parents' place all the time, and while Emily has come, Susan always has an excuse.

The pieces click, and I smirk. "Which brother?"

Susan blushes and shakes her head, hiding her face in her hands as she groans.

"Oh my word!" Emily cackles, and Susan chucks another throw pillow at her head. "You have a crush on one of Molly's brothers!"

"Which one?" I press.

"Ryder," she mumbles, trailing her finger over the fleece blanket to make patterns in it.

I can see it. Ryder is going to culinary school in the hopes of opening a restaurant in Cloverfield. Susan is a prolific baker who's saving to start a bakery. On paper, they make sense.

My mind wanders back to the first time I had Susan over to my house for a meal. It was the twins' birthday, and Mom had ordered us all home from college. She'd let me invite Susan, and it was a night full of games and laughter, cake and presents. Susan came alive that night, teasing Ryder and Ryley as much as I did. She'd fit into our family in a way that few of my friends ever had.

She'd come over more during the school year and even stayed for a few weeks in the summer when her parents had gone on vacation to Europe for their thirtieth anniversary. And after that...

"What happened the summer you stayed with us?" I ask curiously, propping my arm on the back of the sofa so I could better look at her.

"I—"

"Nope! Don't deny it. After that summer, you didn't come to the house anymore. What did my idiot brothers do?"

"Nothing!" Susan stands abruptly, her jaw popping as she grits her teeth. "I'm going to bed. Think about what I said, Mols. Good night."

She flies up the stairs and slams her door so hard the pictures in the living room quiver.

"What just happened?" Emily asked, looking at me in shock.

"I don't know," I admit. *But I'm going to find out Sunday.* Ryder and Ryley are spilling their guts because no one hurts one of my best friends and gets away with it. Not even my brothers.

Saturday drags. Tanner texts me a couple times with questions about the boys and the positions they play. He tells me he's decided to let both Ethan and Willow on the team, although Willow will be a bench warmer this year unless needed. While Reynolds adhered to the strict *no girls* policy, it appears that Tanner really doesn't care. I grin as I reply to his text.

Me: Sounds like a plan

Is that an appropriate response? Why is he even texting me? I hit send and settle back in to grade the horrendously awful book reports. Surprisingly, Seb's is the best so far. Although I don't know why I am so amazed. The kid seems like one who throws his whole heart into whatever he does.

My phone pings, and I glance at it, shocked that Tanner texted back so quickly.

Tanner: What are you up to on this dreary Saturday?

I glance out the window. Raindrops streak down it like tears on a cheek, and the gentle ping of the water dripping from the eaves is a lullaby that makes me yawn, even though it's only ten o'clock in the morning.

Me: Grading papers. These kids have no clue about grammar.

Tanner: Well, it's a good thing they have an amazing English teacher.

Me: Are you saying that Ava is a better teacher than me? ;)

I nibble at my lip as the bubbles of doom appear, disappear, appear again. Why do I care so much what he thinks? It's not like he's ever shown romantic interest toward Ava. And I do want him to be my friend—and friend only. I should be encouraging him to date some nice girl and leave me alone.

I've worked myself up to an upset stomach before Tanner's text pings.

Tanner: You're a lit teacher, Mols. You encourage their love of reading, not writing. Ava is an amazing English teacher and you're an unbelievingly enthusiastic, engaging lit teacher.

Me: Thanks

Warmth replaces the dull ache in my stomach as I stare at Tanner's admiration. Why am I doing this to myself? I should text him and say I changed my mind about the assistant coach job. But I don't. I simply stare at the words of praise as a smile comes unbidden to my lips.

Sunday afternoon, I'm hopping up the steps to our old house and letting myself into the entryway. The stairs curve up on my left, a leafy garland of reds, oranges, and yellows revealing the season. I can hear the chatter of my brothers and mother in the kitchen at the back of the house while Dad and Gramps sit in the living room, watching a baseball game on the TV.

The soft browns and greens of the house are like a warm embrace, pulling me in as the yeasty smell of rolls and cheesy potatoes swirls with the cinnamon candle burning on top of the mantle.

"Hey, old men!" I tease as I kick off my flats and move from the entryway to the living room on my way to the kitchen. Susan sent a batch of Mom's favorite cookies—turtle pecan—and I don't want Dad and Gramps to pounce on them first.

"Hey, ol' lady!" Gramps chuckles, looking me over with that sharp eye that misses nothing. "How's my favorite granddaughter?"

"I'm you're only granddaughter." I bend to kiss his weathered cheek, rough with a bit of scruff. I raise my voice so that it carries through the dining room. "And we both know I'm your favorite *grandchild!*"

"I heard that!" Ryley calls from the kitchen.

Gramps chuckles and pats my arm before returning to watch the game.

I kiss Dad's forehead before heading to the kitchen. Mom leans over a sink full of dishes, and Ryley has a towel in hand as he dutifully dries. Ryder stands by the stove, working on whatever we're having for lunch. It smells like spaghetti, but I'm not sure.

I can't help but remember Susan's warning last night about unrequited love, and a strange pang of anger surges toward my brothers. One of them hurt Susan—or possibly both, I suppose. I wouldn't put it past them. It's something I *will* get an answer to before family dinner ends.

"Hey, Mols!" Ryley grins at me, but it quickly drops. "Woah, what's that look for? What'd I do?"

"It's both of you, and we'll talk about it later." I peck Mom's cheek, watching the twins as I say, "Susan sent cookies."

I normally don't monitor my brothers when mentioning my baker friend. But now I do. Ryder's back goes positively stiff while Ryley's eyes spark with curiosity.

Interesting. I turn to Mom. "They're your favorites."

"Oh, turtle pecan!" Her smile stretches across her face as she turns to dry her hands off on a gray hand towel. "Tell her thanks, and that we miss her."

I smile, but it feels forced. "I will."

"How's work going?" Mom asks, and I don't miss the way both of my brothers relax at the change in topic. Although, Ryder still seems wary.

I'm so confused.

"Work is good. A couple kids are pushing me, but I think they'll come around."

"Let me guess, a Steinfield?" Ryley laughs harshly when I nod. "I hate that family. Do you remember Trent, Ryder?"

Ryder turns and leans against the counter, arms crossed. "That kid was the worst! He was a freshman and on the varsity hockey team. Constantly threw fits when we lost or when Coach wouldn't let him play."

"He was *third string*." Ryley throws the towel over his shoulder and moves to put a bowl away, knocking me with his hip as he does. "That family holds way too much power in this town, if you ask me."

Mom tsks her tongue. "Be nice, you two!"

"Just stating a fact." Ryder shrugs before studying me. "You look tired, Mols. You got raccoon eyes." He runs his fingers under his eyes. "Trouble sleeping?"

"A bit," I admit. "I also hit my head Friday at the Rink."

"What were you doing at the Rink?" Ryley asks, turning his full attention on me. "You haven't gone there in years."

I clear my throat. "I may have...I mean I did, but...well—

"Spit it out, sis!" Ryder orders, his brows scrunching together in confusion.

"I took an assistant coach position!" I blurt.

"With Ava?" Mom's eyes light up, and she clasps her hands under her chin in her excitement. "I heard they were looking at hiring one for Spin!"

Oh, I forgot about that offer. And just…ugh, *Spin*. That horrid figure skating competition team I'd been on in middle and high school when Mom wouldn't let me play hockey. I'd loved skating but doing it against others stressed me out. And Ms. Higgly wasn't the nicest instructor. She made Abby from *Dance Moms* seem tame.

"No, it's not with Spin." I back up into the doorway of the kitchen, leaning against it and dropping my gaze. Why am I so nervous? I'm a grown adult. I can make my own choices about where I work or volunteer and who I spend my time with. But something about telling my overprotective family is making me jittery—like I drank one too many cups of coffee.

Ryder cocks his head. "She's hiding something, Mom."

"Should we tickle her to find out?" Ryley grins, throwing the dish towel onto the counter and advancing.

"You're both twenty-five and too old for tickle fights!" I protest.

"Then tell us what the job is!" Ryley laughs as I squeal and leap back. He manages to catch my arm and starts to drag me toward him and Ryder.

"Fine! I'll tell you! The job is helping Tanner with the hockey team!"

Ryder halts mid-tickle, and I rip free. Another silence, this one eerily ominous, settles over the house, the only sound is the low volume of the TV in the living room. Both my brothers stare at me in disbelief.

Mom, of course, starts to speak. "You took a job working with that no good, cocky, pain in the—"

"Mom!" Ryder warns.

Mom sucks in a sharp breath. She's beyond mad. Her eyes glow with a promise of retribution but whether it will be toward me or Tanner, I'm not sure. Her hands are balled into fists at her side. She's livid. "Do you not remember how heartbroken you were when he just took off?"

"I know."

"He left *you*, Molly Elaine. And you're just running back to him, no questions asked?"

"We're not dating, Mom!" I shake my head. This is why I didn't come to Mom last night. She is freaking out just as much as I thought she would.

Ryder eyes me. "Why *did* you take the job? You've avoided everything Tanner related for years."

"Five, but who's counting," Ryley helpfully interjects.

"I've always wanted to have a part in hockey, but Mom wouldn't let me join the Cougars in high school."

"You're five-foot-three and a dozen pounds over a hundred." Mom turns back to the dishes, but I can practically see the tension radiating off of her—like the road on a sweltering summer day. "Excuse me for not wanting you to get destroyed on the ice."

Ryley snorts as he dries a skillet. "She has a point."

"Yeah, fine. I can accept that." I roll my eyes. "But this is the chance for me to help in a sport I really enjoy. And Tanner is also using my classroom for his office for the next few months while they fix his. So, I don't know. He's kind of just picked up the friendship where we left off. There's nothing romantic going on."

My traitorous mind recalls the comforting hug in my class Friday morning. Oh, and the butterflies. The way Tanner held me after I whacked my head. I push all of it away. There's no need to think about that. Ever.

Ryder—the more observant of my two brothers—studies me intently. "That's it?"

"Yeah." I cross my arms. "Can we eat, please? I'm done talking about my *nonexistent* love life."

Mom huffs a breath that waves the short strands of her hair. "I've been wanting to talk to you about that."

Great. Just great.

"Oh?" I ask as I pick up the basket of garlic bread and move toward the dining room.

"Yes, I heard that Pricilla Markel's son is looking for a date to some office party he has in December. I thought you might be interested?"

"*Markel?* As in Oliver Markel, Emily's *boss?*" I sigh in exasperation. "I am not dating my friend's boss. Absolutely not!"

"But he's single and the guardian of the cutest little girl!" Mom protests.

"No! Not happening. Dad! Back me up here!"

Dad chuckles and pads into the dining room, Gramps behind him. "If Molly says no, Mabel, then that is that."

"Robert—"

"We've been over this." Dad's dark-blue eyes meet Mom's brown ones, and a conversation passes between them.

Will I ever have that? The ability to say a host of things with a mere look? To know another person so well, you can see the thoughts playing on their face? Tanner and I had that. Before he left.

My thoughts are interrupted by Mom nodding once and saying, "Time to eat."

We all help bring the dishes in from the kitchen and settle around the large oak table. After Dad blesses the meal, we begin laughing and passing the food in the organized cacophony I call home. I smile as Ryder regales us with a story about one of the cooking students confusing an ingredient and creating a catastrophe rather than a masterpiece, while Gramps talks about the hockey team and the practices he's watched. It's loud, it's crazy, it's not proper, but it's home, and I wouldn't trade it for anything else in the world.

"That was so good, Mom." Ryley groans, holding his stomach. "I'm going to have to work out all week to get rid of it though."

Mom laughs and waves a hand at Ryder. "He made the sauce. I just boiled the noodles."

"So you're to blame." I elbow Ryder. He went to college for a business degree and now is going to cooking classes in the city over from our small town. He's a great chef, and I know he'll have a thriving restaurant someday soon.

It brings to mind Susan and her declaration—more or less, but I'm calling it that—of unrequited love from one of my brothers. Time to enact Operation Brother Buster! (Yeah, okay, so the title needs work.)

"Mom, go snuggle with Dad," I order as I begin to stack up the plates. "Ryder, Ryley, and I will help wash these dishes."

"Um..." Ryley raises his hand. "Ryley doesn't remember volunteering."

"Neither does Ryder."

Their matching smirks appear, and I return it with a feral smile of my own. "You'll help if you know what's good for you."

They both get a bit wide-eyed—it's not every day I threaten my brothers, who tower a good foot over me and weigh roughly double what I do.

"On it!" Ryder grabs the stack of dishes in front of me and books it to the kitchen. Ryley follows with the pot of spaghetti in his hands.

"Thank you, sweetie." Mom kisses my cheek and then whispers. "And be careful with that heart of yours. I don't want to see it broken again."

I nod and kiss her back before making my way to the kitchen.

My brothers stand shoulder to shoulder, arms crossed, Dad's trademark scowl on their faces. The only noticeable difference between the twins is Ryley has a smattering of freckles across the bridge of his nose.

"Thanks for the help." I flash a smile as I roll up the sleeves of my cardigan and stride over to the sink.

Ryley throws his arm out, halting my progress. "What is going on, Molly?"

"Yeah." Ryder glares. "Why are you mad at us?"

"Mad? *Moi*?" I press a hand against my chest in feigned shock. "Why on earth would I be upset that you've seemingly hurt one of my best friends?"

Ryder's brows lower. "What does Susan have to do with anything?"

"Who said anything about Susan?" I ask.

Both turn a strange shade of white and look at anything other than me.

"Why don't you tell me what happened the summer she stayed here?" I cross my arms. I'm in no way threatening, but Ryder flinches and Ryley looks taken aback. "What did you idiots do to her?"

"I—" Ryley runs a hand through his hair. "I might have tried to kiss her."

"What?" Ryder pales, looking at his twin like he's seen a ghost. "When?"

"Oh, the day before she and Molly went back to school." When Ryder braces a hand against the counter, Ryley's brows rise. "Why?"

"She—she told me she liked me that day." Ryder wets his lips with his tongue. "I ran away."

"You *ran away*?" Ryley smacked Ryder on the head. "Why? Susan was—is a great woman!"

"I know. You don't know how well I know." He looks miserable. "And then she stopped coming here. I ruined it."

I wrapped my arm around him, compassion overriding any desire to beat them both senseless. "She said something about unrequited love last night. Perhaps there's still a chance."

"Molly, stay out of it." He chuckles, but there's no humor in the timbre. "Besides," he looks up at Ryley, "you liked her, too, didn't you?"

"Yeah. She was so full of life, you know? So happy." Ryley looks a little green. "The thing was, I thought she was flirting with me that summer."

I try to remember. I'd been a little preoccupied with forgetting my own heartache, although he'd been gone a year. But what I do remember is Susan teasing Ryley relentlessly, but hanging on every word and movement Ryder made, watching him in the kitchen, helping with the dishes while he worked on dinner. She'd been learning about him the whole summer.

"But man, if she still likes you, you should take the chance and call her." Ryley smiles, looking genuine. "Don't lose out on this chance."

"No." Ryder shakes his head. "I'm not getting into it again."

My brows lower as they both stare at each other, some weird twinlepathy going on between them. "Don't hurt my friend." I laugh nervously. "Come on, we have dishes to do."

We shelve the Susan talk for now, but I sense a simmering storm that has my stomach curled into knots. I hope I didn't open a chapter that was better left closed.

Chapter Eighteen

Tanner

Molly is jumpy Monday morning. She holds the stack of reports she'd graded Friday and Saturday, a look of panic in her eyes when they land on me.

Breathe, I mouth to her as I take my place at the back of the room. She forces a wobbly smile and takes a deep inhale. A chuckle rumbles in my chest as the bell rings, and the kids file into their seats. Laughter ripples around the room and some shoving ensues at the back that I stop with a clearing of my throat. I don't fully understand why Skinner stuck me in here, but with a glance at Molly, I'm glad he has.

She needs me right now. And boy, does it ever feel good to be needed once again by Molly Pruitt.

"Good morning, class!" Molly's voice rolls over the room, demanding attention. It's not that she's forceful. She's simply...Molly. Sunshine personified, eager to teach and help the kids grow.

"I have your reports here that I will pass out momentarily. I must admit," her eyes travel across the kids, "I wasn't overly impressed."

Molly begins to pass out the reports when the door slams open and in stomps none other than Kai Reynolds. He glares at me, then Molly, before taking the only open desk in the class—right in the middle. The room has never been so quiet as he slouches down at his desk, arms crossed stubbornly across his chest.

"Good morning, Kai." Molly smiles at him, and he grunts.

Molly meets my gaze with raised brows, and I shrug. I don't know why he hasn't been in school the last week, or why he seems determined to be a grouch, but I'll figure it out. Like Mom said, I can be tenacious when I want to be.

As Molly slowly passes out the summer reading reports to the kids, she talks through the assignments for the week, explaining each task as she goes. Her skirt, which hits at her calf, swishes as she strides around the room. Her white tennis shoes squeak every once in a while, and she has her hair up off her neck in an artful messy bun.

She's beautiful.

I mentally curse. Rubbing my face, I try to push aside the over-whelming desire to tell Molly the truth—about why I left the way I did and what I really, truly want now that I'm back. But I'm a coward. I don't want to lose her again because of my stupidity. Better to wait and see how things play out.

Laying the final report on the student's desk, Molly turns around at the front of the class and folds her hands in front of her. "Any questions?"

Gloria's hand pops up in the air.

Molly tenses, but her smile remains in place. "Yes, Gloria?"

"A D minus?" She laughs, but it sounds slightly manic. I lean back in my chair, curious as to what her reaction is going to be. "Surely, this must be a mistake."

"It surely isn't." Molly gestures to the whole class. "Truthfully, most of your papers were abysmal. The only semi-decent one is Seb's, and it's still only a B minus quality. I don't know what your last literature teacher allowed, but I don't like what I read in those book reports."

"I always get As and Bs." Gloria protests, her eyes flashing mur-der toward Molly as she stands and leans over her desk. I wouldn't have dared to even *think* about looking at a teacher like that when I'd been in school. It might have also been because I had a righteous fear of my father.

Molly's control is admirable as she meets Gloria's gaze head on. "Not in my class, Gloria. Take a seat. If you want to discuss this afterwards, we can."

The brat waits about three seconds before sitting in her seat. I notice she slips her phone out of her bag, hidden behind her copy of *Tuck Everlasting*. She pulls up the texting app and fires off a message to someone.

I stroll over to her as Molly begins her lecture and tap her on the shoulder. "Phone. Now."

"Mine." She smiles at me, and I barely resist the urge to shudder. The girl is terrifying. Not because she's physically threatening, but because she thinks she can get whatever she wants. I remember kids like her in high school, and I'd given them a wide berth. I'd been popular but not because I was mean. At least, I hope I hadn't been.

"Give me it now, or we can go see Principal Skinner." I hold my hand out, and Gloria huffs as she slaps the phone into my hand. "Thank you."

I move back to my seat, setting the phone on my desk, then turning my attention to Molly as she begins talking about Natalie Babbitt's life. Her eyes skip over Gloria, and more than once, she looks my way. She's engaging, walking, talking, and smiling at the kids with the enthusiasm that can only come from someone who loves what she's teaching. It's the joy that used to be in her eyes when she'd talk to me about the fantasies and romcoms she was reading. Once again, she arrests my attention, and there's nothing to do but surrender.

A buzzing draws my eyes down to Gloria's phone.

Mom: Unbelievable! We'll take care of that. Don't worry.

Unease curls in my stomach. That seems...foreboding. I look up, staring at the back of Gloria's head. What is she up to?

Granted, the text may be about something totally unrelated to the D minus Molly gave her. But I don't trust Gloria Steinfield. I don't trust her at all.

I don't get a chance to talk to Molly during the day. At lunch, she has a meeting with the school counselor about one of her students, and then it's class after class filtering in and out of the room.

When the dismissal bell finally rings, I step over to Molly's desk, gripping the strap of my satchel like my life depends on it.

"You did well handling Gloria." I let my eyes follow Molly's movements as she scoops up a stack of quizzes and sticks them in a folder. She tucks a loose strand of her honey-brown hair behind her ear, her little hoop earring appearing. Her movements are fluid, graceful, and it drags me into a memory.

"Why do we have to go to a figure skating competition?" I ask, zipping up my windbreaker as Ryley throws open the door to the Rink like he owns the place.

Ryder loops an arm over my shoulders and scoffs. "Because our little sis is competing tonight. We always support Mols, 'cause she always supports us."

"Yeah, but see, Molly *likes* hockey," I protest, shoving Ryder off of me. "You don't like figure skating."

"Says who?" Ryder chuckles at my look of mortification. "No, I don't like it, but I love my sis, so." He shrugs and steps up to buy tickets for us.

A lyrical song plays over the speakers, and I catch sight of Ava Kendell gliding over the ice. Ryley is watching her with interest, his arms crossed and his toe tapping in time to the music. When he catches me watching, he smiles sheepishly. "I've always been a little into dance. But don't tell Ryder, or I'll never hear the end of it."

Ryder steps over, tickets in hand. "End of what?"

"Nothing," Ryley and I parrot together before moving into the Rink to find the guys' parents.

They wave us over, perfect seats right behind the bench and up just high enough that we'll get to see all of Molly's routine. I settle down, smiling when Rick clasps my shoulder. "How you doin', boy?"

"Good, Gramps." I smile. "I'm captain of the squad this year."

"I heard! Reynolds has nothing but glowing praises about you."

I smile, knowing that's not the truth. Coach is hard on all of us, but since I'm the captain, he's especially hard on me. He expects a hundred and two percent.

"Here comes Molly!" Ryder grins, leaning forward with his elbows on his knees. The lighting in the rink turns a pale green, and the tune begins.

I recognize it from my time spent in the Pruitts' home. It's *Defying Gravity* from the musical *Wicked.* Molly cuts across the ice in a black and green outfit. The chiffon material flutters around her legs as she skates backwards then turns to glide forward, a leg extended behind her. She does a spin and lands it, a small smile on her face as the music builds. She moves with grace, more than she has in her day-to-day life.

She pauses as the tempo slows, waving her arms up and down before the music cuts to the end of the song. She skates faster and faster around the rink, effortlessly throwing herself into three aerial spins in a row before coming to the middle. Twirling around and around on one leg, she goes faster and faster before throwing her arms into the air, perfectly hitting the mark with a huge grin.

My heart is in my throat as the roar of applause fills the Rink. I can't move, can only stare at the girl I've long seen as a little sister. She breaks, bowing to the crowd, who cheers louder still.

"Wow." I'm finally able to breathe again. "That was amazing."

"Careful, there." Ryder jabs me in the ribs. "Don't be getting any ideas about Molly."

I laugh and shove him back. But if I'm being honest, this is the moment I start to see Molly Pruitt as more than the twins' little sister.

"Hello!" Molly snaps her fingers in front of my face, and I jerk back to reality. Molly crosses her arms and drily says, "Wow, glad I'm so engaging."

"Sorry, lost in a memory." I grin and scratch at my jaw. "What were you saying?"

"I was saying," Molly throws the strap of her massive purse over her shoulder and reaches for her briefcase, "I'm scared of what Gloria might try."

I snatch her briefcase up before she can grab it and gesture for her to move ahead of me. She glares but complies.

"Sweetie's?" I ask.

"Is this a date?" She stops and shuts her classroom door.

I rub the back of my neck. "Do you want it to be?"

"No." She looks up at me, and I forget how to inhale. "I want us to just be friends."

"*Just friends*. Got it. I can do *just friends*." I hand her the brief-case, and she smiles. But it doesn't reach her eyes. Was that a lie? Does she want more? I clear my throat, hoping to break the awkward tension. "So, coffee before practice?"

She shrugs. "Sure. But I'm paying this time."

"Fine by me." I smile, but it feels wooden. Like I'm just going through the motions as I follow her out of the school.

Boy, did that memory shake me. I forgot how much I loved watching her skate. Forgot how much I enjoyed spending time with the youngest Pruitt. And a large part of me wants to be more than *just friends*. As in all of me. All of me wants to be more than friends with Molly Elaine Pruitt.

Chapter Nineteen

Molly

The weeks pass in a blur. Nothing happens with Gloria and her D-minus grade, and for a while, classes are actually enjoyable. We finish our unit on *Tuck Everlasting* and move into an actual high school suggested book—*The Giver*.

Tanner is always in the back, always watching, even as he's working on plays and plans for the team. We've started eating lunch together in my room, prepping for the first official game of the season at the end of September.

Things have fallen into a rhythm—a routine I can depend on. So, when I roll over to the blare of my alarm the Thursday before our big game with my head pounding like the drummer of a rock group, I want to scream. My eyes ache, I can't breathe through my nose, and I think I might choke on the snot sliding down my throat.

I sit up in my bed and almost double over from the cramps and nausea. Fantastic. The mother of all periods decides to strike while I'm also sick. This has got to be the worst form of purgatory you can find.

I fumble with my phone, pulling up the sub contact and texting her that I'll need someone to fill in for me today. Thankfully, I have sub plans printed up already—it's basically study hall with an extra credit assignment for those wishing to raise their grade. I text Tanner to let him know that they're in a thin blue binder in the top drawer of my desk.

Why is there an elephant on my chest? I throw my arm dramatically over my face, wishing the pressure would lessen so my head doesn't feel like a pimple about to pop. There's also a hippo sitting on my ovaries, but it's not as bad as it was the night before when I got home from practice. I'd been able to hide it—mostly—then, but now, I want to die.

After a quick trip to the bathroom to throw on a new pad and deodorant—I can't stand to smell bad even when I'm sick—I stumble back into bed. I want to read, but my eyes won't focus. Clicking on one of my comfort audiobooks and rolling to my side has me drifting blissfully in and out of consciousness until the doorbell rings.

"Seriously?" I groan, dragging myself down the stairs and to the door. I have half a mind to cuss out whoever disturbed my beauty sleep—a head cold on top of PMS needs all the rest it can get. I probably look like one of those demonic gremlins after water gets on them as I fling open the door and all but growl, "What?"

Tanner's brows disappear under his thatch of brown hair. "Well, good afternoon to you, too."

"What are you doing here?" I ask, suddenly all too aware of the oversized Cougars t-shirt and old, holey leggings I'm wearing. My hair probably looks like I shoved my finger in a light socket, and I can feel a cramp coming on that has my eyes watering—although I hope to Tanner it looks like it's just the cold.

"I didn't need to stay all day at work, so I brought you some stuff for your cold." Tanner holds up a grocery sack. "But it's more than just a cold, isn't it?"

I blink at him, my foggy, half-asleep, half-medicated brain not computing. "What?"

He chuckles. "Are your roommates here?"

"No, Em's at work and Susan is...out." *Wow, real intelligent, Mols. Especially when you look like you were hit with a garbage truck. Wait, why should you care? It's Tanner! He's seen you covered in mud* and *blood before. And it shouldn't matter that you're not making sense. You're sick.* I sway, feeling dizzy.

Tanner grabs my arm. "Go sit. I'll make some tea with honey and get you some ibuprofen."

"I'm fine. I don't need you to baby me."

Tanner smirks. "What if I *want* to baby you?"

"You'll get sick," I protest, even as he guides me to the sofa and makes me sit.

Tanner tucks a blanket around me, up to my chin. He's close enough that all I see are his blue eyes as he whispers, "I'll take my chances."

Leaving me with a kiss on the forehead, he disappears into the kitchen.

I know I'm PMS-y, but the hot flash hitting me now has nothing to do with my hormones. Or maybe it has everything to do with them.

I'll figure it out later. My head currently aches too much.

I curl onto my side, my eyes already slipping closed, when Tanner appears with my favorite mug in hand—it has quotes from some of my favorite classic literary authors.

"Here." He squats beside the couch, pressing the back of his hand against my forehead. His brows furrow. "Do you have a thermometer?"

"Bathroom, bottom drawer," I mutter, taking the proffered drink and taking a sip. The tea he's made is minty with a hint of licorice. "What is this?"

"Tea?" He smirks when I scowl before wandering off to find the bathroom that I had so helpfully told him held the thermometer.

It won't kill me, right? I take a sip of the still hot tea. It is sweetened with honey and soothes my aching throat—something I'm incredibly thankful for. I take another sip as I settle into the corner of the couch. My head is propped between the back and the side, and with the blanket tucked up to my chin, I'm quite cozy.

"Found it!" Tanner comes back into the room right as I'm beginning to doze. Does the man not know to leave a sick woman well enough alone? "And here is the heating pad."

"I don't need that." I try to glare, but my eyes water again. Sinus pressure. It's only sinus pressure and raging hormones. It has nothing to do with how sweet and attentive Tanner's being. Nothing whatsoever.

Tanner ignores me and plugs it in. It has a ridiculously long cord, and he stretches it over the back of the couch so that I can hold it against my stomach. He turns me so that my head is propped on one of Susan's decorative pillows, pulls the end table up, and places my mug on it. He then picks up my legs and drapes them over his lap as he settles in on the couch.

"What—?" I have to clear my throat before continuing. "What are you doing?"

"You still like having your feet rubbed, right?" He raises a brow, his smirk making that dreaded dimple appear.

I can't say no, because I do love it. I've always loved it, and he freaking knows it. I throw my arm over my face. Tanner laughs, picking up one of my feet.

"Are these...pickle socks?"

Heat floods my face. I forgot about the socks—a joke between Emily and me because we have a weird sense of humor. They are my sleeping socks. Socks *no one* outside my roommates is ever supposed to see.

"You're just trying to kill me with mortification today, aren't you, Tanner?"

His low, rumbly laugh warms my core more than the heating pad. He begins rolling his thumb against the arch of my left foot. I hiss when he hits a tender spot. I rip it from his grasp, hitting his leg as I scramble to sit up.

He gasps and grabs my ankles again. It's only then I realize what I'd done. I kicked his bad leg. Right above the knee where his tendons had been destroyed and surgically repaired.

"Oh my gosh, I'm sorry!"

He waves me off, rubbing his knee with one hand as he starts rolling his thumb over my foot once more. "It's fine."

"It's not fine! I hurt you and—"

"Lay down, Mols." His tone is level, but his expression dares me to argue.

I don't. Shivering slightly, I tug the blanket up to my chin.

"Why are you being so nice?" I mutter.

"I can be nasty if you want. But you've got a lousy day going on. Period and a cold?" he tsks his tongue and shakes his head.

"I don't—"

"Mols?" Tanner chuckles. "I have Maria and Taysleigh Bradshaw in my life. I can tell. Besides the fact that you took the heating pad without complaining, you also were holding your stomach when I came in. And you keep shifting like your back hurts."

Dang his perceptiveness.

I cover my face with my hands and groan. "Again, kill me with mortification."

"It's not that big of a deal." He rubs my calves through my leggings, loosening the tension caused by my cold. Although, I am beginning to wonder if it's the flu as another chill shivers through me.

Tanner scoops up the laser thermometer and takes my temp, frowning as the display chirps twice. "You have a low-grade fever. Try to get some sleep."

"Thanks, Doctor Bradshaw," I mumble, my eyes already closing. "Are you leaving?"

"No." He grabs the TV remote off the coffee table. "I'll stay until your roommates come home."

Suddenly, in my dazed, tired, emotional mind, it isn't enough to have my legs over his lap. I want to curl against him, have him hold me, and tell me I'll feel better tomorrow. Tears clog my throat at his tender administration. Why is he being so nice to me?

"Tanner?" I whisper past the lump and swelling going on in my throat.

"Yeah?" He's watching whatever he's pulled up on the TV, not really paying attention when I sit up and turn, tucking my head into his lap and draping his arm around me. He tenses for a heartbeat, before tugging the blanket up and laying his hand against my upper arm. "Sleep, Molly. I'll stay as long as you need me."

I'll need you forever, I think, slipping off into the crazed dreams of a sick and hormonal mind.

CHAPTER TWENTY

Tanner

"I'll need you forever," Molly says softly as her eyes slide closed, and her breathing evens out.

I stare down at her. She's a mess, but *my* mess. A mess I want to go through every high and low with. I knew that the moment she opened the door I would stay until I knew she was going to be okay. She looked about ready to cry on the doorstep, despite her clear anger and frustration. And I couldn't walk away. Not this time.

I rub up and down her arm, trying to watch the old sitcom playing on the TV. But all senses are firing on Molly. On her breathing, on the strand of her hair wafting up and down with each exhale. She has her hands curled up under her chin, her eyes moving as she dreams. She's facing my chest, and I move to rub her back as she snuggles deeper down to capture the warmth.

Yeah, she's sick. But somehow, she's still the most beautiful woman in the world. Why did I walk away from this?

Because nineteen-year-old Tanner Bradshaw was a flaming idiot, that's why. He'd hightailed it out of Cloverfield, and though he might have looked back, he didn't turn around—didn't call out to those he'd up and left until he'd had to jump ship and come home with his tail between his legs. Mom and Taysleigh easily welcomed me back. But Molly? Not so much. I know I don't deserve her. Because the reason I ran is the same reason I don't deserve her—I'm terrified. Forever is a long time. And I'm not sure I deserve forever with Molly. But sweet mercy, do I ever want it.

Molly groans, a violent shiver wracking her frame. She wiggles closer, her forehead almost pressing into my stomach. She inhales as deeply as her clogged nose allows and sighs, settling back into soft, congested snores.

Time passes slowly. I flip to the girls' Netflix and turn on some superhero melodrama—because let's be honest, they're horrible—as I wait for Susan and Emily to return to the house. Molly's phone, sitting on the end table, lights up a few times, but I can't move to check it. So, I just sit, rubbing her arm and back as she sleeps, never wanting the moment to end.

The fall shadows have grown long when I finally hear keys jingling and the door swinging open.

"I'm home!" Susan hollers, the sound echoing through the silent house like a cannon going off.

Molly jerks awake, then moans, "Oh, not Sue." But she doesn't move away from me. The blanket shifts as she pulls it up to her chin again and shivers.

"Did the sleep help?" I ask.

Molly's puffy eyes blink owlishly as she looks up at me. "No. I think I might feel worse."

I push up on the couch and am just reaching for the thermometer when Susan steps into the living room and pauses. Her eyes flash but she doesn't move. Just glares. It gives me a chance to study her.

Molly has talked about her quite a bit in the weeks we've spent together planning for the team. Susan's blonde hair is pulled into a high ponytail on top of her head. An oversized green sweater hangs on her thin frame and is tucked in the front of her distressed mom jeans. She has a tote bag thrown over her shoulder with succulents on it. Her gaze goes from her friend's head in my lap to me leaning over her to grab the thermometer.

"What are *you* doing here?" She turns to the bleary-eyed Molly. "What is *he* doing here?"

"She texted me this morning to say she was sick." I ignore the mother of all death glares Susan is leveling at me as I finally manage to get the thermometer and check Molly's temp. It's higher than it was, but still low—barely a hundred.

"Molly, he's your ex!" Susan declares as I sit back and smooth a hand against Molly's warm forehead. "And he's…he's…"

"Taking care of me," Molly mutters. "What's wrong with being babied?"

"By *Tanner Bradshaw*?" Susan challenges.

"Tanner Bradshaw?" A third voice joins the argument. I crane my neck to catch sight of a pixie-ish girl I'm assuming is Emily. Shoulder-length black hair is pushed away from her face with a headband. Next to Susan—who I am guessing is nearly five-foot-eight—she's super short. Her pert little nose scrunches up when she smiles at me, her hazel eyes sparkling in the golden hour glow pouring in from the windows. "Oh my gosh, Tanner Bradshaw is sitting in my living room!"

"With Molly in his lap!" Susan gestures.

Emily peeks over the couch. "Holy cannoli! This is adorable!"

"No, no it isn't!" Susan interjects. "He left her! Took off and now he's snuggling her when she's in a compromised state!"

"Um, excuse me!" I raise my hand. "For the record, she snuggled up with me. I was just going to rub the pickle sock feet."

"You're really going for the trifecta of mortification, you know that, Tanner?" Molly mumbles, getting a chuckle out of me as I smile down at her.

Emily hums knowingly, and when I meet her gaze, she winks. Turning to her irate roommate she says, "I think they're fine, Sue."

"Well, *I'm* not fine with this. Not at all." Susan glares at me again before turning and storming off into the kitchen. I hear cabinet doors being slammed and the sound of pans banging on the counter.

"Is she usually that...?" I ask, tapering off when I don't know how to finish the sentence.

"Territorial? Protective?" Emily snorts. "Oh, yeah. When Susan loves, she loves all in. It takes a lot of trust for that to happen, and when it's broken? It's hard to get it back."

"What did I do to get on the blacklist?" I raise my brows. "I've never met Susan before."

"Yeah, but you hurt Molly." Emily shrugs. "*An enemy of a friend is an enemy* is taken very literally in this house."

"I'm pretty sure the saying is *an enemy of my enemy is my friend*," I state.

"Is it though?" With another wink, Emily sails into the kitchen after Susan.

I shake my head as Molly sits up, her eyes squeezed shut. "I'm going to the bathroom."

"Okay."

She cracks one eye open, her face pale. "I really hope you don't get sick."

I chuckle. "Why?"

"Because the game is Saturday." She rubs her face with a hand and pushes her wild hair out of the way. "The boys need their coach."

"And they'll have you if I am sick." I grab her hand. "We'll be fine either way, Mols."

She blanches further and stands, shuffling to the bathroom. Once she disappears around the corner, Susan is on me again. Her hands are on her hips, a yellow apron covering the front of her. She holds a wooden spoon in one hand, wielding it like a wand from *Harry Potter*. Her ponytail swishes with every murderous stomp she takes in my direction.

"I don't like you," she declares.

"Susan!" Emily appears at her side with an exasperated huff. "Give the poor man a break!"

"I won't!" She waves the spoon in the air. I swear, I'm waiting for *expelliarmus* to fly off her lips. "If he hurts Molly again, I swear I can murder him and leave no evidence."

"Good grief." Emily rolls her eyes. "What have I told you and Molly about true crime?"

"Plenty. But it might prove useful in this case." She levels a glare at me. Seriously, does the woman have another facial expression? Because I have yet to see it.

I raise my hands in surrender. "I solemnly swear I'm not planning on hurting her again. Ever. I was immature and stupid four years ago."

"Oh, and you're so much wiser now?" Susan's fists are back on her hips. "I don't like you."

"A point you've made abundantly clear," I deadpan.

Emily snorts. "*I* like you, Tanner."

"Thanks, Emily!" I grin at the perky girl, and she smiles back.

Susan scowls. "You're not welcome any longer."

"Yeah, he is." Molly shuffles back into the room and pushes past her friends to curl back up with her head in my lap. "He's my friend. He stays."

It shouldn't feel like winning the lottery. Like I was handed a first-place trophy and a million bucks. But it does. It is better than getting the NHL contract, better than the high of winning or seeing myself getting better and better at the game I love. Molly's approval is an adrenaline rush I'll never grow tired of.

Chapter Twenty-One

Molly

I still feel like crap after my nap, but now I'm awake. My legs and neck ache, and while I love curling up on Tanner, I know it's not the most comfortable position for me or him.

With a sigh, I sit up. "Can you make more tea?"

"And risk the wrath of Warden Susan?" he asks in an exaggeratedly loud whisper.

I chuckle. "Ask Em to do it."

He sighs dramatically, a smile twisting his lips as he moves toward the kitchen.

I grab the pillow he'd been sitting against, flopping onto the couch as another round of cramps hit. I am a giant wuss when it comes to being sick. But I am thankful I have good friends who will baby me.

Despite my stuffy nose, the pillow still smells like Tanner. Like the cool freshness of an ice rink and the woodsy, minty cologne he's worn since high school. My fuzzy mind tells me Tanner sat and rubbed my back and stroked my hair while I slept. I want to cry. Why is he being so freaking nice? He has no reason to be this wonderful. Especially since I've been a total jerk. Yeah, we've been amiable as coworkers, but that's it. So, why would he risk getting sick to come take care of me?

Tanner comes back into the living room, and I sniff as I sit up to take the mug from him. "Thanks."

"How are you feeling?" He lowers back down next to me.

"Like I got hit by a garbage truck." I take a sip of the tea. "What is this?"

"It's a tea for sore throats." Tanner lays his arm across the back of the couch. I eye his side, contemplating how far over the line it is to curl up against his side.

I take another sip, squashing the desire even as he props his legs up on the end table. "It's really good."

Tanner raises a brow. "Yeah?"

"Yeah." I smile.

"Mols?"

"What?" I look into his blue eyes. They're warm, soft, comforting. Gosh, his gaze is like the ocean on a hot day, daring me to jump in and take the risk. But just like the ocean, I feel like I'm going to drown. Get eaten by the creatures and monsters lurking in the depths. The lump in my throat now has nothing to do with the flu.

"You can curl up with me again."

"It's fine. I'm fine."

"Molly." His voice is soft again, gentle.

"What?" My voice warbles, tears far too close to the surface.

"I won't read anything into it."

I shake my head. My heart is raw, everything gaping, spilling, nasty, and real on the ground. "I can't."

"Why?" He cocks his head, his brows furrowing.

"I..." A tear slips down my cheek.

Tanner reaches across the gap and wipes it away. "Even if you're a mess, even if you're falling apart, I'm here. My friendship doesn't have conditions."

"Friendship." I gesture between us. "That's all we are?"

"If that's all you want." He sits back. "I'm happy just being friends."

I hesitate for a heartbeat before curling into his side. His arm tightens, and he leans his cheek against the top of my head.

"Thank you," I whisper.

He replies, "Anytime."

Thankfully, there was no school on Friday, and by Saturday, I am back up and around. Tanner never got the flu—the jerk—and when I pull into the Rink on Saturday morning, he is waiting in the lobby with his coffee and a to-go cup for me.

"Feeling better, sicko?" He grins, and I punch him in the arm.

"Har, har. Very funny." I roll my eyes as I take a long sip. A sigh of contentment slips off my lips. "Perfect. You're a saint."

He raises his coffee in a salute. "I aim to please."

I follow Tanner as we head to the locker room where the boys are gearing up.

Willow sidles up behind as Tanner raps on the door.

"Are you all decent?" he calls, cracking the door open just enough so he can see in. "Coach Pruitt and Willow are waiting out here."

"We're good!" Leo's voice rings out over the laughter and jeers as we step into the room.

Tanner does a head count and nods. "Alright, huddle up, team."

The boys scramble to find a seat on the benches that line the locker room. Their gazes are glued to Tanner, much like mine is. He stands at a whiteboard, marker in hand as he reminds them of some of the new plays that he wants them to try today against the Richmond Wardens.

Capping the marker, Tanner surveys the group. "Okay, so this game isn't vital to playoff status. I want you to play well, play hard, but don't be stupid. Use your heads. Luke?"

Our new captain looks up from where he's taping up his stick. "Yeah, Coach?"

"Any words of encouragement for the team?"

Luke's gaze flicks over all of us. I can tell he is terrified, but then he starts talking. "We're a different team than we were last year. We've got new coaches, new players, new teams to face." He pauses, looking at the ground as he gathers his thoughts. "But one thing hasn't changed. We play because we love the game. We play because we want to win, sure. But the thrill and the fun of working together, facing a challenge as a team, that's why we're here." Another pause and Luke stretches out his hand to the center of the room. "We're a team."

Every eye is riveted to Luke. Slowly, one by one his teammates step up and put their hands over Luke's. Even Owen, his jaw tight as he places his hand atop the pile.

Leo looks over at Tanner and me. "You, too, Coaches."

Tanner chuckles, and I follow behind him. Smushing into the circle, my back hits Tanner's chest. I try to focus on what Luke is saying to the boys, but all I feel is Tanner's breath on my neck. On his chest rising and falling. On that smell that I've been thinking of since Thursday.

I'm late raising my hand when we all cheer *Cougars,* and I hurry out to the ice, going to stand behind the bench and ward off my emotions. My cheeks are hot, my hands are shaking, and I want to puke. Why? Why now after five years of nothing? Why is my traitorous body remembering Tanner's touch, his scent, his sheer presence that makes me feel safe? He's not safe! He crushed my heart. Left it broken and dirty on the ground when he took off. And I can't risk letting it get shattered further.

My thoughts are settling, my breathing calming, but then Tanner appears at my side. His brows shoot up under his hair—hair that's a touch curlier than normal. "You okay?"

"Yep! Just fine." My voice cracks, and I clear it as I turn to stare out at the empty ice. "It was just warm in the locker room."

I catch the look he gives me from the corner of my eye. He clearly doesn't believe me. I lick my lips nervously as the boys head on to the ice to warm up.

The opposing team, the Richmond Wardens, warm up on the right side of the ice, the slaps of the sticks against the pucks echoing through the Rink as fans fill the stands. Our team does the same, encouraging one another as popular pop songs boom across the overhead speakers.

I remember competing here. Remember the thrill of the music echoing around the rafters and through my bones. I can still feel the silky costumes against my skin, smell the makeup and hairspray, and hear the cheers as I finish my routine. I close my eyes, soaking in that memory. I miss *that*—that very specific moment when it was just me, the ice, the music working together as one.

And I remember the first time I watched Tanner play.

The first game of the season is tonight, and everyone is in a flurry at home. Ryley and Ryder are running around making sure they have everything while Mom is making cocoa for her and me. Dad already escaped the chaos to warm up the car.

Ryley and Ryder are juniors and are beyond excited to play tonight. I have to admit, I'm pretty stoked to be watching the Cougars too. I pull my beanie down on my head as Mom hands me my travel mug.

"In the car. Now!" she calls up the stairs as I hurry to open the door. The boys thunder down the stairs and out the door on my heels.

We're early to the Rink and one of the first families in the stands. I can't help but grin. the Rink is home away from home. The fresh ice, the whir of the cooler, the smell of Grams making fresh popcorn—she hands me a small bag for quality control, obviously—and the energy that hangs in the air on game day.

Soon, the lights dim, and the boys skate out to warm up. They're good, doing a few warm-up drills and laughing together as they get ready to win. I'm almost pressed against the Plexiglas, watching with bated breath. This is what I miss out on by only figure skating. Because I don't have the comradery Ryder and Ryley have as they practice with their team. They're *partners* while the girls in my figure skating troupe are *competition*. I hate it.

Then the game starts, and I'm enraptured. My brothers are good, but I'm watching number forty-seven. Tanner Bradshaw. Ryder and Ryley have mentioned him. He's a sophomore this year.

Why have I never watched him before?

He weaves across the ice like he was born on skates. He gets three assists and scores two goals. He laughs at and needles the opposing team—and yeah, he gets a couple penalties. But he's the most graceful hockey player I've ever seen. He makes it look easy when I know it's not.

"Wow. Forty-seven is good," I whisper to Dad. His eyes follow Tanner, a small smile blooming on his face.

"He is."

It's not until after the game, when the boys invite Tanner to get ice cream with us, that I realize who he is. He's the kind guy who helped me the first day of school when I'd fallen on my face in lit class.

Tanner invites Ryder, Ryley, and me to play a little two-on-two the next day. And I am right. Tanner is good at hockey. Like, really good.

And that day was when I officially became friends with *the* Tanner Bradshaw.

"When was the last time you skated, Mols?" Tanner asked, obliterating the memory as we sit on the mostly empty bench.

I peel my eyes back open as I chuckle. It lacks all mirth. "A long time. I don't even own skates anymore."

He looks at me. "What did you do with them?"

"I sold them to help pay for books for school." I can't look at him. He's seen me compete before. Ryder and Ryley said he'd been *transfixed*—their words, not mine. I'd carried that comment with me at each competition since, and when Tanner left, I couldn't bear to step onto the ice again.

"You loved skating, Mols." Tanner's eyes widen. "Skating is in your blood. You came *alive* every time you hit the ice to do a routine. Why'd you stop?"

I can't tell him the truth, so I go for as white of a lie as I can conjure up. "Competitions sucked, Tanner. You're all alone in the middle of the ice. One screw-up and the world sees it." I can't look at him. Tucking my hands under my thighs, I lean forward, watching the boys with a sigh. "It was senior year. My first program of the season. My head wasn't in the routine, and I slipped when landing a triple axel. It was humiliating, but having Coach Higgly ream me out when I got off the ice was worse. I placed second, but she hated me for it. I quit soon after that and haven't touched a pair of skates since."

I can't speak for a bit. My heart aches at the memory. The reason my head hadn't been on the routine was because Tanner had left that week. The week of the biggest program of the year.

"I'm sorry that happened, Molly."

"It is what it is. I'd love to see you skate after the game, though."

"I don't do it often." He sighs. "I usually just warm up the leg a bit before the boys get here. It's usually a little stiff after sitting so many hours at work."

"Oh." I startle when he grabs my arm.

"Mols?"

"Hm?" I stare at his chest. If I look at him, I'll be a wreck. I'll break and tell him I stopped competing because the ice and the Rink reminded me of him. Reminded me of his laughter and our times here, skating and kissing when it was only us two in the Rink the nights Gramps worked late.

Stupid, childish desire wells up inside of me. I want to lean in and kiss Tanner Bradshaw right now.

My friendship doesn't have conditions, Molly.

Would *no kissing* be a condition? Because, good gracious, I want him to see me as more than a friend. While I'm still terrified of getting hurt, a tiny sliver of my heart has already forgiven him. And it's that stupid tiny sliver that wants to kiss him senseless and have it be our last first kiss because we agree we are supposed to be together. Forever and ever.

"I think you should skate again." Tanner's voice rocks me back to reality. "Not for a competition or an award but because you love it."

"It was more than just that screw-up, you know."

Why did I say that? And why do I feel out of breath?

I look up and am pulled into orbit by the endless galaxies of his eyes. My heart is galloping in my chest as I step back from Tanner. "I quit because skating reminded me of you. And I didn't want to be reminded of someone who'd walk out and give up on me."

Stop talking! my brain says, but I keep going. "I can't do this right now, Tanner." *Skating or us?* I'm not sure what I'm referring to anymore. My emotions are a pendulum, swinging back and forth to the ticking of a clock and completely out of my control. "I can't—I need time."

"Okay." His fingers tuck a strand of hair behind my ear that escaped the two French braids I'd done them in that morning. "But I'm not giving up so easily on us anymore, Mols."

"I—" Knocking on the Plexiglas behind us has us breaking apart. I clear my throat and turn to see Ryder and Ryley eyeing us with raised brows. Tanner laughs and waves, but my gaze is arrested by someone two rows behind my brothers.

With her saccharine smile in place and cell phone in hand, stands Gloria Steinfield.

CHAPTER TWENTY-TWO

Tanner

A strangled gurgle comes from Molly, and I don't think it's just because of her brothers. I follow her gaze and catch sight of Gloria, who has her phone trained on us with that stupid, false smile on her face.

"We're in so much trouble," Molly whispers, her eyes flicking from Gloria to me and back. "What are we going to do? I can't lose this job, Tanner! I have debts and rent and my car to pay for and—"

"Molly! Calm down. It will be fine." And for the first time in a long time, I truly believe it. There was something about the way Molly had finally told me a bit of how badly I messed up. How broken I'd made her. The vulnerability, the truth of her admission, had speared me right in the chest. Is this the start? The beginnings of mending the giant rift between us?

I'd meant what I said to her Thursday—I'm not about to push for more than friendship unless she wants it. But boy, do I hope we can fix things enough for her to want it.

Molly's sapphire eyes meet mine—halfway to tears as she draws in a shaky breath. "How can you say that?"

"Because it will be. A video from a seventeen-year-old brat against our word that it was nothing? We'll be fine." Or at least, Molly will be. If they want to fire me? Go right ahead. I don't need this job. And I am ninety-nine percent certain that Gloria and her mother don't have a clue about that little fact.

"Okay. Okay, you're right." Molly draws in a deep breath as the boys join us on the bench.

I put a hand to my ear and widen my eyes. "I'm sorry, I'm what?"

"You heard me." Molly smacks my shoulder and crosses her arms, her chin jutting out even as a tiny smirk ghosts across her lips. "I'm not saying it again."

A chuckle rumbles in my chest as our team skates onto the ice for the National Anthem. After that, our first line gets into position for the puck drop. I shift nervously behind the rest of the team.

It's game time.

The boys tear across the ice, and the first period flies by in a whirlwind of slapshots, ice shavings, and the cheers of the crowd. We score twice and manage to keep the Wardens to one. We're not great on the power play, something I'm going to have to work on. I jot a note.

Molly leans over halfway through the second period and says, "Luke and Leo are a powerhouse together. We should keep them on the same line."

I nod, adding that as a note as well.

A few minutes later, Molly is back in my space. Floral and caramel swirl around me, fuzzing my vision for a long minute. I try to focus on what she's saying, but I can't shake the memories. The times in the back of my pickup as we stargazed and stole kisses. Skating around the ice hand in hand as Rick cleaned the locker rooms. The November Barn Dance where I'd first kissed her.

And then you left months later. I shake the thought away. Yeah, I left, but I'm back now. And this time, I'm not going anywhere.

"Did you hear me?" Molly asks as the ref blows his whistle on one of the Wardens players.

"Sorry, I was thinking."

"Yeah, I saw smoke." When I raise my brow at her, she laughs. "I was saying Carter might need a little more one-on-one from us this week. He seems distracted."

"Want that to be your project this week?" I ask as I add it to my growing list.

"No, that should be your job." She crosses her arms and leans against the Plexiglas. Her eyes track the players, her tongue sticking halfway out of her mouth. Her fingers drum against her bicep.

"Why my job?" I turn back to the game, not wanting to get caught watching her. Why is she consuming my thoughts? They should be on this game, on how the boys are playing, what our weaknesses are. Not on how good Molly looks in an oversized sweatshirt and leggings. Nope, definitely not on that.

"You can hit a puck harder," comes her reply, her eyes tracking Wyatt as he cuts across the ice, the puck handled surprisingly well beneath the blade of his stick. "You know a lot of the tricks and how to aim."

"That, and if you did it, it would mean you have to put on skates and actually go on the ice," I lob back.

Oops. I hadn't meant to say that. I hadn't thought before the words left my tongue, but they were a low blow.

Please tell me I haven't just killed whatever bit of friendship was forming between us.

See, old us I understood. I knew how far to press, how far to go before reaching Molly's breaking point. How to tease and rib her into laughter rather than tears. But our dynamic now is completely different. I knew Molly the girl, but Molly the woman? She's a mystery wrapped in an enigma, and I'm not sure I can unravel the twisted threads without breaking them.

Molly looks up at me. "That isn't my fault."

Ouch. I turn back to the game, stuffing down my emotions for later. Right now, I have a team to focus on. That's all that matters.

We win, four to two. The locker room is buzzing as Molly and I walk in. She won't look at me, her arms still crossed over her literary sweatshirt, and her brows are furrowed as she stares at the ground.

I stifle a sigh as I turn back to the team. "Good game, everyone."

Willow grins as she pulls off her helmet. She'd gotten to play the last five minutes and shocked everyone by her aggressiveness—including me. She'd held herself in check during practices, but up against the Wardens, she was an absolute beast. I like her style.

"We'll take this Monday off but be here Wednesday for practice. Coach Pruitt and I have notes we'll go over before hitting the ice. I'm proud of you all. You worked as a team, and it showed."

They all grin, even Owen though he ducks his head to hide it. The guy confuses me, but I can't deny he is a force to be reckoned with during a game.

"See you all at school Monday!" I call as I head back into the empty rink.

A scuff of a shoe against concrete has me turning to face Molly. A silence that's heavier than a weighted blanket settles around us. I don't know what she wants me to say.

I'm sorry? That seems trite, even though I am.

You're right? That's also true, but I don't want to say it—even though I need to.

"You had some good observations on the guys today," is what spills out of my mouth.

If Molly wasn't standing in front of me, I would smack myself in the forehead. *That was so dumb, Bradshaw. You're right would have been a much better opening gambit.*

"Thanks." She's staring at my chest, refusing to meet my gaze. I want to drag her to me and crush her in a hug, wipe away all the hurt. The brokenness. There's so much of it, and it's driving me crazy that I can't fix it; rather, I've caused most of it. I have nothing to give. I want to do something...but what?

"Tanner, about what I said—" Molly hesitates.

"About what? You said a lot of things." I bite my tongue, waiting to hear her out.

Molly swallows and turns to stare at the ice beside us. "I need time."

"To get back on the ice?" I clasp my hands behind my back to keep them from reaching out. My heart is screaming for her. My fingers twitch, wanting to hold Molly again. But I don't deserve to. She deserves a guy who won't run when he gets scared, when he hates the memories and himself too much to stay. I swallow the bile rising and wait.

"Yes." She looks up at me and wets her lips with the tip of her tongue. "And...I need time to figure out what we're supposed to be."

"Can't we just be friends, Mols? Like we were when I was Ryder and Ryley's teammate? Those were good times, weren't they?"

"They were. But I—"

"Tanner!"

My name shouted across the Rink has us both jumping. Ryley charges over, grabbing me into a hug and pounding my back—hard. Ryder is a few paces behind him, his knowing, calculating gaze flicking between Molly and me with curiosity.

"Hey, Ryley!" I thump him back before escaping from his arms. "Long time, no see!"

"Yeah! It's not like you've been home for two months or anything." He mock scowls before turning to his sister with a smirk. "Whatcha talking about?"

"Nothing that concerns you," Molly retorts hotly, crossing her arms and turning away. "I'll see you Monday, Tanner."

I want to call after her, grab her shoulders, and demand *you need time for what*? But that probably won't win me any brownie points. So instead, I watch her go, everything in me wanting to follow.

"Hm, see, I think something *is* going on." Ryley turns to Ryder and grins. "What do you think?"

Ryder nods. "Yep. Spill it, Bradshaw! You plan on hurting our sister again?"

"What?" I turn to the twins, shaking my head as I do. "Don't be ridiculous. I didn't mean to hurt her the first time."

"You take off for Houston without telling anyone." Ryley ticks off the list on his fingers as he goes. "You leave Molly a freaking note to explain, you don't contact any of us again for five years, and oh! You return out of the blue to coach the high school varsity hockey team! And you don't mean to do any of it?"

"No, I meant to do all of it." I cross my arms and glare at my old best friends. "I just didn't think I'd hurt anyone in the process."

"Seriously?" Ryder rolls his eyes. "Maybe you are as stupid as you look."

"Hey now!" Ryley runs a hand through his butterscotch-brown hair as he strikes a model pose. "That title is reserved for me!"

Ryder snorts but doesn't respond to his brother. Instead, he turns to me. "I'm serious, Tanner. You hurt her a lot when you left."

I know. That pesky lump forms in my throat, and I swallow past it, making my eyes water.

"If you hurt her again, so help me, you'll be hurting, too." Ryder studies me. "But I remember there being a warrior's heart in you. You protected her from the jerks that lurked around Clover-High. You stood up for anyone getting picked on. Surely that guy isn't gone?"

I shake my head. "He's here. It's been a long time since he's done anything remotely chivalrous, though."

"I don't know." Ryley taps his chin. "Didn't Em say something the other day about Tanner bringing over cold stuff for Molly?"

"Yeah, and he rubbed her feet?" Ryder smirks. "And made her tea?"

Heat rushes my face. "Anyone would have done that."

Ryley gives a small chuckle. "No, anyone would *not* have."

"I'm confused." I shake my head, not tracking their shifts from welcome to threat to praise. "Are you wanting me to pursue Molly or back off?"

"Depends." Ryder shoves his hands into the pockets of his jeans. He shrugs, pulling taut the shoulders of his leather jacket.

"On what?" I asked, a note of desperation in my voice.

"On whether you plan on sticking it out this time."

CHAPTER TWENTY-THREE

Molly

And the winner is...Molly Pruitt!

Cheers. Roses. Hugs.

The sound of the ice beneath my skates. The spins as the music swells.

Joy.

"No! I don't want to." I stare at the cubbies of rental skates. "I don't."

But my hands reach for the size seven figure skates, seemingly of their own accord.

"Whatcha doing there, Molly girl?" Gramp's warm baritone causes me to spin around.

I gasp, pressing a hand against my chest. "Holy crap, Gramps!"

He chuckles and leans against the doorframe. "Sorry. But you're watching those skates with a look of someone dreading what they're about to do."

"I'm not dreading it. It's just been a long time." I finger one of the laces that's dangling down from the cubby. Proof that whatever kid was working last night wasn't following the manual. I tug the skates out, their familiar weight holding me in place. I swallow. "What if I've forgotten?"

Gramps chuckles. "I think it'll be just as easy as remembering how to reconnect to that handsome young man who you kept glancing at all game."

I glare at Gramps. "It hasn't been easy."

"So, you have been reconnecting?" Gramps strokes his mustache as his lip quirks up.

"Gramps!" I start, but he holds his hand up, halting my protest.

"Listen, Molly girl. I've gone around the sun on this hunk of rock we call Earth eighty-six times, and I've learned some things." He holds up a finger. "First, I learned that your grandmother was the craziest woman for settling down with the likes of me."

I laugh, easily able to imagine Grams rolling her eyes at that.

"Two, the best pizza topping in the world is pepperoni."

That is an opinion our entire family has, and one we laud as fact.

"And lastly," he leans in close and whispers, "I've learned to notice when people are in love. Tanner? He looks at you like you hung the moon. But he also looks at you like you're the biggest mistake he ever made."

"Ouch, Gramps." I clutch my chest, trying to force a smile on lips that refuse to curve upwards. I fail.

"Not that *you're* a mistake, Molly girl. The fact that he walked away. He looks at you like he messed you up."

"He did." I hug the skates to my chest. "He took my heart the day he left, Gramps. Don't you remember?"

"Yes, and now he's back." Gramps taps a pair of skates further into the cubby. "Perhaps this is your chance to practice a little virtue called forgiveness. It's a novel idea and something couples of all ages have to use again and again and again. I forgave your grandmother a million times, and she forgave me a million and one. It's not easy, but what good thing in life is?"

He walks away—going to fix something in the Rink, no doubt—and I tuck the skates under my arm. I listen to the low voices of my brothers and Tanner talking, the echo of it reverberating against the metal supports of the rafters.

Forgiveness. Gramps's words rattle around my head. *It's not easy, but what good thing in life is?*

Was I willing to forgive? To let go of the pain of my past to move into a friendship with the man who'd hurt me—whether or not he ever asked me to?

Part of me isn't. I want to run away this time. To be the one to escape before I get hurt. But...what could I miss out on if I do that? What if there's a chance to redeem this relationship—despite it feeling so fractured that it might never be repaired?

I step out of the rental booth and walk over to Tanner and the twins. My brothers look at the skates in my hands. It takes a minute for them to register what they are and why I'm holding them. But once they do, their eyes widen.

"Really?" Ryder asks, a note of worry in the word.

Clearing my throat, I drop my gaze to my shoes. "Do you think we can—can we try skating?"

"Only if you want to, Mols," Tanner answers, his warm voice pulling my eyes up.

There's a depth of emotion pooling in Tanner's eyes. I don't know what he's thinking. It used to be so easy to tell, and now it's like looking at the pieces of a puzzle. I should know the picture, and, in a way, I do. But it's like there are some new pieces, an extra couple things in the picture that aren't on the box. There are new layers, new depth. And heaven help me, but do I ever want to figure it out.

Taking a fortifying breath, I nod. "I do."

Tanner smiles, and dang it, Gramps is right—that is the look of someone who thinks I've hung the moon. And it terrifies me. What if I'm the one destined to destroy our relationship this time around?

I gesture to my brothers. "You guys want to help?"

Ryley's mouth is hanging open, and he walks around me, poking my cheek, my arm, my stomach before I hit his hand away with a scowl. "Hello, strange robot. Who are you, and what have you done with my sister? You know, Molly Elaine Pruitt? The one who's refused to go on the ice and ran at the very mention of hockey for the last five years?"

"I'm a coach now!" I rebut.

"Assistant coach," Ryder corrects.

Tanner, hands shoved in his team sweatshirt, shrugs. "Co-coach."

Ryder scowls at him. "Jerk."

"Ryder!" I smack him with the back of my hand. "No being rude to my co-coach."

I can feel Tanner's gaze on me. But rather than get lost in his confusing, emotion-riddled eyes, I decide to focus on Ryley, who's squinting at me.

"No, seriously." Ryley shakes his head. "Who are you, and what have you done with Molly?"

With a huff of exasperation, I stomp to the bleachers, tug off my black and white sneakers, and shove my feet into the skates. My hands shake as I tighten the laces, my eyes flicking up to the ice. It's never felt quite so large. Quite so hard and cold and unfeeling.

"You need help there, Mols?" Tanner points at my half-laced skate.

"What if I fall, Tanner?" I glance over my shoulder, hearing Ryder and Ryley arguing in the skate rental box. "What if I'm a giant bruise tomorrow?"

"I won't let you fall, Molly." Tanner leans close, his woodsy freshness wrapping around me.

Good gracious! The man can't know how he affects me, can he? No, that would be ridiculous. Yet why does my pulse spike with every encounter, leading me closer and closer to cardiac arrest? Death by sexiness. Well, there could be worse ways to go.

I hurry to finish lacing my skates before Tanner drops to one knee to do it for me. Tanner Bradshaw. On one knee. In front of me. I'm not sure my poor heart could handle that.

"You ready?" Ryder asks, waddling in his skates toward the ice with a giant grin. He pushes through the opening, effortlessly sliding across the ice like he was born with skates on his feet. I mean, he basically was. I'm fairly certain the twins learned to skate before they learned to walk.

I, on the other hand, wobble on the solid ground. My legs buckle as I grab the boards, staring at my arch nemesis—the ice—as Ryley steps past me and onto it with natural grace.

"Don't be a chicken, sis!" Ryley's laugh echoes around the Rink as I finally step cautiously onto the ice. The skates slide over the ice, and my arms pinwheel as I struggle to find my balance. It's slicker than I remember, and I curse my quivering knees.

"Easy there." Tanner grabs my hands and guides me forward. "Remember how to glide, Molly. There you go."

He encourages me as we skate, and slowly, I look more at him than at my feet. Ahead, rather than down. Eventually, I let go and do a loop around the rink with a grace that surprises me.

"There you go! You got it!" Tanner cheers from where he sits on the boards that are in front of the bench. Ryley and Ryder have joined him, one on either side.

"Try a jump, Molly!" Ryley calls. Even from across the ice, I can see his dark eyes sparkling with pride and a bit of a challenge. We Pruitts are nothing if not competitive.

"Do you want me to break my neck?" I laugh but do a little hop across the ice, the muscle memory stronger than I gave it credit for.

Ryley whoops a cheer, all three of the guys joining me on the ice as they clap.

Tanner skates ahead of me as Ryder challenges Ryley to a race. Tanner turns, going backwards with his hands clasped behind him. "I'm proud of you."

"Thanks." I look up at him and bite my lip. "You're a good teacher, Tanner Bradshaw."

He laughs and bows. "Likewise, Miss Pruitt."

"Gag me." Ryley mimes choking, earning a laugh from everyone.

I pause, looking at the four of us. Emotions clog my throat. It's like old times—me a sophomore, Tanner a junior, the boys seniors. Hanging out on the ice on a Saturday night. Goofing off, playing hockey, creating a new routine. *Friends.*

I'm too emotional for this. I can feel my chest tightening. I found it—that elusive peace I've missed for years. That pang of loneliness is filled when I look into Tanner's and my brothers' faces. But it won't remain. The twins will find their people and leave. Tanner has already proven he'll take off for the first flashy opportunity. Nothing is certain. Nothing is secure.

I force a swallow as I turn and head for the exit.

"Where are you going?" Ryley calls.

"Enough skating for today. Good first time, yeah?" With a twittery laugh that turns to a sob, I hurry off the ice.

CHAPTER TWENTY-FOUR

Tanner

I sit in front of the TV, not really watching the Comets as they play. My mind is on Molly. The look of pure panic as she'd looked between her brothers and me has burned its way into my brain. I squeeze the remote. What was going through her head?

My phone rings, and I jump. Taysleigh's name flashes across the screen.

"Hey, sis," I say, trying to push Molly to the back of my mind.

"Congrats on your first win, Coach Bradshaw!" she screams, and I jerk the phone away from my ear. And she says the kids are loud.

"Thanks, Tays."

There's a pause, then, "What's wrong?"

"What do you mean?"

"You're normally stoked after a win. Like...*ridiculously chatty for Tanner* talkative."

I snort. "Because you're an expert on me all of a sudden? Besides, who's to say that's not a *Tanner the Hockey Player* trait instead of *Bradshaw the Coach*?"

"Because I'm your big sister, and I know these things." She sniffs. "What happened between Molly and you, hm?"

"What?" I laugh, but it sounds nervous even to me.

"Tanner?" She draws my name out, waiting.

"Fine! She told me she hasn't skated since I left."

"Ouch."

"Yeah, but then after the game, she hit the ice, even did a couple of her old moves." I pause and rough my hand over my face. "Tays, after she did that, she froze. I watched as she looked between me and her brothers. And then she ran away."

"Oof. She sounds like you."

"Thanks a lot, Taysleigh. That's real helpful." I roll my eyes and lean my head against the back of the love seat. "But I can't help but wonder...what if that's all our relationship is going to be? One of us always running away?"

"Have you apologized yet?"

I wince. I know I should. It's at least half true. I'm sorry for *how* I left, but I'm still not sorry for leaving. I wasn't ready then to be what Molly needed right out of high school. Now...maybe I'm still not what she *deserves*, but I want to be. I want her to have a choice this time.

"Tanner?" Taysleigh's voice shakes me back.

"No, I haven't."

"Maybe start there," she suggests.

"But what if I'm not?"

"Not what?"

"Not sorry? Because I would have hurt her, Tays. One way or another. I was an arrogant jerk right out of high school. She deserved better then." *And maybe she still does.*

Taysleigh sighs. "Tanner, I don't know what she did or didn't deserve; just like I don't know what's going on in that thick head of yours now. But are you sorry for hurting her?"

I nod, then remember she can't see me. "Yeah, I am."

"Then apologize!" Another dramatic sigh. "I swear, you and Jacob are two peas in a pod."

I chuckle. "You have claimed you married the emotional doppelgänger of your brother. More than once."

"Don't remind me." She groans.

We talk a bit longer, about the kids, Jacob's job, and the game. After we hang up, I check my texts, surprised to see one from Ryley.

Ryley: Hey man! It was great hanging today. Would you like to come to dinner Sunday afternoon? It might not be...warm, hosting wise. Mom is still royally ticked at you for hurting Molly, but I would love to have you there. So would Ryder. Anyways, up to you! Just know the invite is out there.

Ha. I stare at the message, my thumbs doing a little dance over the keypad as I think about what to say. Do I accept the invite and risk the wrath of Mrs. Pruitt if it means showing the twins and Molly that I plan on sticking around this time?

You're not going to run anymore, Tanner James Bradshaw. You're a man now. A wise one. You know a good thing when she runs into you. I smile, the memory of slamming into Molly in the hall at the faculty meeting flitting through my head. Watching her teach, teasing her at Sweetie's. Working together, planning together, laughing together.

Yeah, there is tension. An underlying hesitancy on both our parts. But there's a lot of good there, too. But how do I eradicate that little bit of wall that remains?

Apologize! Taysleigh's voice echoes through my head. Well, that's highly annoying! When did my sister become my conscience?

Me: Hey man! I'd enjoy that. It's been a long time since I've seen your parents. Is there anything I can bring?

My thumb hesitates over the send button. Is this really worth it? Is Molly worth all this struggle? This uncertainty?

Another heartbeat passes, and I click send.

I stand on the Pruitt's front porch feeling incredibly stupid. I hold a bottle of sparkling peach juice in my hands—the fanciest drink I could find at the dollar store in town—and am attempting to find enough courage to knock. Or ring the bell. Or whatever I have to do to alert the people inside that I'm outside, freaking out.

It's just the Pruitts! Rick likes you; so does Ryley or he wouldn't have invited you.

Taysleigh's annoying voice whispers through my head, *Apologize, Tanner!*

"I will, yeesh. Shut up," I mutter as I ring the bell. The doorbell chimes, and a yappy little bark starts up.

"Sara! Hush up!" Ryder yells over the barking. He pulls open the door as he pushes a small white dog—whose tail is going a mile a minute—out of the way with his foot. "Hey, man! Glad you could make it."

"Thanks for inviting me." I shift the bottle to my other hand and clear my throat. "I brought a drink."

"Oh, this is Mom's favorite."

"Yeah, I remember." My face flames when Ryder's brows raise. "Anyway, can I come in?"

Ryder flings the door wider and bows like he's a butler. "Welcome to the Pruitt abode."

"You've been spending too much time with Ryley," I state flatly as I kick off my shoes.

Ryder grins and gestures for me to follow him through the living room—where both Mr. Pruitt and Rick are snoring on the couch while a hockey game plays in the background—and past the immaculately set dining table to the kitchen.

Mrs. Pruitt is standing over the stove, stirring what looks to be gravy with a vengeance while Molly washes the dishes with equal gusto. Both women glare at their respective tasks, and Ryley stands to the side with wide eyes, silently drying the dishes Molly all but slams onto the mat.

When he sees us in the doorway, he mouths *help me* and nods to both his mother and sister.

Apparently, Ryder's idea of helping is to throw me under the bus. "Hey, Mom, Molly. Tanner's here. And he brought sparkling peach juice." Ryder stalks through the warzone like a general. He opens one side of the double-door fridge and sets the drink on the shelf. "Wasn't that nice of him?"

"Oh, yes." Mrs. Pruitt smiles, but it lacks all warmth and sincerity. In fact, it looks a bit like a wolf stalking its prey. "So nice."

I gulp and smile back. This is more terrifying than facing off against the Seattle Krakens in the Western Conference finals. "Thank you for the invitation, Mrs. Pruitt."

"Ryley decided to do it without consulting me." Mrs. Pruitt's mouth thins to a dangerous line. "If it were up to me, you'd be eating on the back deck with the dog."

"Mom!" Molly turns, her cheeks red, her eyes flashing. "Ryley invited him, and if I'm fine with Tanner being here, you should be, too!"

Mrs. Pruitt sniffs and goes back to her gravy. I'm suddenly very afraid to eat anything she's made.

Molly flashes me an apologetic look after glaring at her mother's back. She returns to the dishes, and I ease up beside her. "Can I help?"

She looks up at me, a strand of her hair brushing her temple. "Sure. Grab the towel from Ryley."

I turn toward her brother, but he's already thrown the towel, and it hits me square in the face. It's sopping wet.

"Thanks for that," I mutter, wiping at the water on my face with the sleeve of my cardigan.

"Yeah, you had something right there." Ryley gestures to my whole face. "Thought I'd help."

I shake my head and take the spatula Molly has just finished washing to swat at her brother. He jumps back with a cackle and scoots around me and his mother to retreat to the living room. I dry the utensil and look to Ryder for where to put it.

"Drawer, there." He points to the one right next to his mother.

Pulling on every ounce of courage I have gathered from my NHL years, I open the drawer and put the spatula in its place. Mrs. Pruitt doesn't say a word as she pulls the gravy off the stove and carries it into the dining room. I turn back to Molly at the sink with a soft exhale of relief.

Molly smirks at me as she whispers, "Her bark is worse than her bite."

I lean close so Mrs. Pruitt can't hear from the dining room. "That doesn't bring me much comfort, Mols. Her bark has halitosis and probably some gum diseases."

Molly snorts and then coughs, her smile large and eyes watery. She stifles another giggle which leads to another snort which has Ryder looking at her curiously. His puzzled expression has me chuckling, and soon, the two of us are laughing nearly silently with tears trailing down our faces as we struggle to pull ourselves back together.

"Dinner!" Mrs. Pruitt calls, and I fold the towel and hang it on the rack to dry as I follow Molly and Ryder into the dining room.

My palms get sweaty when Rick and Mr. Pruitt step in from the living room with Ryley. Is it hot in here? Because I'm pretty sure I could melt into a giant puddle. This is a lot. My chest feels tight. I'm not ready to face down this family that is thick as thieves and includes a few members who hate my guts.

Ryley guides me to a seat between Molly and him. Rick and Ryder sit across the table, beaming at me in a slightly freaky way. Why are they smiling like that? However, it's counteracted by Molly's parents—who are glaring at me from either end of the table.

As the food is passed, Ryder starts up a conversation. "How are the Comets doing this season, Tanner?"

It feels like a punch to the stomach. I really don't know. I've watched one game, and I didn't pay any attention to it because I was preoccupied with thoughts of Molly. Besides, the team dropped me the moment they discovered I wouldn't be back. I'm not worth the time anymore when there is young blood on the team and new friends to make.

I swallow the bite of mashed potatoes and shrug. "They haven't really kept in touch since I've been back in Cloverfield."

Mrs. Pruitt scoffs. "Imagine that. They only wanted you for what you could do. Sound familiar, Molly Elaine?"

"Mom," Ryder warns.

But Molly cuts him off. "Enough with the passive aggressiveness, Mom. What are you trying to say?"

"I don't want him in this house!" She jabs a finger at me. "You're welcoming him back with open arms after he hurt you, Molly."

"And I'm sorry for that, Mrs. Pruitt." I look at her and hope she sees the truth. The depth of emotions that color the words, even as it feels like there's a vise around my chest. "I'm sorry for the way I left. It was wrong to leave Molly a note and take off. I should have faced her like a man."

"Dang right," Mr. Pruitt mumbles.

"But..." This isn't how I had planned this apology going, but this is my chance. I look at Molly. Big mistake. The pain on her face etches a deeper cavity in my chest, and my inhale is shaky. "I'm not sorry I left. I hurt you, Molly, and for that, I apologize. But I needed to leave. We needed a chance to grow and mature. I—I think even if I had stayed, we would have ended up broken and hurt."

"You can't know that!" Mrs. Pruitt scoffs.

"No, I can't." I meet her fiery gaze with my own, a long-sought peace wrapping around me. "But if Molly is willing to give us another shot, another chance at friendship at least, I'm willing to take it. If your sons want me to hang out with them, I will. Because you can never have too many true friends."

Ryder grins from across the table with a nod, and Rick hides a smile of his own behind his hand as he leans his chair back on two legs.

"I'm asking for forgiveness for the way I hurt you. All of you." I lay a hand on Molly's shoulder. "But especially you. It wasn't fair. Will you forgive me?"

Molly's throat bobs. "Come with me."

She pushes away from the table and heads to the kitchen. Slowly, I follow. As we step out onto the back deck, I feel a heavy foreboding biting at my heels.

CHAPTER TWENTY-FIVE

Molly

He's sorry for hurting me but not for leaving? My ears ring as I brace my hands against the railing. The leaves race across the backyard, rustling as they chase each other down the hills and the road. The yellows, reds, and oranges blur as tears fill my eyes.

The door closes, and I sense more than hear Tanner lean against the railing.

"Okay. What's up?"

I turn and jab my finger against Tanner's surprisingly solid chest. "You left me behind and went off to Texas to play hockey and date movie stars and models, and you never looked back! Now you're sorry, but, oh! Not for leaving. Just for hurting me?"

I can't help the blasted tears that push into my eyes. I turn to escape, but he grabs my shoulders, his thumbs drawing soft circles that send fire racing down my limbs. "I looked back, Molly. Over and over again. But it didn't seem fair to pull you into a life you didn't want."

"How did you know I didn't want it? You never asked. Maybe I would have—"

"Yeah, you would have, Mols. You would have up and gone off to Houston with me. Gotten into some college miles away from here that you would have hated, but you would have gone for me. For us. Besides that, I know you would have hated every moment of dating an NHL player. You don't like flashy, and that's what my life was in Texas."

He starts to pull away, but I clasp my hands over his wrists, holding him in place. A dog barks, a kid screams down the block, the wind blows some of my hair into my face, but I don't acknowledge any of it. Don't see anything but the depth of Tanner's eyes, and the way he's staring into mine.

When I don't let go, don't move out of his space, he whispers, "Mols?"

"Why didn't you ask me, you stubborn know-it-all?" It's a whisper that ends on a sob. I'm so mad at him for leaving, yet I don't want to let him go. I want to push him away because letting him get close runs the risk of getting hurt again. But I know that if he chooses to walk away now, the damage will already be done.

Tanner's throat bobs at my question. "I told you—"

"No, that's not the truth. Not all of it, anyways." I step closer, his broad shoulders blocking some of the chill of the wind. "Even when we were dating in high school, you never let me in on the big choices. You always made them alone. I want to know why."

"I..." His eyes close, and he tightens his grip on my shoulders. "I was—I *am* afraid."

The admission startles me. That wasn't the answer I was preparing for. He'd never been a controlling monster like some of the guys my friends dated. But Tanner held his cards close, only letting me see when he'd already made up his mind. Like when he moved to Houston. But that was...fear?

"Fear of what?" He doesn't look up at me. The longer he's silent, the more I need to know his answer. My stomach tightens as I step closer. "What are you afraid of, Tanner?"

I think I'm going to be sick by the time he sighs and says, "I'm afraid of you, Molly."

Another sucker punch. The air whooshes out of me, and I close my eyes.

Two for two, well done.

I moisten my lips with my tongue, trying to gather my thoughts, but the only word to escape is an ineloquent, "What?"

"I'm scared you'll leave. Or choose someone else. Someone better than me—because heaven only knows what you saw in me in high school. And I'm so good at running from what scares me. What hurts me. The thought of you leaving terrified me. And I thought that if I did the choosing, if I chose hockey and left, then it wouldn't hurt as bad, and I wouldn't have to deal with *that*."

"*That* being...?" I open my eyes and study his face.

"Rejection, I guess." He shrugs, still staring at the paint chipping off of the deck.

"But you chose to reject *me* before you even knew if I would reject you, Tanner."

"I know. I regret it every time I look at you, Molly. Every time I think about you. Oh gosh, if you only knew how often I laid in bed while in Houston and thought about you, you *would* run away. I'm a fool. A giant idiot, and I—" he doesn't finish, but he finally looks up. Something shines in his eyes—something that looks a lot like tears.

"Don't." I reach up and cup his cheek. His five o'clock shadow scrapes my palm, and I run my thumb over his cheek and dash away a single tear. "Don't live in regret anymore. You were right at the table. We both needed that time to become who we are."

He sniffs. "You are pretty great."

I smile, but my words are cold when I say, "But if you ever walk away from me again, I swear I'll—" My gaze flicks to his lips a moment before I close the distance between us.

It is thunder after the lightning. Low and rumbling and comforting. It is coming home after a long day to a warm cookie and a cup of coffee. It is toe-curlingly delicious and warm. There is no frenzy. No taking. It is all giving. It is longing and hoping and loving. All I want and everything I never thought I'd have again.

Tanner tugs me closer. His kiss deepens for a moment before he sighs and begins to trail little kisses, featherlight, across my jaw and cheek before burying his nose into my neck.

"Oh, Molly," he breathes.

It won't last, my head chants the words even as I bury my face against Tanner's chest and twine my arms around his waist. He will eventually find something better than Cloverfield and me. Ride off into the sunset without a backwards glance once more. Gone all over again. A new woman or a new job. A better life is out there for Tanner Bradshaw, I know. It is only a matter of time before I, Molly Pruitt, am left behind again.

Tanner's hold on me tightens. "What are you doing to me, Pruitt?"

I shiver at the huskiness in his voice. *But if anyone asks, it's the autumn breeze.* "I don't know. Are you experiencing palpitations?"

"Terrible ones." His words hold a grin.

I can't help but smile against his cardigan. "Are there hot flashes, too?"

"Worse than a middle-aged woman."

"Wow, rude!" A burst of laughter escapes. "Oh, and I'm sure there's weak knees?"

"They're shaking like palm trees in a hurricane." He nods as I lean back, his grin mirroring mine. "What's the diagnosis?"

"It's serious." I work to school my features to neutrality, but I'm not sure I manage it all that well. Not with Tanner grinning at me with his dimple and blue eyes. If his legs were palm trees in a hurricane? Mine are sinking in quicksand. I clear my throat.

"Don't keep me in suspense, Doctor Pruitt." His arms tighten around my waist.

Heat climbs into my cheeks. The way he's looking at me, the way he makes me feel and act? I know what *my* diagnosis is, and there's no way I am telling him it.

"Molly?" Tanner's brows furrow. "What's wrong?"

"Nothing. Never mind. Let's go eat."

I turn for the door, but Tanner cuts in front of me. "Nuh-uh. You don't get to start this little game and quit when you get uncomfy."

"*Uncomfy*? What are you, a tween girl?" I cross my arms and attempt to ignore the twinkle in his eyes.

"Molly." He drags my name out, a goofy grin on his face.

"Fine! I was going to say it sounds like you have a crush. Happy?"

The insufferable man laughs. "Only a crush, huh?"

My traitorous brain replays the mind-numbingly epic kiss, and I drop my gaze to the slats of the deck. "Yeah. Just a crush."

"Interesting." He hums. "Because I'm fairly certain it's a bit more than that."

"What?" I look up so fast my neck stiffens.

Tanner's lips purse, the smile vanishing. "Yeah. I'm pretty sure I'm halfway in love with you, Molly Pruitt."

I can't swallow. My mouth is the Sahara Desert in July. If my legs were quicksand before, now they've been struck by lightning and turned to glass. I can't move, I can't think.

I'm halfway in love with you, Molly Pruitt.

But he can't be! This wasn't supposed to happen. No amount of kissing is going to fix the broken mess that is us.

"Say something, Mols." Tanner laughs, but it's nervous like he doesn't know what to do after his confession.

And I don't either. Because the thought of him loving and caring for me terrifies me half to death. It makes me want to run away—just like he said he is afraid of me doing. But at the moment, Tanner is between me and the escape door.

Some of my fear must show on my face because Tanner grabs my hand. "Listen. I don't need this to be reciprocated at this very moment. I don't need to hear you say you're in love with me or that everything I did is forgiven. Heck, I'm happy just being your friend because I honestly didn't think you'd even give me that."

"Well, that's good," I squeak out.

He smiles—good gracious, does it do funny things to my breathing—and says, "But I do want you to know that if you try to run from me, I will chase after you. If you hide, I'll find you." He drops his gaze to my fingers, squeezing them as he takes a deep breath. "You can even try walling up your heart again, Mols, but I'm pretty good with a sledgehammer. I'm not asking for anything this week. This month. Even this year. I'm not asking for anything, Molly, except...please, let me pursue you again. You're worthy of that."

He wants to pursue me?

Someone hand me a dictionary because I can't find my words. Speechless. He rendered me absolutely speechless. I stand there like a fish out of water, my mouth opening and closing as if I'm gasping for air.

Knowing his work here is done, Tanner smiles before turning and holding the door open. "I'm taking that as an *all right* to the pursuing thing."

I shake my head. "What does pursuing entail?"

He chuckles as he steps back into the house. "I guess you'll just have to wait and see."

Chapter Twenty-Six

Tanner

Molly silently follows me back to the table. Her cheeks are flushed a pretty pink. I hope that's from our kiss and not the wind that is blowing outside. As we settle back at the table, Ryley cuts a glance to his mother before, ever so subtly, puckering his lips. He jumps as I kick him under the table, and Molly's eyes go wide. Ryley simply chuckles and resumes eating.

I feel like an imposter, like a puzzle piece that almost fits, but isn't quite right. One shade is off, one side a touch too short, and it feels like you'll never find your place again.

With a muffled sigh, I shove another bite of potato into my mouth, my stomach churning. I replay the kiss. She'd kissed me, right? I glance out of the corner of my eye. Molly is looking at me, a tiny smile on her face. That's a good sign, yeah?

I dated while on the Comets, but never more than one date per girl. Because none of them compared to deep-blue eyes and spunky personality I had left behind. Some had money. Some had fame. None of them had the freckles and the smile that made me melt inside like snow on a warm spring day. None had that spark of energy when talking about something they really loved. None of them were Molly.

Mr. Pruitt clears his throat. "Tanner, can we go for a walk after dinner?"

My stomach does a flip as I nod. "Yes, sir."

"Good." He eyes me like I'm a dangerous animal.

Molly's hand finds mine under the table, and she squeezes. I'm not sure if it's a warning or an encouragement. Neither bodes well for me.

I shove my hands into my jacket pockets to keep from fidgeting as I walk down the street with Mr. Pruitt. I want to bolt, but I keep my gait level, following after the man as meekly as I can.

"So. You're interested in my Molly again, hm?"

I clear my throat. "As friends, for now, sir."

"Hm. But what if she wants to be more than friends?" Mr. Pruitt stops walking, and I turn to face him. We're about two blocks from his house. Two blocks from my car and a quick exit. I smooth my sweaty palms against my pants. "You going to take off again, son?"

"I—"

"Listen here. Molly is a grown woman. She can make her own choices. But I am, first and foremost, her father. I won't let you hurt her again, Tanner. If that means running you off, so be it. I love my daughter and her beautiful precious heart too much to let you destroy it again."

"I won't hurt her, sir. I—I was an idiot to walk away before. I told her that." *And then she kissed me*. I run a hand through my hair and rub my neck. "I don't understand what she saw in me in high school. What your boys saw. But I want to be that man again. Only with a whole lot more wisdom and gentleness."

Mr. Pruitt has his arms crossed, his dark-blue eyes squinting as he stares at me. "I'm going to be keeping my eye on you, Tanner."

"Please do, sir." I shove my hands back in my pockets as he starts walking again.

His brow raises, and he grunts what sounds like approval, although it's hard to tell. "Dad said you were different." He rubs a hand over his goatee. "And I accept your apology from earlier, just so you know."

"Thank you, sir."

"You've changed. You're not nearly as cocky as you were five years ago."

I chuckle. "An injury that shatters your dreams gives you a lot of time for introspection."

"Good. Good." Mr. Pruitt grins but sobers quickly. "Just you be careful with my Molly." He wags his finger at me. "I'm trusting you with my most precious treasure."

"I will be so careful, sir." *I don't want to lose her again.*

With a nod, Mr. Pruitt turns around and heads back toward the house. "Ryder should have that apple crisp ready by now."

"Sounds delicious," I say, even as my stomach tightens. Because Molly is there. How do I show her that I won't run? That I'm not planning on ever leaving her again? Yeah, I'm afraid. But this time, I'm jumping in headfirst, and there is absolutely no turning back.

I sit in the back of Molly's classroom the next day, clicking my pen as her students file into the room. I can't think straight. Can't take my eyes off Molly. She sits at her desk, her glasses on the edge of her nose as she reads the final chapter of *The Giver*. Her sweater sleeves cover her fingers as her eyes slide across the page, her lips quirking up as she soaks in the escape of Jonas and Gabriel from their utopian prison.

I pick up my phone and snap a picture, as enchanted with her obliviousness to the world around her as she is with the world in her book.

The warning bell rings, and the class pours in. Gloria flounces to her seat, her heeled boots clicking across the tile in a grating staccato. I clench my teeth. She acts like a queen. Just once, I'd like someone to knock her down a peg. Or twenty.

Kai shuffles in, and I feel the urge to talk to him. He looks horrible, with greasy hair and dark circles under his eyes. He glances at me and scowls.

I keep my eye on him as Molly launches into her lecture about the ending of *The Giver*. But now, I can't seem to focus on her voice. What's wrong with Kai? Surely, it's not just me replacing his grandfather. It can't be. Something else is going on with this kid.

The period ends, and I step up to Kai, who is still slumped in his seat.

"Hey, man. We'd love to have you back on the team."

"Didn't make the cut, did I?" His lip curls back as he looks at me like I'm gum stuck to his new shoes. "Besides, I hear you have a new kid. The enemy."

"Ethan helped us win the last game. He's a great addition to the team. And I think you could be, too, if you wanted." I cross my arms, trying to get a pulse on this kid.

Kai scoffs. "Yeah, not with you as coach."

"Why? Because I replaced your grandpa?" I spread my arms out wide. "He retired. I took over. I didn't kick him out of his place, Kai."

"Newsflash, Bradshaw! I don't care! I don't care about you or hockey or anything else because life sucks! Do you have dead parents? Huh? Dead sister? Because I do. And the only family I have left is my grandpa, and he's dying too! He's dying, and I can't do a damn thing about it!"

He pushes past me and out the classroom door, slamming it hard enough to knock a picture frame off one of Molly's shelves.

"Tanner?" Molly's hand lands on my arm. "What just happened?"

"I think I touched a nerve." I rub the back of my neck. "Funny thing is, I can relate a bit to that." I look down at Molly. Her gaze is warm.

"Tanner—"

I hold up a hand to halt whatever she's about to say. "Yeah, I know. I shouldn't have pushed him so hard."

"That's not what I was going to say." She smiles. "You care. You're showing him that, even if he doesn't like it. And I was going to say you should go after him."

"Oh...right." I pat her hand before stepping toward the door. "Better see if I can go find him."

Molly nods as her juniors file in, and I hurry out the door. Popping my head in Ava's room, I ask if she's seen Kai. She hasn't, so I begin roaming the hall, finally ending up in the office with Mrs. Maize, who pages him.

The kid doesn't show. Panic bubbles in my chest. He'd been mad. Really mad. Mad enough to do something stupid.

Worry lines Mrs. Maize's forehead as she calls the resource officer to the office as I pace. Skinner leans in the doorway, his bushy brows lowered.

"You don't have any idea where he went?" Skinner asks as Officer Charlie sits and takes notes.

"No." I shake my head and clasp my hands behind my neck. "I was trying to get him to join back up with the Cougars. He yelled that he hated me, that I didn't understand, and that his—" I swallow and look at Skinner. "Did you know Reynolds is dying?"

Skinner slowly nodded. "Yeah. It's why he retired. He's got cancer, Tanner."

"And no one bothered to inform me of this...why?"

"He didn't want anyone to know." Skinner meets my gaze, sorrow lining his eyes. "But he must have told Kai."

"Yeah. He did." I grit my teeth. "What kind of cancer?"

"Skin."

I swear. Tears push into my eyes—the same cancer as Dad's. I swallow a lump in my throat as I look at Charlie. "No idea where he might have gone?"

"When he's taken off before, it's usually been over to the Rink."

"Then that's where I'm going." I pat my pockets, thankful my keys are still there, before I hurry out of the building and to my car. My mind decides to replay my final moments with Dad. Holding his hand, singing his favorite songs. Mom, Taysleigh, and I telling him how much we loved him. Him telling us how much he loved us.

I'd made it home just in time. Anger still simmers in my chest that Mom and Taysleigh hadn't told me sooner. I would have taken time off. The league would have let me come home. But Dad had loved watching me play on the Comets. Had loved seeing me pursue my dream. He told me that, minutes before he was gone.

I pound the steering wheel with my palm, pinching my eyes with my fingers before I climb out of the car and hurry into the Rink. It's unlocked, and I see Rick standing by the ice watching a young man race across it like all the demons of hell are on his tail.

"He came pounding on the door," Rick explains. "I know he should be in school, but there was something in his eyes that told me he needed to skate it out."

"Yeah." I can't say more as I watch Kai go back and forth. Sweat drips from his forehead, but I sense it's more than perspiration. I know that look. That wild panic that makes you want to run, run, run, and never look back. Never turn around. But you do because you can't help longing for what's behind.

I grab the skates Rick hands me. A knowing smile twitches his mustache before he disappears back into the bowels of the Rink. I lace them up and head onto the ice.

Kai skids to a halt, throwing up a wave of ice as he does. "What do *you* want?"

"Some people at school are worried about you."

"Who? You?" The kid sneers, running a hand through his hair. "You only care that I'm not on your team."

"No, man. I care about you. I know what it's like to lose a dad, and I know what it's like to lose someone to cancer. It sucks, man. It really does. But running doesn't fix it. Trust me. Running only makes you lonely. Isolated."

He scoffs and crosses his arms. "I don't believe you."

"Fine. You don't have to. But I'm not giving up on you."

He looks at me. "I don't like you, Bradshaw."

"You're not the first person to tell me that, and I'm not asking you to." I grin at him. "How about we play a little one-on-one?"

"You got a stick?"

"There's some in the locker room. First to three?" I ask with a raised brow.

A light that has nothing to do with anger sparks in Kai's eyes. "You're on, Bradshaw."

We play hard. Sweat soaks through my dress shirt as I battle it out with the boy who is mad at the world. I manage to work out some of my own frustrations and hurt onto the puck as well.

The score is six to eight—Kai winning—when we finally stop and grab the sports drinks Rick left on the bleachers.

"You play hard, Kai." I take a swig and wipe at my forehead. "I'm impressed."

He smiles, and I'm rendered speechless. It's dazzling, white and straight and lightens his black eyes to an almost purple hue.

"Thanks, Coach."

"Does this mean you want to play for me?" I don't look at him, focusing my eyes on screwing the lid back onto my drink.

Kai passes the shaft of his stick from one hand to the other. Just when I think he's not going to answer, he whispers, "I'm going to be in the system if Grandpa dies within the next two months."

I press my lips together, not saying a word.

"And once I'm out of there..." His throat bobs. "I don't know what I'm going to do, Coach. I have no family. No friends who'll take me in."

I think of the basement. Of Mom and our two guestrooms upstairs. And I know she'd say the same thing. "I'll take you in, Kai."

"What?" He looks at me, utterly bewildered. "Why would you care about the kid who...who was such a jerk to you?"

"Because there's a little bit of jerk in all of us. I've pushed people away, and they've let me come back; come home." I clasp his shoulder. "There are plenty of people who want to help you, Kai. You just needed to be brave enough to reach out."

Chapter Twenty-Seven

Molly

I worry away the rest of the school day, barely able to focus. Tanner doesn't pick up when I call at lunch, and I barely manage to eat my peanut butter sandwich without choking.

Once three o'clock hits, I hurry to my car. Still no text. I drum my fingers on the steering wheel before pulling out and heading to Sweetie's. His car isn't there, so he has to be at the Rink. At least, I try to tell my nervous stomach that.

He didn't leave you, Molly. He didn't. My chest tightens, and my throat aches as I order both a vanilla and a caramel latte. At least, I think that's what I order. My brain seems staticky; the only thought resonating is that he could be gone. Again.

Settling the to-go container on the seat, I pull out of the café and head toward the Rink.

I scan the parking lot, silently pleading, *Please let his car be here!*

And there it is! His car. Tears press against my eyes as I unbuckle and hurry toward the building. It takes three tries to get my key in the lock because my hands are shaking so badly, and I almost trip over my own boot-clad feet stepping into the cold air of the Rink.

Tanner is sitting on the bleachers, talking to Kai. I finally draw in a deep breath as I hurry forward.

"I'm here for you, man. Even if you just need to talk. And we *can* have you on the team this year. You might be benched for a good chunk until you can prove yourself, but I want you here. You've got skill."

"Thanks, Coach." Kai smiles—a full-fledged, teeth showing smile—before standing. He turns, and that guarded look drops over his face when he sees me. "Miss Pruitt. Sorry for, well, you know."

"All is forgiven, Kai." I smile, hoping it doesn't look sympathetic. I know that's probably the last thing he wants. It was the last thing I'd wanted when Grams had died.

"Thanks." He nods at me, then Tanner, before heading out the door.

I hand Tanner his latte, unable to stop the tremble in my fingers. Why did my brain automatically assume the worst about him? He didn't leave. He is standing here in front of me. Helping a hurting kid, no less!

Stupid, stupid brain!

"Hey." Tanner grabs my hand that's holding the latte. "What's wrong? You look upset."

"I—I couldn't get ahold of you." I roll my eyes. "It was stupid."

"What was?"

"My...panic." Heat climbs into my cheeks.

Hurt flashes across Tanner's face. "You thought I'd left?"

"I..." I can't lie. Can't say it hadn't crossed my mind. So I shrug. "I wondered. But I knew you said you wouldn't. And I...I trust you."

You do. You trust him. If anyone is going to walk out, it's going to be you. You're not going to get hurt first this time.

I pause, staring off into space as I run that thought through my head again.

I'm going to be the one to hurt Tanner. I'm...no! I shake my head. *What is wrong with me?*

"Molly?" Tanner takes both coffees and sets them on the bleacher. "Molly, what's wrong?"

"I don't know!" I want to scream as he pulls me to his chest. "I was scared you'd left and then my head...these horrible thoughts."

"It's okay." He smooths his hand against the back of my head. "Do you want to talk about it?"

"I thought...I was thinking that if someone was going to leave, it would be me first this time." I shake my head. "I don't want to leave. Why am I thinking about leaving?"

"Because we're both runners, aren't we?" Tanner tips my chin up. "We run away from pain, from trouble, from conflict?"

"Yeah." I chuckle. "I avoid all of that like the plague."

"So do I," Tanner says.

"How do we fix that?"

"Instead of running away from each other"—his hand settles on my waist, drawing me closer— "what if we ran toward each other?"

My hands slide up and around his neck. "Yeah?"

"Yeah. What do you say?"

But he doesn't give me the chance to reply. Our lips meet. His are still as warm as they had been on the deck the day before. Still gentle and searching. If this is what running toward Tanner is going to be like, I'll be running to him for the rest of my life.

Our lattes get cold.

Tanner grabs his as he links his fingers with mine. "Want to come over to my place for dinner? Mom told me this morning she's making lasagna."

"I'd like that." I hesitated in the doorway. "Tanner, are we dating?"

A mischievous twinkle dances in his eyes. "Are we? Or are we kissing friends?"

"What?" I laugh.

"My mom tells the story of a friend from college who had a guy who was her *kissing friend*. They weren't dating, but they'd make out together."

"Ew!" I say with another laugh.

"So, are we a thing, Mols, or are we kissing friends?" He puckers his lips, and I bump him with my shoulder.

"I suppose we're a thing, Tanner James."

He smiles, swinging our clasped hands as we reach our cars.

"Do you remember the way to my house? Or should you ride with me, and I'll bring you back here tonight to get your car?"

"I remember." I slide into my car and watch Tanner walk to his.

We are dating. I'm still scared something might happen, but Tanner wants to make this work. Make *us* work. And I can't help but grin as I follow him out of the Rink parking lot. In fact, my cheeks kind of hurt from all my smiling.

The road we wind down is as familiar as mine. It's the dead-end street with the old basketball hoop at the end. The cornfield that's waiting to be harvested. The white, ranch style house with the green shutters. The swing between two towering maple trees. The flowerbeds that wrap around the front of the house.

This had been a second home for one glorious year. A place to feel accepted and valued. I loved coming over here after school to warm cookies, hot cocoa, and study dates with the cute senior who cared enough to pay attention to me.

A knock on my window has me releasing my death grip on the wheel and stepping out to Tanner's side.

"Sorry." I wipe my damp cheek with my fingertips, surprised that I'd started crying. "I guess it hit me harder than I thought."

"What did?" Tanner asks as he interlocks our fingers. "My house?"

I nod. "It was another home my junior year. Then you left, and I didn't feel like I belonged here anymore."

"Mols." His grip on my hand tightens. "I'm sorry."

"It's fine."

"No, it's not." His brows lower as he looks at me. "Please...I know it's slightly selfish, but I need to hear you say you forgive me."

Have I not said that? I think back over our conversation on the deck and realize I haven't. I haven't told him I forgive him.

"Tanner." I turn to face him, grabbing his other hand. I think through everything that's happened in the last month and a half. All our ups and downs. The hurt—the bitterness—it doesn't ache quite as badly as it had. I look forward to seeing Tanner every day. Enjoy planning and working by his side for the Cougars. It feels—as cheesy as it sounds—like I've found my home. My soul-mate. I didn't think I believed in them until he came crashing back into my life, and I realized I would never find another person I love as much as I love Tanner Bradshaw.

I look up at him, tears coming yet again at the realization, and whisper, "I forgive you."

Tanner tucks a strand of my hair behind my ear. "Thanks, Mols."

He makes to pull away, but I tighten my grip on his hands. What he'd said on the back porch—it had freaked me out then, but now...

"Tanner?"

He looks down at me, his eyes warm and full of peace. He is at peace with this, with us. So why do I feel so unsettled? So nervous to say what's on my heart?

Because you said it before, and he left.

I swallow the panic and choke out. "I'm pretty sure I'm halfway in love with you, too."

His face doesn't move. He doesn't react. But his pupils dilate as his gaze flicks to my lips. The longest silence known to man stretches between us, and my courage dwindles. Had I said the wrong thing? Spoken out of turn? But he'd said he was content with just friends. How else was I supposed to tell him?

"Mols?" he finally rasps out.

"Yes?"

"This isn't—" he shakes his head, the vacant look evaporating. "I wasn't expecting that so soon."

"What?" I throw my hands up, stepping away from him with a grunt of exasperation. "What are you talking about?"

"Thought it would take a bit more pursuing." He chuckles. "Listen, this isn't a rebuff. Molly." He grabs my hand and pulls me around when I turn toward his front door. "I know I've done nothing to earn it, but do you trust me that this isn't a rejection?"

"I tell you I'm falling in love with you, and you stare me down." I try to tug free, but his other hand snags my hip. Sarcasm laces my words as I say, "Yeah, sure, I trust you."

"Molly." He chuckles and kisses my forehead. "I know you care now. And when I tell you I love you, you're going to react the same way."

"Am I?" I ask dryly.

"Yep." His nose brushes mine. "Because you're never going to see it coming."

I scoff but don't pull away as he once more links our fingers and leads me to the front door.

"I'm home!" Tanner calls, mimicking the way he used to enter the house when we'd come over after school.

His home is just how I remember it—though a bit of updating has happened in the kitchen area. The brown couches, the lodgey feel, the open kitchen with his mom puttering around in it. That's all the same. And the smell...lasagna on the stovetop being kept warm while the yeasty, buttery scent of garlic bread in the oven blends with the smell that is Tanner's mom. Earthy with the sweet scent of lavender.

It smells like memories.

My chest tightens, but I refuse to cry again today, so I force a smile as Mrs. Bradshaw turns from the stove. Her eyes flick from Tanner to me to our clasped hands. Her brow raises even as a knowing smile slides onto her lips. "I wondered how long it would take."

"Mom!" Tanner lays a hand over his heart in mock shock.

"Tanner!" His mom laughs as she mimics the action. "You used to ask about Molly every time you phoned home when you were in Houston. Don't even try to deny it, Tanner James! I have the records to prove it."

"Prove I asked about Molly?" He raises a brow when I giggle. "What's so funny?"

"This conversation!" I shake my head with another laugh. "I've missed this."

"Then you should have brought yourself over more often, Molly." Mrs. Bradshaw holds her arms open. "Come here, my dear."

She folds me into her arms, a tight, air-stealing hug that is absolutely perfect. Oh, how I missed this! I hug her back before easing out of her hold.

"Thank you for having me over. Although," I glance over my shoulder at Tanner, "I'm sure he didn't ask."

Mrs. Bradshaw laughs. "He didn't, but I always make enough in case Taysleigh and the kids drop by."

"Which they often do." Tanner's arm slips around my waist. "So, I knew we'd have enough."

"Well, everything smells delicious!" I proclaim as we sit down at the dinner table.

After we're all served, Mrs. Bradshaw leans forward. "Now, tell me all about the last five years, dear."

"There's not much to tell, Mrs. Bradshaw," I say, after swallowing the most heavenly bite of lasagna I've ever had—not that I'd ever tell Mom or Ryder that!

Mrs. Bradshaw waves her hand like she's shooing a fly. "It's Maria, dear. You're twenty-two, for pity's sake!"

"You remember how old I am?" I ask. My mouth hangs open when she nods, and those pesky tears prick at my eyes once more.

Maria's gaze softens. "I've always remembered. I remember that you love peanut butter cookies dipped in chocolate milk. I remember you loved English and literature. You helped Tanner pass those classes."

I laugh as I watch Tanner's ears turn red.

"You loved to run barefoot through the grass, you always snuggled Polly when you were over because your mom wouldn't let you get a cat, and your favorite food was my homemade pizza."

The tears are now running down my cheeks. Apparently, today is the day to get them all out of my system. "How do you remember all that? *Why* do you remember all that?"

"Because you were just as important to me and Marcus as you were to Tanner." Maria lays her hand over mine. "And never forget that whatever happens in the next five years, you are *always* welcome in this house, Molly Pruitt. Never stay away so long again."

Tanner is smiling at me as I stand and hug his mother once again, unashamedly crying on her shoulder. My heart, which I hadn't realized was quite so bruised, hums contentedly in my chest. Everything is falling into place. Everything is straightening out.

And that scares me ever so slightly. Because what will happen now?

CHAPTER TWENTY-EIGHT

Tanner

After a night of laughter, cookie making, and game playing, I walk Molly out to her car.

"Thanks for tonight." She smiles up at me, and I swear the moon glows in the blue of her eyes. "I needed this, and it was amazing, and you were amazing, and—"

"No more *ands*." I pull her to me, and she laughs. "Seriously, this was cathartic for me, too."

"Oh, the hockey man is using big words. What's it mean?" Her nose wrinkles up, her glasses wiggling with it.

"It means therapeutic or healing, so you can un-scrunch that nose of yours, ma'am."

"*Ma'am* makes me sound like an old woman." She pushes against my chest, but I don't let go. Rather, I tickle her sides, getting a squeal of protest followed by giggles. "Tanner, let me go!"

"But I don't want to." I press my lips to hers for a quick peck, enjoying every moment of being near Molly. I have missed her. Craved her. Gosh, I see her every day and still miss her when she isn't nearby.

"Well, Susan may call the police if I'm not home in the next twenty minutes. And she'll definitely name you as number one suspect. But," Molly's arms slide up and around my neck, "a few more minutes won't hurt."

She pulls my head down, kissing me deeply. My hands settle on her waist as she leans against the side of her car. Oh, this is heaven. This is bliss. This is what I never thought I'd have again.

"Molly," I breathe as we come up for air. I lean my forehead against hers, feeling lightheaded from that world-altering kiss.

"Good?" She chuckles as I nod, bobbing her head with my own. She smiles. "Good."

Another kiss later, and she's slipping into her car and heading for home. I rub the back of my neck, wondering how in the world I got so lucky as to earn her heart again.

The high from the night before is immediately shattered when I step into Molly's classroom the next day. The look on her face tells me that the caramel latte I'm holding won't be enough for whatever is going on.

"What happened?" I ask, hurrying to her desk.

She leans her forehead against her hand, turning her phone toward me. "Have you seen this?"

I glance down and do a double take. "Is that—?"

"Us. Last night. Outside your house on your *dead-end street*." Tears make her eyes glassy. "Who would do this, Tanner?"

"Gloria," I growl. Adrenaline courses through me, the same feeling I get right before slamming an opposing player into the boards making my skin prickle. I lock my hands behind my neck, refusing to give in to the urge to pace.

"Even if it was Gloria, we can't go accusing without proof. And this?" She bites her lip. "Tanner, what if it is grounds for dismissal? They're never going to fire you, but they'll fire me!"

"No, they won't." I glare at her, anger curdling the little bit of coffee I'd drank that morning. "Because if they do, they'll lose me."

"You'd quit your job for me?" Molly's tone tells me she doesn't believe it. And I can't say I blame her. I wouldn't believe me.

"Listen, Mols." I come around and sit on the edge of her desk. "I don't need to work. I do it 'cause Dad always said it keeps the brain sharp." A wave of longing hit me. I wish Dad were here. Wish he could show me what the heck I'm supposed to do—both with this mess and dating Molly again. I rub the back of my neck. "If they fire you, I'm gone. I've been thinking about this since you told me Gloria was threatening you with our friendship. And if they do end up firing me, I really won't care, because you'll still be my girlfriend. Hey." I cup her cheek when she tries to turn away. "Molly, we're not giving up that easily."

"Is it really worth it?" Her voice cracks, and she won't look at me.

The words lodge in my throat. Does *she* not think we're worth it? I may be willing to fight for us, but she needs to want it. I need her to want it. It takes me three tries to get out, "Yes, it is. You're worth a whole lot of trouble to me."

Molly scoffs, crossing her arms. "You can't even say *I love you*. Or acknowledge when I say it."

"Love doesn't run away."

"No." Her eyes are hard when she looks at me. "It doesn't."

The bell rings, shattering the moment. The seniors pour in, all whispering and laughing as they look between the two of us. Another flash of anger spears through me, both at Molly's comment and at whoever had taken that picture. I lean close and whisper, "This conversation is not over. We're tabling it until later."

"Fine." She glares at her phone before clicking it off and smiling at the class. But it's forced, her eye twitching as she stands before them. "Good morning, class!"

"Good morning, Miss Pruitt." Gloria is all teeth as she smiles between us. "Or is it Mrs. Bradshaw now?"

A couple of the kids snicker, and I have to force the growl to remain in my throat.

"That is quite enough, Gloria." Molly's voice is colder than Antarctica in the winter. "That is none of your concern, and you will respect my wishes for my personal life to remain just that—personal. Now, please open up your copies of *The Great Gatsby* and read the first two chapters *silently*, and then we will discuss them."

Molly writes the page numbers on the whiteboard before slumping into her desk chair. My heart tightens. This isn't right. This wasn't how things were meant to go. This was supposed to be our happily ever after at last, right? So why does it feel like everything is suddenly falling apart?

As Molly begins to talk about *The Great Gatsby*, my phone pops up an email notification. Skinner. What does he want? I clench my fists as I begin to read:

Tanner and Molly,

Please see me in my office following the first period. There are some matters we need to discuss.

William Skinner

Well, that isn't good. Will he fire us? I meant what I told Molly. If they fire her, they lose me. If they lose me...well, the team might suffer, but I won't regret it. Not if I have Molly. And besides, I could always start a hockey league in the area. Something outside of the school. Maybe even a girls' league?

But the thing is, I do like working in the school. Getting into the community has been pretty great. Plus, having Molly near me each day is a bonus. Seeing her light up when teaching makes me smile, and the thought of losing that causes my heart to ache. But if what

Gloria said a few weeks ago is true and there is some archaic rule about coworkers dating, we probably don't have much of a choice.

Besides, my head argues, *you'd much rather lose seeing her every day at work than lose her completely, right?*

I meet Molly's eyes from across the room. Her face is pale, and I can tell she's just read the email.

We're fine. I mouth, and my heart really believes that.

We're going to be okay.

Molly grabs my hand right before I step out into the hall. One of the aides is filling in for a study hall while we go and talk to Skinner.

"Are we going to fight this?" she whispers. "Can we?"

"It's a dumb rule." I squeeze her fingers.

"But is it worth it?" she asks again, her gaze flicking between my eyes as she subconsciously pushes her glasses up with the side of her finger.

"I'm not running this time, Mols. *We're* not running from this. We weren't making out during school hours, we won't let it interfere with our ability to be professional, and no matter who's in there or what they accuse us of, we're a team. Remember what Luke said to the boys on Saturday?"

She smiles up at me and some of the panic and anger leaks from her expression. "I was a little distracted Saturday."

Oh, that's right. Because during the pep talk, she'd been smashed against my chest, smelling like floral and caramel. I loved every minute of it.

"It went something like, *the thrill and the fun of working together and facing a challenge as a team, that's why we're here.*" I brush one of her perfectly curled strands of hair behind her ear. "We're a team, this is a challenge, and we're facing it together. And newsflash," I lean in close, ignoring the giggles of the few kids already in her room, "I play to win."

An *aw* catches my ear. I lean back quickly—no use getting in even more trouble—and hold the door open for the now crimson Molly.

"Show off," she mutters, and I chuckle as we head toward Skinner's office.

But even after all my bravado, my muscles still tighten and my stomach flips as we step past Mrs. Maize—who casts a sorrowful look in our direction—and into the office.

Skinner stands behind his desk, his bushy brows low. Across from him, in the wingback chairs that are situated in front of the desk in a semicircle, sit not only Mr. and Mrs. Steinfield but also Mr. and Mrs. Tucker—Owen's parents. Both couples are ramrod straight, and if looks could kill, Molly and I would both be piles of ash on the ground at their feet.

"Look!" Mrs. Steinfield points to our clasped hands. "They're not even trying to hide it! This is a blatant disrespect for the rules!"

"Clearly they care more about their relationship than their jobs and *our* children," Mrs. Tucker agrees with a nod.

My brows shoot up as I look first at Mr. Tucker then at Mr. Steinfield. The former was pinching the bridge of his nose as if they'd already been through all of this. "Claire. We haven't heard from Tanner and Molly yet. And for the record"—he looks at us with a shrug— "it wasn't on school property where that picture was taken, was it?"

"No, sir, Mr. Tucker. It was at *my house*." I look over all the adults. "A place that should be fine for Miss Pruitt and me to kiss each other if we see fit."

"The rules state—" Mrs. Steinfield begins, but I cut her off with a slash of my hand.

"Why should the school policies dictate my life outside of work?" Heat fills my chest, blurring my vision. I'm righteously *pissed off*. Not only is this a total witch hunt, but it's possibly ruining any chance I have of rebuilding my relationship with Molly. And I won't stand for it. "If I want to date Molly Pruitt—if I want to *marry* her—why is the school telling me I can't?"

"Because the rules state—" Mrs. Steinfield tries again, but Molly interrupts her.

"That rule was never stated in the files I filled out when I was hired. How old is that policy, Mrs. Steinfield? And how far back did you and Gloria have to dig in an attempt to get me wrapped around your finger?"

Silence. A long, loud, deafening silence settles over us all. Mrs. Steinfield's mouth opens and closes like a landed fish, while Mr. Tucker hides a grin behind his large hand.

"Well—" Mr. Steinfield clears his throat. "The fact remains that it *is* a school policy. Skinner? Are you going to fire Molly Pruitt or not?"

"Now, wait just a minute—" Skinner's hands are shaking as he raises them in the air.

"You're going to fire Molly?" I scoff when both women nod. "Fine then. If that's the way you want it, I will be quitting."

"What?" Skinner's mouth falls open as does Mr. Tucker's.

I shrug. "I don't need this job; I took it because I want to see the boys excel and grow in their love and passion for the sport I've dedicated my life to. But if you're going to attempt to stonewall Molly out of a job she was born to do, then—"

"Tanner!" Molly's voice interrupts my tirade.

"What?" I turn sharply to her, looking down to see a tiny smirk on her lips.

"Calm down."

A glance around the room shows that everyone else is staring with open mouths at my pronouncement. I clear my throat. "Sorry. But my point is—"

"I think you made your point perfectly clear, Mr. Bradshaw." Mr. Steinfield adjusts his tie, looking a tad paler than he had before. "But Claire's argument is also valid. It's a school policy. If we bend this one, how many others will we be forced to change?"

"I repeat my early statement: I quit." I ignore Molly's tightening grip on my hand. "Molly keeps her job as the literature teacher, and I'll resign as the hockey coach."

"Now, wait just a minute—" Skinner starts again.

Mrs. Tucker glares at him. "That's perfectly fine by me."

"Not me," Mrs. Steinfield declares. "It's not just about the stupid policy!"

Oh, she's going to admit the *real* reason now, huh? Funny how desperate a weasel gets when it's cornered.

"Then, by all means. Do tell, Claire." Mr. Skinner folds his hands on top of his desk, calmer than he had been minutes before. "What is the big issue?"

Mrs. Steinfield jabs a finger at Molly. "She's been giving my daughter lower marks all of the first quarter because she hates her! It's discrimination, plain and simple."

Skinner nods once then gestures towards Molly. "Miss Pruitt, you have the floor."

All the parents swivel to glare at Molly.

This should be interesting.

CHAPTER TWENTY-NINE

Molly

I gulp as every eye in the room latches onto me. A bead of sweat tickles its way down my back, and it takes every ounce of self-control to not squirm. Why is staring down a classroom full of teenagers less terrifying than this?

"Well?" Mrs. Steinfield raises a condescending eyebrow at me. "What do you have to say for yourself? Nothing, right? Because you can't justify treating my daughter like dirt!"

"I have plenty to say, Mrs. Steinfield." I struggle to keep my frustration from being unleashed. Tanner has done enough tongue-lashing for one day. Instead, I draw my shoulders back trying to remain calm, despite the rolling tempest building in my mind. "I gave your daughter Ds and Cs because that is all her papers deserved."

Mrs. Steinfield splutters. "Why, you little—"

"Furthermore, Principal Skinner." I turn to the man who has a sheen of sweat over his bald head. "I have proof, and plenty of eyewitnesses, that Gloria has threatened me in class. I have it from a good source that she's blackmailed teachers into altering her grades which is the *only* reason she's passed the classes she has. Though, I will admit. I'm a touched confused," I turn toward the other couple in the room who are staring openmouthed at me, "why you're here, Mr. and Mrs. Tucker? Owen has absolutely nothing to do with this, does he?"

The innocence of the question catches the couple off guard. I tighten my hold on Tanner's hand, trying not to fidget as the Tuckers look at each other, then at the Steinfields, then up at us.

Principal Skinner clears his throat. "Actually, Owen Tucker was the one who brought the photo to my attention."

"He what?" Tanner sounds positively terrifying. I feel him straighten, his whole bearing going alpha male in this moment. It is, admittedly, hotter than anything I've ever witnessed in my life.

Skinner clears his throat, drawing my attention away from Tanner's sexy protectiveness and back to the matter at hand. "Yes. Well. Seeing as the kiss in question wasn't on school property, I won't be pursuing any disciplinary action."

"Oh, you won't?" Mrs. Steinfield grins and taps her maroon manicured nail against the desk. "David, should we *suggest* that William here be reconsidered for the job of principal at the next board meeting?"

"Yes," Mr. Steinfield agrees. "Along with the *firing* of two incompetent teachers!"

My stomach heaves. Pressing my free hand to it, I swallow tightly. "If that's what you want, fine. I'm not breaking up with Tanner. While I love my job, if the kids don't think I'm a fair teacher, then there's no reason for me to stay."

Tanner nods. "But know this, Mr. and Mrs. Steinfield, Mr. and Mrs. Tucker. Both of your children are sneaky and deceitful."

Both couples' mouths fall open.

Tanner raises a hand to stop any comments. "If you want them to be liked and respected, maybe work on teaching them to *be* respectful and kind to those around them."

"Why, I never!" Mrs. Tucker exclaims, pressing her hand against her chest.

"Well, maybe you should!" Tanner snaps. "You're losing a great teacher because your kids are too selfish and spoiled to care about anyone and anything except themselves. And ironically, the ones they're hurting are themselves. Molly *cares* about your kids. Cares about teaching them. Me? I care about hockey—a game that teaches teamwork and responsibility, for sure. But they'll play for, what? Four years? Eight if they're lucky? Molly's lessons will go on for years." He looks down at me. "I know I've carried quite a few with me for a long time."

"Oh, please." Mr. Steinfield rolls his eyes. "Spoken like a lovesick fool!"

"A lovesick fool you can't control." Tanner grins, a wild light in his eyes. "So, fire me. Fire us. We don't need you or your little power trips. I've about had it with your bratty kid and his disrespect for me and my authority. Your loss if we don't make it to state this year." Tanner shrugs and looks at the now very sweaty, very pale Mr. Skinner. "Are we done here, sir?"

"Er...yes. Yes, we're done." He licks his lips and waves us out of the room.

"Am I...can I go back and teach, sir?" I ask. "Or do I need to pack my things?"

"For now...um, you may return to your classroom." Skinner shrinks when all the parents glare at him. "We'll talk more later, Tanner, Molly."

"Yes, sir." We parrot before stepping outside the office doors.

I slump against the wall and struggle to inhale. I'm going to puke. I'm going to have a meltdown. I'm going to...to...I don't know what. It is barely the start of the second quarter, and already, I am getting the kids ticked at me. I expected it, sure, but not this soon.

"Hey, we'll be okay." Tanner nudges my shoulder as he leans against the wall with me. "If they fire you, you'll just have to marry me so I can support you."

"What?" I look up at him. He's insane! He still can't say *I love you*. "Don't be an idiot, Tanner."

"I'm serious!"

"Tell me you love me before you propose." I scoff and push off the wall. "Let's get back to the natives."

The day is the absolute longest. Gloria and Owen glare at Tanner and me anytime they pass us in the hall. And here I thought Owen had gotten over his crappy attitude. Guess I was wrong. Again. All I want to do is crawl under a rock and cry for a year—and I hate crying. When will this nightmare be over?

Finally, it's time to go home. But I can't find the energy to move, slumping into my desk chair and closing my eyes against the world.

The scent of a forest and spearmint washes over me, and I sigh as Tanner asks, "Hey, what's your favorite fast food?"

"Huh?" I open one eye, looking up at him. "Why?"

"I have a plan." He grins, not waiting for my response as he says, "Meet at my place at six."

"Why?" I call after him as Tanner hurries from the room, ignoring me.

"Men," I grumble, jumping when I hear an "oh" from the hall.

Tanner pokes his head back in, his dimple appearing as he grins. "Dress warm!"

Then he's gone again. I shake my head. He's far too chipper for a man about to lose his job. Yeah, *he* may be filthy rich from his time in the NHL, but not all of us have that luxury. I have student loans to pay. I have rent and food worries. Ugh, car insurance.

I rub my temples. All of that is a tomorrow worry. Tonight, I'm going to do what Tanner wants—dress warm and meet at his place at six.

What does the crazy man have up his sleeve tonight?

"What do you mean all that he told you was to dress warm?" Emily bounces on the edge of my bed, Baby Charlotte in her arms. Her boss, Oliver, is working late, so Emily brought Charlie over to our house so she could get some chores done here. The little girl snores softly on Emily's shoulder.

I pull on one of my thermal hiking shirts and then a t-shirt of one of my favorite bands—*The Gray Havens*. Over all of that, I shrug on a cardigan and my windbreaker.

"Wow. You're taking this warm thing to a new level." Susan smirks from where she leans against the doorframe. She sobers quickly. "Are you really back together with him?"

"Yep." I grin, clearly a fool in love. But will Tanner ever love me back? I press my lips together. He'd been the one to say he was halfway in love with me. But when I said it back...nothing. I shrug. "It may end badly, but I'm finally ready to risk it. This time, I have even more friends to support me."

"But with the same guy?" Susan's brows raise, telling me she thinks I'm nuts.

Maybe I am. But it also feels *right*.

"I think it's cute," Emily says. "Second chance romance!"

"That only works in novels and chick flicks!" Susan rolls her eyes. "Not in real life."

Emily gestures with her hand, still holding Charlie secure with her arm. "I beg to differ with Exhibit M."

"M?" I ask, pulling my favorite beanie on. Black knit with a brown pompom.

"Exhibit Molly, of course." Emily grins. "Kiss him senseless tonight, Dolly Molly!"

"Or be sensible and don't." Susan rolls her eyes as Emily breezes out the door and down the stairs. She starts to follow, then pauses to say. "If this works out, I'll be happy for you, Molly. Honestly. It's just..." She sighs. "I'm not sure I believe in happily ever after anymore."

"It'll come for you, Sue." I step over and pull her into a hug. "I really believe we all have a happily ever after—one way or another."

Tanner grins as he opens his front door for me. "Come on in! I'm just getting one more blanket from Mom."

"A blanket? What are we doing?"

"Watching the sunset and then stargazing!" Tanner presses a hand against his chest. "I even took the truck to get its oil changed right after work."

"You still have the truck?" My mouth falls open when Tanner nods.

"It's in the garage, right next to Mom's SUV."

My memory rewinds to the first time we'd laid in the back of his truck. To the memories of our first kiss and how happy we'd been that night. Now, Tanner's choosing to recreate that. I fall a little bit more in love at that very moment.

Tanner hands me four pillows and drapes a blanket over my head like a veil. "Ready?"

"I suppose." I laugh as he attempts to carry a picnic basket and about six blankets over his arm. "So, stargazing, huh?"

"Yep." His grin makes his dimple appear.

I can't help but smile back. It's infectious, like a yawn but instead of making me sleepy, it sends butterflies swirling inside my stomach. What is this feeling? I haven't felt this way since competition skating. The nervous energy that has me bouncing on the balls of my feet.

Tanner puts everything into the back seat before holding the door open for me and helping me scramble in.

My hands are clammy, and I wipe them against my pants legs as Tanner turns over the engine and backs out.

"Are we going out to Farmer Richard's?" I ask as Tanner reaches over and grabs my hand. It makes me jump a little as he brings it to his lips.

"Yep." He glances at me out of the corner of his eye. "Calm down, Mols. This isn't a big deal."

But it *feels* big. Like another turning point in our lives. Is this where he leaves again? Where I leave? Tanner said it himself. We're runners. Could this be where we break it off for good? Go our separate ways as much as we can after breaking our hearts anew? Yeah, *I* think we're soulmates. And that's what makes this so scary. I press my free hand against my stampeding heart, willing even breaths as we drive in silence to the barn outside of town.

A brisk wind blows, but Tanner has come prepared. Two of the blankets are heated with a battery pack, and he flips it on as he lays the pillows and blankets out in the bed of the truck. Then Tanner grabs the basket of food and hops up. Offering me a hand, he pulls me up into the truck and then down beside him. Draping one of the heated blankets around my shoulders, he kisses the tip of my nose.

"Stop worrying," he chides gently.

"But what if—"

"Hey, *what ifs* aren't guarantees. It's paying for tomorrow's possible problems with today's joy. Forget about it."

"That's hard." I shiver, pulling the blanket tighter around me.

"Nah, not really." Tanner throws his arms wide. "This is us forgetting about today and tomorrow and enjoying right now!"

I laugh. "Okay. Maybe I can try."

"Good." He grins and pulls out a thermos. "Here's some hot cocoa. And this—" he pulls out a bag of fast-food hamburgers and fries. "This is about the worst food ever, and it's probably getting horribly gross and cold, but—"

I lean over and give him a quick kiss on the lips. "It's perfect."

Tanner's dimple appears again as he cups my cheek and kisses me back. After a few minutes, we break apart and snuggle in to watch the sunset as we munch on burgers that are a touch cold, drink cocoa that's hot enough to scald our tongues, and simply forget about the day.

Tucked against Tanner's side as the stars wink into view, I realize that I am pretty nearly, perfectly happy. He holds me, securely yet gently, his head resting against mine. He tugs the blanket up higher. I wiggle closer. He shifts and slowly, I look up. He's staring at me with a burning gaze that warms my core faster than any heated blanket.

"Molly." He says my name like it's worth more than rubies. His eyes study me like I'm a masterpiece and slowly, oh so painfully slowly, he says, "I. Love. You."

He doesn't move to kiss me. Doesn't move to cup my cheek or crush me in a hug. He simply stares at me like I'm the *Mona Lisa*, and he's an art collector.

I want to tell him I love him. That I never want to leave his side again. But my words choke on a sob as I lean my head against his shoulder and cry.

"Did I say something wrong?" Tanner asks, bewildered.

"No." I shake my head. "What you said—it was perfect."

"Then why are you crying?" A note of a laugh taints his words, and he eases me back, wiping away the tears with the pad of his thumb.

"Because Tanner." I laugh. "I may lose my job, and if that happens, I don't know what I'll do. But you finally said it and—" I grab his face and kiss him, falling across his chest as he deepens it. It may have been hours but is probably only minutes when I finally pull back and curl against his side. "I love you, too, Tanner James."

He chuckles, a little breathless as he says, "After that kiss, you better."

I can hear his heart under his jacket, racing as wildly as my own. The stars blanket the navy sky as the last rays of the sun paint the horizon purple.

And right then? I am perfectly, completely, incandescently happy.

CHAPTER THIRTY

Tanner

It is close to midnight when we pile back into the cab of the truck, shivering a bit but grinning like we're in high school again.

Molly grabs my hand as we drive down the road, the radio softly playing a country song. Abruptly, she orders, "Pull over, Tanner."

I obey without hesitation, and she turns the crank to roll down the window, turns up the radio, and grins at me as she hops out of the truck.

"What are you doing?" I laugh as I follow her around to the truck bed.

She scrambles up and waves for me to follow, her smile crinkling the corners of her eyes. "I'm not ready for tonight to end."

The light of the full moon illuminates our little bubble as *My Person* by Spencer Crandall croons around us. Molly loops her arms around my neck, slowly swaying us to the melody. Her grin lightens the blue of her eyes, and she looks...settled. Like she's been gone on a long trip and at last, unlocked the door to her home. As if being here with me, on the side of the road by an empty cornfield, is exactly where she'd choose to be out of anywhere in the world.

"How'd I get so lucky to get you back?" I whisper, emotion tightening my chest.

"You came home. And I'm really glad you did, Tanner James. God bless the player that messed up your leg."

I chuckle. "Blessing in disguise. Because you're way better than a multimillion-dollar contract."

Her brows raise, and she says, "You're just figuring this out now?" She tsks her tongue. "And here I thought you were smart."

"Oh, I'm plenty smart, thank you." I smirk. "Because I'm not letting you out of my sight, Mols. Never again."

I convince Molly to stay in Mom's guest room upstairs instead of driving home. Sure, her apartment is only like five minutes from my house, but the thought of her driving home tired has me tied up in knots.

"Need anything?" I ask in a whisper, leaning against the door to the bedroom.

Molly shakes her head, her eyes already half-closed as she hugs me.

"No. I'm perfect."

"You better get into bed before we do something stupid."

Molly nods against my chest but doesn't move.

"Mols."

"Fine." She steps back, and I bend to press a light but lingering kiss on her lips. "Tonight was perfect, Tanner."

I couldn't agree more. "Good night, Molly Elaine."

"Good night, Tanner James."

I smile as I shut the door, leaning my forehead against it before forcing my feet to carry me down to my space in the basement. But instead of climbing into bed, I pull open one of my drawers and grab the little red box nestled among my socks.

Popping it open, I stare at the single diamond set in a thin silver band. The ring is almost five years old. Five years of it going with me to every game, nestled in my duffle bag. Every trip with the team over breaks, every hotel, every house, every bus ride. It was me holding on to the part of me I'd left behind in Cloverfield.

Is it too soon? It feels too soon. But we have a history. We had who we were before I left, and we have our lives now. Is it possible to bring them together and create something beautiful? Build something together that will last for the rest of our lives?

It's too late to think about this tonight. I'm too tired.

Snapping the lid closed, I set the box on my nightstand and get ready for bed. Tomorrow, we'll find out if we have our jobs.

One big life change at a time, Tanner. One big change at a time.

Molly is up before me and leaves a note on the fridge that she'd run home to get ready for work. A strange pang of disappointment at not seeing her with bedhead hits me, but I shove it away as I get dressed.

Because I will get to see it. Someday, I will marry Molly Pruitt and love her for the rest of my life. I'll wake up to morning breath and bedhead. I'll make her caramel lattes from home and cinnamon rolls from a can. Kisses and snuggles. Baby cries and children's laughter. I want it all. And I want it with Molly.

By the time I'm ready for my day, it's still early enough to go grab our favorite coffees from Sweetie's. Something tells me we're going to need a little fortification for this day.

Sweetie looks up as I push into the shop, her eyes sparkling as she turns back to the person in front of the counter.

Molly. How is it possible to miss her after seeing her a mere five hours before? It's like I'm a ship at sea, lost without my anchor to hold me steady. How'd I go five years without her?

Molly turns and grins at me. "Looks like we had the same thought this morning. Too bad for you, I've already paid."

"Well, it was your turn anyways." I chuckle.

Sweetie's gaze sweeps between us. She opens her mouth to ask, but I beat her to it with, "Yeah, we're dating now."

"About dang time." She mutters something in Italian as Molly blushes with a nervous giggle.

"She's all mine again." I wrap an arm around Molly's waist and press a kiss to her temple.

Molly smiles up at me, and I swear I stop breathing.

"No matter what," she agrees.

"Some of the kids were talking yesterday about a mess happening at the school. Are they really trying to fire you?" Sweetie asks, her brows lowering as she looks at us.

"Yeah." Molly's smile falls. "But it'll be fine. I'll find...something."

"*Stupidi idioti,*" she mumbles before picking up her phone.

"What are you doing?" Molly laughs nervously.

Sweetie grins; it's slightly vindictive and unlike the normally perky shop owner. "I'm calling in a favor, *mia cara.* Just leave everything up to me."

CHAPTER THIRTY-ONE

Molly

Tanner twines our fingers together as we head inside Clover-High. We're immediately stopped by Luke, Carter, and Leo. All three cross their arms, staring at us.

"You're quitting?" Carter accuses.

Tanner shrugs. "Only if Principal Skinner and the schoolboard say they're firing Miss Pruitt."

Leo looks at me. "Are you still going to coach if they fire you?"

"I—I don't know." I shake my head, hating this helplessness. I'd had my life perfectly planned, ordered out for the next twenty years. I was going to teach. Save. Eventually buy my own place when I could afford it. Have a nice car and maybe a cat.

Yet, life had other plans. It brought Tanner back. Brought me to a place where I had to lean on someone else. Trust someone else.

Are you going to run from it, Molly Elaine? Or are you going to learn from it?

Ugh, why did my conscience sound like Mom?

Mom. Did she have any idea what was going on? I'd filled Susan and Emily in that morning. But Mom? She won't like this. She'll say I should dump Tanner and keep my steady, dependable job.

But at this moment? I'm feeling anything but steady and dependable. I'm feeling slightly reckless. Rash. And for once, it doesn't fill me with dread.

"Well, if you do quit, Coach," Luke smiles, "you should start your own team. Or a league. We'd all join."

"Heck yeah!" Leo punches the air. "We'll stick it to 'em!"

Carter raises a brow. "Have you been watching *Newsies* again?"

Leo shrugs. "I may be trying to decide if I want to try out for the school musical."

"Guys." Luke rolls his eyes. "Not the time."

"Right!" Leo looks at us. "We're with you, Coaches! We're not letting the best teacher and coach in the world get booted out of here."

"Thanks, fellas." I smile sadly. "But we might not have a choice. If the board votes us out—"

"When's the board meeting?" Luke asks.

"I don't know," Tanner admits.

Leo snorts. "Let me talk to my dad. He's an officer *and* one of the board members. If they haven't posted it, then—"

"They have." Carter shows Leo something on his phone. "And it's happening tonight. But look. It seems like they posted about it one week before the photo."

My cheeks warm at the thought of the boys having seen that photo. Tanner squeezes my fingers.

"How is that possible? Were they trying to fire Miss Pruitt before that?" Luke asks.

"I have a feeling that Owen was going after Coach, Gloria after Miss Pruitt, and they ganged up together." Leo runs a hand through his sandy hair. "Owen has hated Gloria for as long as I can remember. And then all of a sudden, he's running with her? It just didn't make any sense."

Carter huffs a breath. "Well, this says that it's an open session." He looks up, a calculating look to rival Sweetie's in his eyes. "Leave this to us, Coaches."

"Yeah!" Leo pumps his fist again before turning to the twins. "What's the plan again?"

As they huddle up, Tanner steers me around them and into my classroom. Taking my coffee cup, he sets it on his desk and lets his bag thump into the chair. He locks his hands behind his neck as he turns back around to me. "You ready for tonight then?"

"No." I cross my arms over my chest. "But I meant what I said to Sweetie. No matter what, it's us. I'm tired of running from things that *might* hurt me. You were right last night."

He raises his brow, his smirk appearing. "Oh? And what was I right about, pray tell?"

"Worry is paying for tomorrow's possible problems with today's joy." I take a deep breath and nod my head at him. "And I'm done with that."

"Good." He looks at me with pride, and I turn away with a shudder. "What? What'd I do?"

"Nothing, but if you keep looking at me that way, we *are* going to get in trouble."

He snorts, and then he's wrapping me in a hug from behind. "Eh, I'll take the chances."

"Tanner!" I laugh, trying to elbow him to get him to let me go.

"Okay! Fine, I'll be good!" He releases me and hands me my coffee.

"Thank you." I chuckle as I take a long sip and move behind my desk. Later, we will have to worry about the Steinfields and the Tuckers. We'll have to deal with all the accusations—of discrimination, improper conduct, and broken rules. But that's a later worry. For now, I'm going to do what I love most.

I'm going to teach.

Tanner watches me all day. His smile is a steadying presence, his gaze my due north. I grin and go through my lessons with an ease that surprises me. I should be nervous, but I'm not. Before I know it, the final bell of the day rings.

It's then I look around my classroom. At the coffee motif, the cozy lights, my teal desk mat, and chair. Tears press in the corner of my eyes, and it takes Tanner gripping my shoulders to calm me down.

"You'll be back." He slides his arms around me, pulling him to his chest. "I know it."

"You have more confidence in the outcome than I do." I laugh, but it sounds hollow.

Tanner tightens his hold. "We've got people behind us."

"Three boys and Sweetie."

"And your roommates. And my mother. Have you told your brothers?"

I snort. "Tanner, this is Cloverfield. I guarantee you everyone and their dog has heard by now."

He laughs and turns me around, settling his hands on my shoulders. "Seriously, Mols. We'll be back. I just...I have this feeling."

"And if you're wrong?" I whisper.

"If I'm wrong," he looks me in the eye, completely serious, "then we'll cross that bridge when we come to it."

With a steadying sigh, I nod, grab my bag, and follow him out to our cars. We were supposed to have practice today. Would anyone even show up?

Impending doom settles on me as I drive to the Rink. I was so sure nothing could touch me last night. Whether it was the high of telling off Mrs. Steinfield, my date with Tanner, or something else,

I'd felt invincible. But now? I park and lean my forehead against my steering wheel once I park.

"We're going to be fine," I declare to the emptiness around me, pushing away my doom. We would make it so. Tanner and me against the world, right?

Taking another steadying breath, I stretch, twisting my neck left then right, and nod once before stepping from the car.

Tanner is leaning against his, smiling that dimpled smile that makes my heart skip a beat—does that sound as cheesy out loud as it does in my head?

"Ready?" he asks.

"Yep." I grin, linking my arm through his as we head into the Rink.

The chill, the slight scent of sweat and popcorn, the swish of skates and laughter...

"Wait, what is that?" I ask, dropping Tanner's arm and hurrying to the edge of the ice.

It takes a full thirty seconds for my brain to process what I'm seeing, and when I do, I laugh in disbelief.

There are a ton of students from Cloverfield High on the ice, skating and teasing one another. More sitting in the stands. Laughter and conversations swirl around us. There has to be close to half of the student body here. I press my hand over my mouth as I stare.

No way. I shake my head as Tanner slips his arm around my waist.

"Wow," he says.

"Hey, look! The coaches are here!" calls a voice, and everyone turns. Up skate the thirteen boys and one girl that make up the Cloverfield Cougars. They grin at one another as they stop near the edge of the ice.

"Coaches," Luke glides forward.

"Luke." Tanner nods for him to proceed, and the captain smiles.

"We're here to say we support you and Miss Pruitt. We respect both of you—you've given us no reason not to. We want you to stay our teacher and coaches, and we're all" —he gestures to the kids— "ready to say so at the board meeting tonight."

"Really?" I ask, pressing a hand to my chest. My voice is thick. "You're all serious?"

"Very." Carter nods. "You've been here for us. You've gone to bat for us, fought for the team, and helped us win for the first time in forever."

"We might even have a shot at state." Wyatt shrugs. "You're a great coach, Coach Bradshaw. It's stupid that they're willing to lose you just because you're dating Coach Pruitt."

"Besides." Leo wiggles his brows, and I cover my laugh with my hand. "I kinda ship it."

"*Ship it*?" Carter smacks the back of Leo's head. "What the heck?"

"It's a thing!" Leo defends.

Luke clears his throat to cut them off. "If you want us to, we have your back, Coaches. That's what a team does."

They fall silent, and I swear everyone in the entire Rink is holding their breath, leaning in to hear what we're going to say. I look up at Tanner to find him mysteriously glassy-eyed, and I know his answer.

I wrap my arm around Tanner's waist as I say, "Thank you all. We appreciate the support."

"We're going?" Leo asks, eyes dancing.

"You're going." Tanner clears his throat with a chuckle. "Let's go to a board meeting!"

CHAPTER THIRTY-TWO

Tanner

My knee bounces under the table, the nerves I've been able to suppress all day rearing their head as I sit by Molly's side. She keeps glaring at my knee as it shakes our chairs ever so slightly with its jiggling.

"Tanner," she finally hisses. "Hold still!"

"I can't." I look at her, feeling rattled. "This is terrifying."

She snorts and shakes her head. "Now who has to calm whom?"

"A kiss for good luck might help?"

"Not here!" Her eyes scan the room. The school board sits at the front of the conference room in City Hall. The table stretches from wall to wall, all seven members spaced out. Files and papers are scattered across it, but the members are more concerned with talking among themselves at the moment than reading the agenda.

A few of our friends are scattered throughout the chairs. Emily waves at us, smiling sweetly, while Susan has her arms crossed and is staring straight ahead.

"Hey, you two!" Ryley slaps my shoulders as he sits down behind me. "Puked yet, Tanner?"

Ryder comes up behind him, moving more slowly as he looks forlornly over at Molly's roommates. But he directs his words to Ryley. "Try to act older than your IQ, Ry."

"Ouch, *little* brother." Ryley chuckles as his eyes scan over the board members. "So, where's the snake in heels who wants to fire you?"

"She's not on the board," Molly says, jabbing her thumb over her shoulder. Claire Steinfield stands straight and proud, a small smirk of victory on her lips as she talks with Dawn Tucker. "I swear she makes her daughter look like a saint."

I snort. "You got that right."

Ryley winces. "I remember Trent Steinfield from high school. I have a feeling neither child can do any wrong."

"Ha. Right. Absolutely no wrong," I say, my knee bouncing up and down, up and down, up and down.

"Tanner!" Molly grasps my leg, and a new energy enters my bloodstream. "Calm down. You're making me nervous."

Breathing in deeply, I hold it as I grab her hand and thread her fingers with mine. On the exhale, I say, "Sorry."

"Wait, so that picture was real?" Ryder grins and smacks Ryley on the arm. "Called it! Pay up!"

Ryley glares at Molly and me, like it's somehow our fault that he lost a bet.

"Wow, glad we're a source of entertainment." Molly rolls her eyes, but her smile doesn't waver, even when the chair head—Mr. Steinfield himself—calls the meeting to order.

My eyes scan the crowd. The room looks pretty empty. Sweetie sits a few rows back, a smug smile on her face. Her nephew is beside her with his girlfriend—they'd been freshmen when I'd graduated, and I vaguely remember seeing them at the Rink before.

On the back left side of the room are Rick and Mr. and Mrs. Pruitt. Instead of glaring at me, Mrs. Pruitt has her disapproving scowl trained on the back of Claire Steinfield's head.

Emily and Susan. Ryder and Ryley. Ava and a handful of other teachers. None of the kids are here yet. I wonder if they'll bother to show.

I swallow down my trepidation and turn back to Mr. Steinfield.

"We called this meeting today to discuss the abysmal behavior of two of Cloverfield High School's staff. Molly Pruitt's position is being called into question due to evidence that she marks grades lower than they should be due to discrimination. We have five different reports here, all with low marks that were submitted by students Gloria Steinfield and Owen Tucker. Please come forward and give your statements."

Gloria walks up first, and I have to curl my hand into a fist to keep from screaming at her—something that wouldn't help either of our cases. Gloria smooths a hand over her pale-pink dress slacks and straightens the collar of her cream-colored shirt before pulling a small frown at the other board members. "I have had to deal with Miss Pruitt's dislike for a quarter of school! Last year, I got all As and Bs in my literature class. But this year..." she sniffs, pulling a tissue from her pocket and dabbing at her eyes.

I roll mine with a small scoff of disbelief. Were the council members going to fall for this act? I glanced down the rows. A few were reading the reports that Molly had graded and that, in my opinion, were done far more leniently than they deserved. Their brows lowered and raised depending on what they were reading. Good. Perhaps they'd vote sanely.

The door creaks open as Gloria begins talking again. I glance over my shoulder, my mouth falling open as Kai enters with Coach Reynolds by his side. At least, I think it's Reynolds. He...doesn't look good. My throat tightens at his sunken cheeks, the bags under his eyes, and the slow, pain-filled moves. Why is he here?

Reynolds looks at me, a small smile of pride on his face as Kai leads him over to Sweetie and her nephew. I am beyond confused.

Gloria's voice breaks through my thoughts, turning my attention back to the drama unfolding before the school board. "And then when I tried to ask about it, she freaked out! As if it were wrong to simply ask about the grades!" Another sniff. "Please, make the *wise* choice and get rid of her! She's a horrible teacher!"

With that, she turns from the front, and her pout turns into a smug smirk as she looks at us before taking her seat.

"Owen Tucker?"

He ambles to the front, looking a bit pale as his gaze rakes over the board. "Yeah, she gave me low marks on work I really did try my hardest on. I know she has a thing for Coach Bradshaw, but I didn't think she'd take it out on me for not liking the guy." He nods and then turns back to his seat, not looking at Molly and me at all.

Interesting.

"Anyone to speak on behalf of Molly Pruitt?"

Ava stands, but before she can move from her row, the door to the conference room bursts open. In pours the students who'd been at the Rink that afternoon, moving down the aisle until Luke, Carter, and Leo push their way to the front of the group and face the board members.

"We're here on behalf of both Molly Pruitt and Tanner Bradshaw—our coaches." Luke's voice rings loud, clear, and confident. Like the leader he is. "We think they're both amazing teachers and inspiring coaches. They encourage us, they protect us, they're fair and upright."

"Fine, fine." Steinfield waves his hand at the boy. "But we're talking about Miss Pruitt, currently. Not Coach Bradshaw."

"With all due respect sir, but isn't that why we're here?" Luke gestures to everyone. "Our teacher and coach got called out for having a relationship *outside* of school hours. They were essentially stalked by one of *our* classmates, and now they're in danger of losing their jobs because of it."

"And?" Steinfield cups his chin in his hand. "The point?"

"The point is we don't like it." Carter steps up. "We think it's wrong to tell them they can't be in a relationship, especially when we didn't know anything about it until we saw that picture."

One of the other board members looks over the kids with pursed lips. "Is this true?"

Every last one of them nods.

"Interesting," she looks at Steinfield. "I'm confused then. I believe that the rule for the district is that the children aren't supposed to know when the staff are in a relationship together. It says nothing about them *not* being in a relationship at all."

"Well—" Steinfield splutters before another board member interrupts.

"As for Miss Pruitt's grading of Miss Steinfield's papers, I must agree with her. This is horrendous writing. I think the Ds she gave to *your* daughter, Steinfield, are far fairer than what I would have given. This is clearly F quality." The member looks at Molly with a definitive nod of approval.

"The issue here—" Steinfield tries again.

"The issue here," a third member, whose arms are crossed over his chest, says, "is that your little princess has her undies in a twist because she might have to work at something for once in her life."

"I object!" Mrs. Steinfield jerks to her feet.

"Oh, shut up!" a board member hollers before the whole room descends into chaos.

Molly looks at me, her eyes wide, and I burst into laughter. Had we actually won this fight?

It takes a good fifteen minutes and a security guard escorting a hysterical Mrs. Steinfield from the room for everything to settle down again.

The board votes for Mr. Steinfield to relinquish his chair position to the next senior member—who just so happens to be Leo's father, Lucas Drake—for the remainder of the meeting. Besides Leo, Lucas has two other kids in the high school, and all of them love Molly's class.

"Miss Pruitt," he begins, interlocking his fingers and placing them on top of the table. "I do apologize if this meeting has caused you unnecessary stress."

Molly inclines her head. "It's quite alright, Mr. Drake. I'd just like to put this mess behind us, if we may?"

Lucas smiles. "I agree. I move that we vote to keep Molly Pruitt on as our literature teacher at Cloverfield High School. Any further complaints against her shall be thoroughly investigated before another board meeting is called."

"Second!" calls another member.

"The motion is seconded. All in favor?" Mr. Drake's eyes sparkle as a resounding *aye* fills the conference room. "Any opposed?"

Not even Mr. Steinfield says anything.

"The motion carries!"

"But what about Coach?" Luke pushes forward, fire in his eyes as he looks at me. "He isn't guilty of anything if Miss Pruitt isn't!"

"But that wasn't the only charge against Mr. Bradshaw." Lucas looks pained as he meets my gaze. "We've had quite a few complaints filed by parents and ardent supporters of the team against the way you've been coaching. Some have also accused you of favoritism, Mr. Bradshaw."

Molly stands, her hands balling into fists. "If he shows favoritism, Mr. Drake, it's because he favors the team's hearts over their wins."

"May I speak?" a raspy voice I know so well asks as Coach Reynolds pushes to his feet. Kai supports him as he hobbles to the front, and the kids part like the Red Sea did for Moses.

"Of course, Co—er, Mr. Reynolds." Lucas inclines his head. "Go right ahead."

"Many of you don't know this because I haven't publicized it. I haven't wanted pity, but it's time for you all to know. I have cancer. I'm dying."

My chest tightens, and Molly slips her hand into mine, her brows furrowed.

"Well, one of my biggest fears was what would happen to Kai when I pass." Reynolds clears his throat, his eyes watering and when he speaks, his voice cracks. "The other day, Kai told Coach Bradshaw about my cancer. About his uncertainty. Tanner offered him a place to stay for as long as he needed."

Molly gasps, and she looks up at me, a new light in her eyes. "Really?" she whispers.

"Yeah."

"That's amazing. Oh, Tanner, that makes me want to cry." Molly wraps her arm around mine and leans her head against my shoulder.

"If Tanner should be accused of anything, it should be for loving all of these boys too much." Reynolds looks at me. "You've grown into a fine young man, Bradshaw. I was proud of your career success, but I'm even prouder of who you've become in here." He pounds a fist against his chest, and it takes everything in me not to cry in front of all these people. "You did good, son."

"Thanks, Coach," I manage.

"Well," Lucas clears his throat. The whole board looks pretty misty-eyed. "Thank you for that stunning endorsement of character, Mr. Reynolds."

Kai looks over at me and says, "Coach, if they fire you, I'm going to whatever team you start next."

"Me too, Coach!" Carter cries, and soon the entire team is chanting and swarming us. They take up positions in a circle around Molly and me, crossing their arms and reminding me of a band of knights protecting their royals.

"Okay, okay!" Lucas chuckles once one of the board members whistles so that silence descends. "I move that we keep Tanner Bradshaw on as hockey coach for the Cloverfield Cougars. Any further complaints against him shall be thoroughly investigated before a board meeting is called."

"Second!" four members say at the same time.

"All in favor?"

Everyone in the room cries, "Aye!"

"Then the motion carries." Lucas grins at us as he bangs the gavel.

A cheer rings through the room. I turn and scoop Molly into my arms, spinning her around as she laughs.

"Told you you'd be back," I whisper in her ear.

"Know it all," she teases, right before I kiss her with zero remorse while her students, parents, brothers, friends, and the entire school board look on.

Chapter Thirty-Three

Molly

A few weeks later...

"Where are we going?" I ask. Tanner had swooped into my house to kidnap me, amidst Emily's laughter and Susan's eye rolls. Thankfully, I'd been getting ready for the barn dance out at Farmer Richard's farm already, so it wasn't a huge shock that he'd arrived early.

What was a shock was when Tanner tied a blindfold over my face—after tucking my glasses into his shirt pocket—with a chuckle. He then scooped me up, despite my protests about his leg getting strained, and carried me to his truck.

"Tanner?" I persist when he doesn't answer.

"You'll see, Mols." He chuckles and kisses my cheek. "Trust me."

My heart leaps into my throat when I realize—not for the first time—that I do. The last few weeks with Tanner meant talking through a lot of our past. About the running, the abandonment, the fear of getting hurt again. We talked about our futures and our hopes and dreams. We even went to a counselor together. The conversations surprised me. Many of our dreams were the same, with a few that were specific to each of us.

They also showed me that, despite everything we'd been through, we hadn't changed as much as I'd feared. We'd grown wiser, stronger, and more confident in who we were and what we were called to do. But at the core, we were still Molly and Tanner. I was growing to like the sound of our names together.

The cold November night bites into my cheeks as Tanner helps me out of the truck. He leads me over a gravel path and up into a warmer space. He settles his hand against my waist, pulling me closer.

His smile is in his voice as he asks, "Do you remember the first time I kissed you, Molly?"

I swallow as *My Person* by Spencer Crandall starts playing from somewhere. "It was at the November Barn Dance after we'd escaped and went stargazing."

"Yeah, it was." Tanner leans his forehead against mine. "And do you know why that scared me?"

"No." My voice cracks, and I can feel the blindfold collecting my tears.

"Because I was so sure I didn't deserve you. You're a wonderful woman—strong and brave and loving. And who was I to get to love you?"

"Tanner—"

"I know now, Mols. I am the luckiest man on Earth because I get to call you my person. I want to do life with you from now until the day I die, never to run away again. So, Mols," he steps back and says, "take off the blindfold."

Slowly, my fingers shaking, I pull off the blindfold and gasp. Tanner is down on one knee with a tiny red box between us and a nervous smile on his face. My hands clasp over my mouth. I can't believe this is happening.

"Molly Elaine Pruitt, will you marry me?"

"Yes!" I fling my arms around him, laughing as he scoops me off my feet and spins, his chuckles filling my eyes with tears.

Once he's set me back on my feet, he opens the box with a nervous smile. "Want to try it on?"

I gasp again, my eyes watering as he slides the ring onto my finger. One diamond set in a thin silver band...it can't be. "Is this the one I showed you the summer before my senior year?"

"Yeah." His throat bobs as he stares down at it. "It went to every game. Every hotel, every bus ride. It was the past I couldn't outrun and didn't want to lose."

"You haven't." I wrap my arms around his waist and hold on tight. "Never again, Tanner."

"Good."

I jump when a voice hollers out, "What'd she say?"

"She said yes!" Tanner shouts back.

The lights go up as cheers echo. I laugh as the students from Cloverfield come out of the shadows. I'd known that Susan was going to have a table of cookies for the dance. Only they aren't solely the autumn ones I'd seen her working on at the house. Wedding-themed cookies are mixed in with the pumpkins, scarecrows, and leaves, a testament to some sneakiness on her part.

Emily waves from where she stands behind Ryley at the soundboard, a camera in hand that I know has captured my proposal. Ryder grins on the other side, a video camera pointing our direction.

Everyone is here. Ava, Principal Skinner, and the other staff from the school; Sweetie with coffee and cocoa for all of us, Mom and Dad, and Maria Bradshaw. It's everyone I love and care about, and who loves and cares about Tanner and me.

I step back as a popular pop song blasts through the speakers. The kids hit the dance floor with gusto and no small amount of laughter. Tanner pulls me out of the mob and to the fringe of the dance floor. He tucks me against his chest, crossing his arms over my shoulders as he presses a kiss to my temple. "So, what do you think, future Mrs. Bradshaw?"

"I think I'm the happiest person in the world."

Emily snaps a picture of us with a grin before fishing her phone out of her pocket with a scowl.

"Nope, you can't be." Tanner sighs contentedly. "Because that title belongs to me."

Epilogue

Emily

I smile as I snap a picture of the newly engaged couple—my best friend and the hockey coach. They're absolutely adorable. Susan may be a skeptic, but I knew from the moment we walked in on Tanner snuggling a sick and cranky Molly on the couch that their second chance at romance would work. He looks at her like she's everything he's been searching for and yet the very thing he didn't know he needed. I love it.

I love *them*.

And clearly, Tanner loves them too because he roped everyone into helping him pull off the proposal of the century.

And it worked! Molly never suspected a thing. I knew the moment her eyes widened when she took off the blindfold that a proposal was the last thing she expected tonight of all nights.

I wipe at a tear, smiling happily for my friend and her fiancé—dang, that's gonna take some time to get used to!

My phone buzzes, and I pull it out of my pocket. I scowl as the name *Oliver Markel* scrolls across the screen. My boss. I sigh. He probably can't find something for Charlie—his goddaughter.

"Yeah, Mr. Markel?"

"How many times have I told you to call me Oliver?" he asks in reply, the distant wail of an enraged Charlie the background ambiance.

"Lots, and I'll continue calling you Mr. Markel, cause calling you Oliver is way too weird."

"I'm too tired to argue with you right now." He sighs, and I can picture him rubbing his green eyes with his thumb and index finger. "Do you know where Charlie's spare pacifier is?"

"Top drawer of her dresser, next to her hats and headbands." I shift the phone so I can hold it with my shoulder as I snap pictures of the student body surrounding Tanner and Molly, attempting to drag them to the dance floor as *Shut Up and Dance* blasts through the speakers. I can barely hear Oliver shuffling over the line—although I catch the screech of the drawer opening all too clearly before his relieved sigh rattles through the phone speaker.

"Thanks, you're a lifesaver. Where are you?" he asks as the wailing gets louder before it cuts off with a smacking of lips against the pacifier.

"The high school dance." I snap a few more photos.

"Should I be worried?" The sound of the squeaking glider echoes through the phone now. I must be on speaker.

"Nah." I chuckle. "My friends got engaged tonight, and I'm here to take pictures. Speaking of—" I watch Tanner finally give in and allow Molly to tug him back onto the dance floor. "I got to go."

"Okay, Em. See you in the morning."

The line goes dead, and I pull my phone away from my ear and stare at it for a long moment. That was...new. Why did his using my nickname fill me with such...warmth?

Yikes. That's not good. Not good at all.

But I'll worry about that later. Right now, my best friend is engaged, they're having the night of their lives, and I have a job to do.

Time to celebrate the heck out of the future Mr. and Mrs. Tanner Bradshaw!

THE END

Acknowledgements

With each story I write, I realize more and more how many people it truly takes to craft a book into the best it can be.

Thank you to the team at Quill & Flame for taking my little hockey/teacher romance and giving it to the world.

Thank you to my family—Dad, Mom, Andrew, Clara, Abby, Alex, Allison, and Azariah—for putting up with all my brainstorming and story ideas. I love you all 3000.

Thank you to my writer friends—Amber, Anna, Crystal, Nathanial, Rachel, Vanessa, plus everyone else who listened to me gush about my hockey player and literature teacher and all their drama. You all are the greatest!

And thank you to the Master Storyteller—the True Author of love, the One who perfected second chance romance, and who never gives up nor runs out on me. Thank you for giving me the gift of storytelling, and for filling these pages with the evidences of your mercy and grace!

IF YOU WANT TO READ MORE BOOKS LIKE

On *Thin Ice*

QUILL & FLAME PUBLISHING HOUSE HAS YOU COVERED

HEAT WITHOUT THE SCORCH

Quill & Flame
PUBLISHING HOUSE

www.quillandflame.com

www.ingramcontent.com/pod-product-compliance
Lightning Source LLC
Chambersburg PA
CBHW060858210726
48293CB00006B/1858